Shadows of the Blues

God Bless
Whitney

Whitney J. LeBlanc

Outskirts Press, Inc.
Denver, Colorado

Outskirts Press, Inc.
http://www.outskirtspress.com

Paperback ISBN: 978-1-4327-1475-8
Hardback ISBN: 978-1-4327-0920-4

Outskirts Press and the "OP" logo are trademarks belonging to Outskirts Press, Inc.

PRINTED IN THE UNITED STATES OF AMERICA

Library of Congress Control Number: 2007934870

Acknowledgements

I wish to thank the following people.

My wife, Diane has been a positive force throughout the years of our life together. She has been supportive of every creative endeavor that I have attempted. She has especially encouraged, critiqued and prayed for my success as a writer, and so have my children. For this I am blessed.

My editors Nina Catanese and Beth Skony have guided me word for word through the structure, form and proofreading of the manuscript. It was a pleasure working with them.

I am thankful for friends, Roberta Shade Tyson, Thomas D. PawleyIII, Winona Fletcher, Ted Shine, Lydia Sindos Adams, Aloha and Robert Collins for giving love, inspiration, research and proof reading assistance during my second writing adventure.

Thanks and appreciations are extended to the estate of Leslie Pinckney Hill for our citing of his unpublished poem.

- Whitney J. LeBlanc

Dedication

To Diane Hambrick LeBlanc

Also by Whitney J. LeBlanc

Blues in the Wind

Contents

Prologue

Shadows of the Blues is a continuation of my first novel *Blues in the Wind.*

The saga of color, race and religion that plagued the Fergerson/ Broussard families in that novel continues in *Shadows of the Blues*. That was the legacy left by the colossal fornications of their forefathers, and so it is destined that these families deal with these conflicts in perpetuity.

The bigotry of a racially obsessed society continues to follow. The yoke of skin color continues to influence personal values. The conflicting tentacles of religious beliefs, some imposed by the masters, and some inherited from the motherland, continues to confuse and bewilder. Yes, the sins of their fathers had cast the inescapable shadows in which they must now live.

In *Blues in the Wind* we discovered that Martha Broussard Fergerson was beautiful. She was the desire of any man and the envy of every woman. She maintained the life that she was taught to believe a good Catholic should live. However, she was never able to overcome the loss of wealth, stolen from her great great grandfather, by Judge Kenneth Estilette. She could not tolerate the devil's music and she alienated her blues-loving brother--drove her daughter Lala into a hasty marriage to escape abuse--caused daughter Velma to seek the affections of men for money--forced her husband from her bed and burdened the life of daughter Rosa with the stigma of abortion.

Martha's husband, Phillip, bore the greatest burden when she lost her mind. He was the one called whenever Dr. Comeaux had a problem with Martha not wanting to sleep in the ward with colored patients, or wanting to have "a girl" push her wheelchair, or demanding any of the other privileges that she had become accustomed to enjoying. Love between them had faded and died over the years as Phillip watched this beautiful Creole become an evil, revengeful, prejudiced image of her former self. For him she was the mystery of all mysteries. As much as Phillip wanted a divorce, Martha kept him in the marriage, and no longer loved him because he joined the church of the "heathens." Eventually, Phillip became resentful that he was forced to lurk in the shadows to be with the woman he loved while pretending to be the loving and dutiful husband of a mentally ill wife.

At the time of Martha's commitment to the asylum, her eldest daughter Velma was living in Chicago, and had established a lucrative business of providing pleasure for men seeking outside love, while masquerading as a schoolteacher. Although her expressed feeling of not wanting "to see Mama like that," was an honest reflection of how she felt, she was also reluctant to return to Estilette because of the cloud of shame that had caused her to leave. So she was convinced, there was not much point to coming back to visit mama in the hospital.

Because Lala had inherited her mama's Creole beauty, she was a victim of Martha's hatred for blues music and the *"niggers"* who loved it. Lala never got over the public humiliation of being slapped by her mother in a crowded blues tavern. She got married to escape Martha's wrath, and lived in Kansas City for five years. When she left her husband and returned home, to escape the same kind of abuse that had driven her away, she discovered that Martha's resentment had never declined. She could not forget or forgive the treatment she received from Martha's hand, and never traveled the seventy-five miles to visit her mama in the hospital.

Rosa, the faithful churchgoing image of Martha, made frequent trips to the hospital. Although Martha did not always recognize her, Rosa prayed the rosary, supplied candles and answered the needs for special foods, clothes and personal attention. But ever-present was the fear that a word in a conversation would bring back the memory of what had happened with Tante in the back woods cabin. The abortion was their secret and Rosa wanted to keep it so. However, no amount of denial could completely eliminate the shadow of that dreadful truth from Rosa's mind.

Martha's son Bobby was destined to fulfill Phillip's dream of becoming a doctor and making lots of money. But he died from a mysterious illness at the beginning of his residency. Martha's resentment of Bobby's marriage to the dark-skinned Ruth, rather than the white heir to a family fortune, was the main reason she blamed Ruth for her son's death. It was also the inducement of the "accident," which Martha claimed was caused because her rheumatoid legs could not stop the car in time. This was an act of evil that would change Ruth's life forever.

John Broussard was Martha's brother. The people who played the Blues called him *"Lightfoot."* Martha hated the nickname and she hated the people, she called *"niggers,"* who gave him the name. She had contempt for the music, she called *"gut-bucket,"* and she hated the voodoo religion of his wife, Naomi. Even though Martha was his sister, Lightfoot made every excuse not to visit her in the asylum, and the guilt he felt was because she had nursed him back to health when he was crippled by a fall from the church steeple. He was grateful for that, but did not feel it was enough to cause him to ignore the evil of her nature. He was convinced that Martha had made the bed to which she found herself confined.

And so it was, with the people who mattered most in the life of Martha Broussard Fergerson, the daughter of Joseph Broussard, Grand daughter of Antoine Broussard Junior, and heir to the fortune of, great great grandfather, Antoine Broussard, Senior.

Chapter 1

Nightmares and Shattered Dreams

1954 - Phillip Fergerson left the BB King concert walking on a cloud. He had a belly-rubbing, finger-popping, and foot-stomping good time. He floated Alicia to her car through crowds of people reaching out and grabbing, trying to get a piece of her flowing garment. When they reached the gold Cadillac parked in a shadowed island of moss covered trees, he gave her a passionate kiss as his penis pounded against her body in rhythm with the beats of his heart. After prolonged wishes that they could be together more often in less public places, Alicia drove off and his love juice exploded into a pulsating trickle down his leg.

The moment Phillip entered Hell's Castle, which had the earmarks of home, he knew something was wrong. The lights were burning brighter than ever before, stacks of dirty dishes were all over the place, and the smell of burning candles attacked his nostrils. He entered the fiery furnace to a scene that made him vomit everything he had eaten. Shrimp and crawfish floated along with corn and potatoes on a flaming river of unbearable stench.

Candles of every description covered every inch of Martha's alter. She was kneeling under the crucifix, and her naked back and ass were crisscrossed with lesions of oozing blood. Candle wax dripped on her bowed head as she clung to the armrest of the kneeler with her left hand, and dangled a buggy whip from her right.

Phillip grabbed the whip and began slashing her body.

Sheriff Cat Bobineaux emerged from the flames of the candles and snatched away the whip.

* * *

Phillip sat up in a panic. His face was covered with sweat. The night sounds drifting in through the window, along with the cool breeze brought him back to reality.

He had had another nightmare.

Phillip could feel his heart beating against his ribs as he stood, trying to see clearly the time on the clock, which was lit by moonlight shining through blowing curtains. It was three-fifteen.

It was a horrible dream. Raw. Vulgar. Frightening. The worst he had ever had. All of his repressed feelings had finally come rushing out of his subconscious. His guilt over his affair with Alicia Wallace was taking a toll.

They had been lovers in graduate school at Iowa years before she joined the faculty at Southern University, and when she reentered his life, his love for his wife Martha had already faded away.

The night that he found Martha scarred and bloodied was the same night that he and Alicia had attended a blues concert at Martha's brother's club, The Black Eagle. Lightfoot knew about the growing estrangement between

Phillip and his sister, and he helped with seating arrangements so that Alicia and Phillip being together would seem accidental.

Sixty-five year-old Phillip stood in the cool breeze of the window as his mind's eye drifted back. It was fourteen years earlier, and he had entered the bedroom to discover Martha holding his jacket in one hand and a picture in the other.

"Who is this woman?"

He replied impatiently, "A friend from graduate school."

"What is it doing in your pocket?"

"It's just a picture."

"I know that. How did it get there?"

"Why are you searching through my pockets?"

"I'm taking your suit to the cleaners. Where did this picture come from?"

"It's an old picture, it doesn't mean anything." Phillip snatched the picture out of Martha's hand and walked out of the room.

Martha followed, yelling, "That's what you say, but I don't believe it. There must be something going on between you and that woman. But whatever it is, I want you to know you will never be free to be with her as long as I'm alive."

Although Phillip knew Alicia was not the cause of his loss of love for his beautiful Creole wife, he still felt the guilt. Tonight's recurring nightmare was another of the troublesome issues that crowded his life.

He realized there was not much he could do about anything this early in the morning.

*   *   *

Stephen Estilette strolled up the brick walkway of a two

3

story white clapboard house in the colored section of Estilette Louisiana, which was named for his family. He picked up the newspaper, dated May 18, 1954, on his way up to the gallery surrounding the house as roosters crowed along with church bells calling people to worship.

He held the screen door open with his back while he banged on the door.

After repeated blows, Stephen checked is wristwatch. Phillip was usually up with the ringing of the bells. Then Stephen slapped the door; maybe an open handed whack would be more easily heard. After the third whack, the door opened.

Rosa Fergerson wore a pink cotton robe over a faded flannel gown which hugged the tops of her slipper slides. A greasy scarf covered her curler filled head. She had an attractive Creole face but was not as beautiful as her mother, Martha, or her youngest sister, Lala. She was Phillip's pious, church-going daughter who was bordering on spinsterhood.

She said, with a sleepy astonished look, "Why Mr. Estilette, what's the matter?"

Stephen walked in, asking, "Is your Papa awake?" He leaned slightly to the side as his eyes glanced down the long dark hallway connecting the parlor to the rest of the house, then he straightened his six-foot athletic body and turned to face Rosa as she closed the door.

"I don't know, I just woke up. Was that the church bell ringing?"

"Yeah, it's six o'clock." He slapped the folded *Times Picayune* against his thigh. "I've got some news. Could you get him up?"

Rosa moved quickly down the hall, calling back over her shoulder, "Have a seat in the kitchen."

Stephen turned left into the second doorway as Rosa

disappeared into the shadows of the long, picture-covered hallway.

Stephen Estilette, the owner/publisher of the Estilette Chronicle, bore the name of the town that Judge Estilette, his great-great-grandfather, had established. His family and the Broussard family, into which Phillip had married, shared a history that went back to 1845, so this house was familiar territory, and Stephen felt right at home.

After spreading the newspaper on the table, he sat opposite the chair at the window that he knew Phillip preferred, clasped his hands behind his head, and leaned back with a smile. His short-sleeved white shirt revealed the muscular biceps of a man accustomed to athletic activities. He lifted weights, played tennis and golf, rode a bicycle, and climbed mountains when he was able to take a break from running the newspaper.

He and Phillip were an odd couple in this Louisiana town of 50,000 people, one-third of whom were colored. They were friends. Front-door-visiting, wine-drinking, honest-to-God friends. Phillip trusted him with his most prized possession, his son Bobby. In 1938, Stephen hid Bobby in his attic to keep him safe from the racist crackers who had killed Bobby's friend, Pee-Wee Hill.

Since then, Stephen and Phillip were bonded as brothers.

"What brings you over here so early in the morning?" Phillip said as he entered, knotting the sash of his robe. His unshaven face, the color of a paper bag, had a look of concern as he tipped his head to focus his glasses. Although slightly heavier, he looked to be the same age as Stephen, who was 55, ten years younger.

Stephen gave the *Picayune* a push, then Phillip picked up the paper and read the headline: "High Court Bans School Segregation 9 to Zero."

He pumped his fist in mid-air and said, "Hot-damn, it's about time."

Rosa moved to Phillip's side and read over his arm. "Well Thurgood Marshall finally won a case before the Supreme Court."

Phillip nodded, "He sure did. It's a great day this morning." Then he kissed Rosa on the cheek and continued; "Now what you say we celebrate with some coffee?"

"Glory be to God. I believe he's the first colored man to ever do that." She said as she headed to the stove on the far wall of the spick-and-span kitchen. Having been taught by her mama, Martha, that cleanliness was next to Godliness, Rosa never left a dirty dish or a speck of dust. Now that keeping the house had been shifted to her shoulders, she did everything as she knew her mama would have wanted. She slid her hands down the sides of her robe and then reached up to the shelf for the can of *Community Coffee with Chicory*.

Stephen said, "I wanted to be the first to tell you, so I could watch your reaction."

Phillip took his seat with a broad smile. "Well, what do you see?"

"The thrill of a victory."

"Yes Lord. Thanks for waking me up."

"When I saw your paper outside, I knew you were sleeping late."

"Rosa usually gets me up at six when she leaves for church." Then Phillip turned in the direction of the stove, and said, "Rosa, you're late for mass."

Rosa replied, "I was too tired to go today."

Phillip whispered to Stephen, "She's having a hard time sleeping since Martha's been in that hospital."

"I know it must be rough on y'all."

6

Phillip shook his head and mumbled, "You don't know the half of it." Then he contemplated whether he should share the nightmares and the other agonies that he and the family had been through in the last ten months. Martha's breakdown had prompted little white lies, which the family chose to tell rather than reveal the embarrassing truth of flagellation – the reason Dr. Rossini ordered that she be sent to the institution.

After a few seconds, Stephen brought him back to the matter that had motivated his early morning visit, "How do you think Fontenot's gonna take this?"

"Like all the others. It's gonna be a hard swallow, especially for the Superintendent."

"Well they might as well get used to it because times are changing."

"Now you know white people as well as I do, and you know they're not gonna take this lying down. They gonna do everything possible to delay or even stop it if they can."

Stephen shook his head and said, "That won't do any good. It'll just be putting off the inevitable."

"You know that, and I know that, but it's gonna be a bitter pill for the white folks in this state, or maybe even the whole country."

Rosa brought a tray of coffee and fixings to the table. "I heated the left over biscuits and have some of Mama's fig preserves. Just help yourselves."

She put the biscuits in the center of the table, poured three cups of coffee, and took a seat. As she swallowed her first sip, she asked, "Mr. Estilette, how did you come by knowing what was in the paper so early? They don't throw the papers 'til five-thirty."

Stephen answered with a smile, "There is some advantage to being the owner of a newspaper. I got a call last night from the editor of the *Picayune*."

Rosa laughed and said, "I was just wondering. I thought that you might have second sight."

"I wish I did. I could have saved your Papa from that beating he got when he tried to vote."

Phillip waved his hand, "Now y'all just stop that. There's no need to go back to '48. I want to talk about what's happening now. This is May. Do y'all think we gonna have integrated classes by September?"

Rosa said, "I sure wouldn't mind if my classes were integrated."

Stephen replied, "That's easy for you to say. You're Creole, you're used to being around colored and white. But there're a lot of people in this town that don't feel easy about having their children in the same classroom with . . ."

Phillip interrupted, "Niggers!"

Rosa gasped. "Papa!"

Her disapproving tone brought an apologetic smile to Phillip's face.

"I know we don't use that word in this house, but let's face it, that's the attitude that a lot of people have."

Stephen said, "You're right. I wasn't going to say it as bluntly as you, but that's the attitude that's out there."

Phillip continued, "And it's going to ruin this country if it's not changed. This is the right time for that change."

"If I were the superintendent of schools, I'd put you in charge of this transition. You've worked with both the white board members and the colored teachers, and you've got the experience to make integration work," Stephen said.

Phillip fell out laughing and he slapped the table. His mind's eye flashed to the time when Fontenot did not lift a finger to help when he tried to vote. "Man, that's what I like about you. You're an optimist. Impractical as hell, but an optimist just the same. I'm glad you're not Fontenot, you'd get me killed."

"Why you say that?" Stephen asked.

"Whoever is leading the implementing of integration is in the line of fire."

Rosa remembered the courage it took to face the mob of racists that beat her father when he tried to vote for Truman, and she said, "Papa, I know you're not afraid."

"No, I'm not afraid. I'm just not as optimistic as Stephen."

"You just said you were in favor of integration."

"I am, but I'm also realistic. It's gonna be a tough uphill fight to get this accomplished."

Stephen said with conviction, "But integration is just what our schools need. It's the key to achieving everything that's good in this country."

"I still say we're headed for rough waters."

Rosa drained her cup and got up from the table. "I've got to get dressed. I can't sit here talking all day; I got a lot to do. Nice to see you Mr. Estilette, even if it was so early." She added as she left, "Give my regards to Miss Esther and Alex."

Stephen poured another cup of coffee as his mind's eye raced through some of the controversies that he and Phillip had weathered in the past: The storm of letters to the *Estilette Chronicle* and the hundreds of cancelled newspaper subscriptions because of his editorial condemning the beating that Phillip had endured, the legal fight they undertook to get Phillip reinstated after his suspension, and the years of friendship in defiance of color boundaries.

"Now I want to know if you're still planning to retire?" Stephen asked.

Phillip chuckled softly. "I guess you know me well enough to know I've been thinking about that."

Phillip had been an educator for forty years. He had

planned to serve as principal for another five or ten years, but Fontenot had left him with a bitter taste in his mouth when he had failed to support his effort to vote. Phillip knew he could not count on the superintendent to do the right thing, so he had decided to retire, but now that school integration was the law of the land, he was having second thoughts.

He continued, "I haven't made up my mind yet. I've got a meeting with Fontenot in a few weeks, and I'll see what he has to say about this Supreme Court decision thing. Well hell, man school integration is what I've been working for all these years."

"Just remember what you said earlier: Fontenot is just like all the others."

"I'm not likely to forget. I've got a lot to consider."

"I know you do. So I'd better be getting on back to all that work piled up on my desk." At the door, Stephen added, "I sure am sorry about Martha. Give her a kiss from me when you see her."

Phillip nodded his head and watched Stephen drive off. He wondered if Stephen's great-great-grandfather's actions could have been one of the things that had driven Martha crazy. Judge Estilette had taken back most of the four thousand acres of land that he had sold to Antoine Broussard, contending that the sale was a mistake and declaring that men of mixed blood could not legally own property. Martha had kept alive the hope that one day the land would be reclaimed by her family and the wealth returned. It had become a lifelong obsession.

* * *

Phillip filed his request for retirement three weeks later, having come to the conclusion that the Board of Education would never allow him to serve as principal of a school with a racially mixed faculty and student body. Although the Supreme Court decision was a victory, Phillip knew that the attitudes of the white people in power had not changed and it would require many years and many more battles to accomplish integration. He was tired of fighting, especially after the last five years of legal battles to get reinstated. He didn't want his remaining years to be an ongoing struggle to integrate; he wanted to be remembered for the victories already won in the education of Negroes -- especially his program of in-service-teacher-training. Even though Fontenot had stolen the idea and pretended it was his, the Negro teachers knew who had really created the program.

So when Fontenot asked, why he was retiring, Phillip simply said there were personal family problems to which he wanted to devote more time. By now, the whole town knew of Martha's affliction, so it was not necessary to say more than that.

William Fontenot, a man with a reputation for knowing how to handle people, especially Negroes, shook his head in agreement and said, "I understand. If this is what you feel you have to do, I will not ask you to stay on."

"Thank you Mr. Fontenot. That's very considerate."

"Let's have a cup of coffee for the thirty-five years you were principal of the colored school." Fontenot reached over and pressed the button on his intercom. "Donna, bring Phillip and me some coffee."

Phillip had never, in all of the years he worked with Fontenot, been offered a cup of coffee. He would not even try to guess the reason that it was being offered now. Fontenot had always been a chameleon, so it was impossible to tell why he did anything.

Phillip figured to use this opportunity to get some idea

of Fontenot's thinking, and asked, "What do you think of the Supreme Court decision?"

Fontenot pushed his chair back from the desk and stood at the window next to the six-foot ficus. He seemed like a dwarf. Although Napoleonic in stature, Phillip had heard that he cast a long shadow in the political and educational arenas of the city and the state. After a few seconds of thought – *How should I respond to the most intelligent colored man I've ever met?* – Fontenot sat on the edge of the desk, looking down at Phillip. "I don't think I'm going to be around when the decision takes effect."

Donna, straitlaced, and bosomy with horn rimmed glass dangling from the chain around her neck, entered with two cups of coffee. She put one into Fontenot's hands; the other was slammed down on the desk with such force that the coffee spilled out into the saucer. Neither she nor Fontenot made any recognition of the incident, but Phillip knew the action was an expression of resentment to serving him coffee. She turned quickly, making sure their eyes did not make contact.

Fontenot continued, "Like you, I've decided to retire."

"Retire? But Mr. Fontenot, you've got that new school going up out there in Magnolia Heights that will carry your name. I would think that you'd like to be around to make sure it was done proper."

"It will be done proper. I'm sure of that."

Phillip reached over, picked up his coffee, and with obvious ceremony poured the coffee from the saucer into the cup.

"What do you plan to do? You're my age and in good health." Phillip added with a smile, "Planning to play a lot of golf?"

This was the most casual conversation that Phillip had ever had with Fontenot. Mostly they talked about the needs of the colored school. Now, he was angling to get him to reveal more about himself. Phillip realized that Fontenot had avoided his question, and he was curious about why he was retiring. Was it because he wanted to avoid implementing the Supreme Court decision, or was it because he felt that if he did, he would be thrust into a never ending fight with the Board of Education? It could have been either.

Fontenot laughed. "I always plan to play a lot of golf."

Fontenot extended his hand. "Phillip it's been good having you work with me. You're a credit to the colored people of Estilette, and it will be tough finding your replacement. I hope your wife gets better soon."

After the abrupt dismissal, Phillip walked out of the office, down the stairs, and out past the door of the Registrar of Voters office, which held so many unpleasant memories. He was weary of dealing with the likes of white folks. Now his life would be plunged into another sea of troubles: Martha.

Chapter 2

Secrets in Friendship

1954 - Julee, Martha's best friend, called to ask Phillip to take her to visit Martha in the hospital. She had gone last month but wasn't allowed in because she was not considered to be family, although she considered that their Creole heritage, first communion, confirmation, and the sharing of tea and secrets of the heart had made her family.

The Louisiana State Mental Hospital, located in Pineville, was about eighty miles from Estilette. It was established in 1902 and at that time was considered one of the most successful institutions of its kind in the South. Now the ravages of time, lack of upkeep, and patient overcrowding had taken its toll, and terms like "crazy house," "asylum," and "institution" were used frequently to describe how the general population felt about the place.

Ten months earlier, when Julee first learned that Martha was in the "crazy house," she was devastated. Martha was in isolation at that time, so she could not visit. All she could do was pray.

Then Julee's ill-fated, one hundred fifty mile trip from Scotlandville to Pineville in a taxi only increased the urge to see her now. She said to Phillip, "Martha been on my mind since the day she went into that place, and I can't call or write, so I sure would appreciate if you took me to see her when you go."

Julee was only a few years older than Martha, who was sixty. She was born blind, and her parents sent her to the School for the Blind at Scotlandville, where she remained until she was twenty-five. After the deaths of her parents, she returned to Estilette and lived in the family house alone. She supported herself on a combination of cash inheritance, money she made from teaching music, and a part time position on the faculty of the School for the Blind.

Julee refused to wear the dark glasses that identified the blind, and the blue-gray membranes of her eyes surrounded by the café au lait coloration of her skin gave her face an eerie appearance. Many who spoke with her could not stand to look at her face, but she was able to perceive their reaction from the direction and distance of their voices, and she considered them insincere. Except for her eyes, her face was kind and gentle, accented by a large mole in the middle of her chin.

The next week, Julee settled into the passenger seat of Phillip's '52 Ford. Her hands clutched a lace handkerchief and rested lightly on the Bible held in her lap. Phillip glanced at her stoic face and figured she intended to bring solace with a reading from the good book.

Julee was an amazing woman. She was independent and could do things even sighted people found challenging. She played the piano, crocheted beautiful scarves and doilies, and once familiar with her surroundings, she could get around as well as anyone with seeing eyes. Phillip had heard she could tell the difference between a one and a five-dollar bill, but he never understood how that was possible.

Julee asked, "When's Rosa gonna get married?"

Phillip shrugged. "I don't know."

"It ain't healthy for a woman to be alone too long. How old is she now?"

Phillip thought for a second. "Thirty-six."

"Almost forty and never been married, something's wrong. I know she's not one of those women who likes other women, and she's an attractive and talented girl, so why ain't she married?"

"I wonder about that, too. She spends all of her time teaching school and going to church."

"Does she have any men friends?"

"None that I know of."

Julee continued with sincere interest, "She needs to get out and meet new people."

"That's exactly what I tell her. From time to time, I've suggested that she go to the *fais-dodo* or bingo."

After a long silence, Julee asked, "What happened to her?"

"Nothing, as far as I know. What do *you* think happened?"

"I don't know. That's why I'm asking you. You married to her. I'm just her friend, but she don't tell me everything."

It was now clear to Phillip that Julee had shifted the subject to Martha. He was hopeful that maybe she could bring some new light to this darkness since they were such good friends.

"Miz Julee, that's been a mystery to me. I've been racking my brain ever since I found her all bruised and bloody from that whipping."

"Oh, that was about sinning. Good Catholics did that in

the Middle Ages. We were taught that was one way to repent for sins. But I can't imagine what sinning Martha did, or thought she did to cause her to do something like that. I told her she put too much faith in the Catholic church as the answer to everybody's needs, but that was when we were talking about you."

"Talking about me?"

"Yeah, she was upset that you left the church and joined 'the heathens.' You know she doesn't have much toleration for any other religion except Catholicism. That's one thing I don't like about our church: When they get hold of you at an early age, they got your mind for the rest of your life. I started reading the Bible to figure out some of these beliefs for myself. I do believe that God punishes us for our sins, but that's for Him to do, not for us to take upon ourselves."

"Well, something caused her to lose her mind," Phillip said.

"You must know something about what was going on when she got sick."

Phillip had no intention of revealing his affair with Alicia. Although he felt that could have been one of the things that drove Martha crazy, he was sure it was not the only one.

"All I know is when I found her she had whipped herself bloody, and, like you say that was about sinning. But I also know that she never got over her Papa's death and the loss of the family estate."

The remainder of the trip was occupied by their individual thoughts about what to expect from Martha when they got there.

The drive in past flower beds covered with weeds and peeling paint on the buildings confirmed the neglect over the years.

Phillip and Julee waited silently in the reception room. After several minutes, Julee said, "What's it look like in here? It don't feel and smell too friendly."

Phillip looked around, sighed, and said, "There's a table with six chairs where we're sitting. Across the room in front of us are two benches under the windows, which are open but covered with locked heavy wire mesh. The wooden floors are bare, and there's nothing on the walls except the peeling paint that was once olive drab but now it's" Julee interrupted, "The color of baby shit--and the place smells like it, too."

"That's the way it is with these public hospitals. But this is the best we have."

"I just hope and pray she doesn't have to be here too long."

An attendant entered with Martha in a wheelchair, parked it, and left. Martha looked at her husband and her best friend but showed no signs of recognition.

She looked different than she did the last time Phillip visited four weeks ago. Her deep-set gray eyes were losing their luster, her delicate creamy skin was splotchy, and her black gossamer hair had more gray. The most beautiful Creole that Phillip had ever seen was changing right before his eyes.

Phillip kissed her on the cheek. "That one's for me and here's another one from Stephen. He sends his love."

Martha slowly raised her hand and wiped away the kisses; it was not the first time she had rejected Phillip's greeting. She looked right through him as if he was a sheet of glass.

Julee stood and moved her cane around until she found Phillip. She whispered, "Is it all right for me to speak to her?" When he said yes, she tapped her cane until it encountered a bench under the opened window, and she sat down with regal dignity.

"Martha, how are you?"

Martha struggled to get out of her wheelchair and limped over to where Julee sat.

Phillip could see that her rheumatism was worse, and she had lost some pride in her appearance. There was never a time when Martha would leave the house without looking her best. Now it didn't seem to matter that her blouse was unbuttoned and her slip was showing. It was not easy for Phillip to watch the beautiful woman he once loved slowly fade away before his eyes.

Martha sized up Julee and said, "Who are you, some kind of queen?"

"I'm Julee, your friend. Don't you remember?"

"I don't remember too much."

"Now how do you account for that?"

Martha ignored the question. "Can I sit down here? I can't stand up too long, I got rheumatism."

"Why sure, if there's space."

Martha looked at her with surprise. "You can't see, can you?"

"You know I've been blind all my life."

Martha settled next to Julee. "I once had a friend who was blind."

Julee wanted to get back to her question. "Why can't you remember? Is it because you don't want to, or because you've gone senile?"

Martha laughed. "Senile? Lord, no. Ain't nothing wrong with my mind."

"Except that you try to shut things out. Let me see how you look now, it's been a while since I had a good look at you."

"Are you crazy? You're blind."

"I am blind, but I'm not crazy. Now be still." Julee

waved her hands around until they touched Martha's face. As Julee delicately traced the facial details with her agile fingers, Martha was silent and still.

Julee finished her perusal and said, "Your hair needs combing, your eyes are puffy from lack of sleep and you got some wrinkles that you didn't have before. But so do I. We're both getting old. And your lips got the turn of a sourpuss. They don't smile much."

"Are you sure you're blind?"

"You can pretend you don't know me, but I know deep down in your heart that you do."

Phillip listened and watched carefully. Martha was mildly different--calm and quiet, almost as if she was tranquilized.

Julee asked, "Phillip, do you see my pocketbook there on the table?"

Phillip brought the purse to Julee, then he sat opposite the ladies to better observe.

Julee opened her purse and took out a small bottle. "I brought your favorite perfume."

Martha opened the bottle of *Evening in Paris,* breathed in a healthy whiff, then dabbed a little behind each ear. Her bearing took on a majesty that Phillip had not seen in a long time.

Martha said with sincere gratitude, "Thank you. What is your name?"

"Julia Donatto. You call me Julee."

"I once had a friend by that name."

"And I had a friend named Martha. What is your name?"

"Martha."

"Ain't that something we both have friends named the same?"

Martha asked, "What you come here for?"

"To find out how you are doing."

"I'm doing fine. How are you?"

"I also came to find out what happened."

"What happened about what?"

Julee was determined to get Martha talking about her condition, and she asked patiently, "What happened to cause you to be in this place?"

"Oh, this is just my rest home. I'll only be here for a short time until He says I can go home."

"Who is he?"

"You don't know who He is? Then you must not be Catholic."

"Now, you know I'm Catholic. What makes you think Jesus is going to tell you when to go home?"

"Why are you asking me all of these questions? I know that you're blind, but you must also be hard of hearing or just stupid. I just told you this is my resting place. It's like purgatory until He's satisfied that my sins are forgiven."

Phillip watched Julee's membrane covered eyes roll around under their lids and her lips pucker into a tight knot that disappeared with a deep swallow of pain. He knew her well enough to know what she was feeling. His mind's eye shifted back ten years to that day when Julee had come over to tell them that Vel had turned Julee's house into a cathouse. Martha, of course, had insisted that Vel did not own a cat. Julee's eyes rolled around today the same as they did when she explained that the smells of liquor, sex, and smoke in her house were like fingerprints to the sighted. Phillip knew as he watched that this was another occasion when Julee's pain was brought on by someone she loved.

Julee dabbed her eyes with her handkerchief, reached over and found Martha's knee and patted it softly. "There's no point in getting catty, I'm just trying to help. And I

21

gather from what you say that you're in Purgatory because of sin."

"We all sin."

"There's a price to pay when we sin, but I'm concerned about you and I want to help you find the self that you once were."

"What does it matter to you?" Martha asked.

"You're my friend, and I love you."

"Don't speak love to me. I don't have any friends. I had a husband once, but he's gone to that woman."

"Your husband is right over there."

Martha shook her head. "I don't know who that man is, but I do know that he's not my husband."

Julee was not making much progress. Martha was not responding as she had hoped she would. Then she said, "I'm gonna read something to you so you'll be reminded that when you walk the path that the good Lord has set, you will live and prosper in the way He intended."

Martha frowned but said nothing.

Julee directed Phillip, "Bring me my Bible."

Phillip knew Martha would not take too kindly to being told she had done something wrong, but he was curious about what Julee had in mind.

Julee opened the Bible and her nimble fingers began tracing the Braille. She read: "This is from Deuteronomy twenty-eight, fifteen. It says here, 'If you do not obey the Lord your God and do not carefully follow all of his commands and decrees, the Lord will send on you curses, confusion, and rebuke everything you put your hands to until you are destroyed and come to sudden ruin because of the evil you have done in forsaking him. The Lord will strike you with wasting disease, with fever and inflammation, with scorching heat and drought, with blight and mildew, which will plague you until you perish. The

22

Lord will afflict you with madness, blindness, and confusion of the mind. At midday, you will grope about like a blind man in the dark. You will be unsuccessful in everything you do.' "

Phillip watched Martha closely. When the words "madness and confusion of the mind" were spoken, there was a twitching movement in her body as if stuck by a pin. What Julee had read was getting through. Maybe Martha had begun to realize that something she had done had caused a curse. Julee had opened the Pandora's Box of Martha's soul.

Martha asked, "Is that why you blind?"

Martha's question struck like a bolt of lighting. Julee held her face straight away.

Martha was not finished. "You got a curse on you, too? My friend who's got a name like you was blind just like you. And she had a curse on her that came from the sin of her father."

Julee's clouded eyes rolled around, and her nimble fingers scanned the tops of the Bible's pages until she found the passage she was looking for.

She took a deep breath and said out loud what her fingers were reading, "John nine: 'As he went along, he saw a man blind from birth. His disciples asked Him, 'Rabbi, who sinned, this man or his parents, that he was born blind?' 'Neither this man nor his parents sinned', said Jesus, 'but this happened so that the work of God might be displayed in his life.' "

Martha straightened up and said, "I don't give a rat's ass what you read in your book. All I know is the father of my friend who's got a name like yours, fornicated with evil women and he gave the disease of syphilis to his child, who was born blind. I still ask if you got a curse on you like my friend."

Julee rose, clutching her Bible and waving her cane. She found Phillip, took his arm, and said, "Let's get out of here. I will not be insulted further."

Martha went to her wheelchair and followed them to the door.

"Why you running away? You just read from that Bible that God puts a curse on those who don't follow his commandments. Now we have something to talk about."

Julee stopped and turned. "All the years we've been friends, I've never said anything hurtful to you about how or why your Papa died, and I know plenty. So why you want to wash my face with the sins of my father is more than I can understand. It just makes me think that maybe deep down inside you're not the friend I thought you were."

Martha continued her tirade, "Yes, I've sinned, but I've punished myself for that, and when I go to confession, I'll be forgiven. But your sin is not your sin, and you got the nerve to come in here all high and mighty, pretending to be a friend and accusing me of breaking the commandments."

Julee had no expectation that her visit would end like this.

The door slammed shut, leaving Martha alone in the reception room.

Phillip could feel Julee's body quivering as he led her toward the exit.

She tightened her hold on his arm and said, "I didn't think she would strike out at me for telling her the truth."

Phillip considered saying, *What did you expect Martha's reaction to be? After all, even though the two of you know each other's secrets, to hear them spoken and laid out bare and naked is a horse of a different color.* But he kept these thoughts to himself and said softly, "With her mind disturbed like it is, there's no telling what she will say or do."

Julee murmured, "That's not much consolation for all the years of love between us. To think she of all people would believe that gossip about my Papa after all this time."

What Julee called gossip was what Martha had heard as truth about how the Creole, Ray Donatto, had caught syphilis while carousing at the juke joints with the black-skin ladies of the evening. Phillip figured that truth was as difficult for Julee to hear as it was for Martha.

As they passed the reception desk, Dr. Comeaux came out of his office.

"Oh, Phillip. Glad to see you. I was just thinking about calling. I've got something to talk over with you. Have you got a minute?"

Phillip looked at Julee's stern face. The blue-gray membrane-covered agates shifted nervously back and forth, and he thought maybe she could use some time alone.

He said softly, "The doctor wants to talk to me. I'll leave you on the bench right here near the reception desk. I'll have the lady bring you some water."

Julee nodded and swallowed her tears.

Once they were in Dr. Comeaux's office, the doctor swung his chair right to left, and then back again until finally he brought his fingertips together and said, with grave concern, "We have a few problems with Martha. As you remember, she refused to sleep in the ward with the other colored patients, so when Dr. Rossini gave me the background of her Creole heritage, we tried to accommodate her wishes. But now we have a new problem. She insists that a special assistant be with her at all times to attend to her needs and push her around. We simply don't have the budget or staff to give this kind of special service to any one patient."

Phillip's heart skipped a beat. He anticipated that the doctor was getting ready to turn Martha out. He knew how difficult she could be, and she had given them trouble ever since her first day. Phillip waited.

Dr.Comeaux leaned forward and continued slowly, "If you would agree to pick up the expense of a private attendant, we can meet Martha's demands to make her stay here as free from stress as possible."

Phillip asked, "How much would that cost?"

"Thirty dollars a month."

Thirty dollars was a lot of money in 1954, especially now that Phillip was not working. He expected that his retirement pay would be about three hundred dollars a month so this unexpected expense would surely be felt. Phillip thought for a moment, realized that he had no other choice, and agreed to pay the extra fee.

Dr. Comeaux continued, "Martha talks a lot about the past, about her father and a brother who plays a harp that she wants to hear again. I get the feeling there's something that she wants to share with her brother that may unlock what she's hiding from me. I can only get so far, and then she shuts down. I was wondering if you could ask her brother . . . what's his name?"

"John Broussard."

"John . . . to come out for a visit."

Phillip could not figure why Martha wanted to see Lightfoot. She hated him. She hated his wife, Naomi, her blackness and her practice of voodoo. None of it made any sense--but neither did Martha. Phillip agreed to get John to come for a visit.

As the doctor stood, he asked, "How did the visit with her friend go?"

Phillip shook his head. "Not good. At first, she didn't remember Julee at all, and then she said some insulting things about her friend's father."

"I'm sorry to hear that. Her memory goes and comes, to serve whatever purpose that she has locked in her confused mind. Sometimes she sounds almost normal, and then she lapses into fantasy."

Chapter 3

Truth in Confession

954 - Lightfoot savored the last bite of bacon as his admiring eyes followed the rhythm of Naomi's ass. It still aroused his manhood, but not as often as it once did. Her ass was firm and round and flowed down and merged with her beautifully shaped thighs. Her breasts were like luscious ripe mangoes, and she moved with the grace of an African princess.

She was the best pussy he ever had. She was kind and gentle and listened to his problems and understood his desires. He loved everything that she was, and everything that she was, Martha hated. She was night-black with nappy hair. She hadn't finished high school and fitted Martha's description of low-class. She even practiced voodoo, but nevertheless she was all Lightfoot needed, and he regretted that now there was so much to do that there was not enough time left for making love.

Naomi sashayed from the sink and stood next to Lightfoot at the table. She asked with impatience, "You done?"

He nodded his head, and she took away his plate.

On the way back to the sink, she suggested, "I know you're planning to fix that toilet today."

Lightfoot had been putting this off for several days now and didn't figure another day would matter that much, so he bit the bullet. "Naw, I'll fix it tomorrow. I'm going to Pineville today."

Naomi turned viciously, put her hands on her hips, and said, "I thought we had this out before and decided that you had enough of Martha's shit."

"Phillip said . . ."

Naomi interrupted and aggressively took a step closer, "I don't care what Phillip said."

Lightfoot continued, "Well it's been a while now since he said she wanted to see me."

"She never wanted to see you when she was in her right mind, why you figure she wants to see you now?"

"I had this dream . . ."

Naomi rolled her eyes, turned, and headed back to the sink. "Shit."

Lightfoot ignored her comment and continued, "You know how it is with Dreams... Well I was sittin' under the pecan tree playin' my harp, and the devil come up out of nowhere and put a saddle on my back and started riding me down the bayou road, and the owls were screechin', and the devil was laughin', and Martha was burning in hell."

Naomi looked back with anger and said, "She oughta burn in hell."

Lightfoot went on, "You know as well as me, when the devil rides you and the owls scream, that's a sure sign somebody's gonna die."

Naomi's response was more of a statement than a question. "And you feelin' guilty!"

"Naw, ain't that 'tall, but after all, she's ma sister."

"And blood's thicker than water!" Naomi flung the wet dish towel, and it landed on his head, dripping the smelly, greasy water down his face. She pulled off her apron, slammed it to the floor, and headed for the door, "Go on then, see yo crazy, white-thinking sister, but that toilet's gonna be spilling shit 'till you get back."

Martha and Naomi hated each other, and just like before Naomi and Lightfoot were married, Martha still created discord between them. However, Lightfoot remembered how Martha had nursed him back to health when he fell from the steeple of the white Catholic Church. The doctors at the hospital were in a hurry to treat the injured white people, and after discovering he was colored, they set his leg wrong and turned him out. He had no money, was out of work because he was crippled, and Martha took him in. He never forgot that.

And he never forgot that Martha hated the nickname given to him by the "niggers," as she called the blues people. Since his left leg was shorter than the right, he walked on the ball of his left foot and left a half-print in the dust. He had attracted a loyal following of blues lovers, and "Lightfoot" was a nickname given out of affection. An accordion player named Freddie expressed best what was generally felt: "Man, when Lightfoot plays the blues, it's like a bolt of lightin' just struck the roots of a tree. It go way down deep. He can play some blues. He can play a train so real, the peoples along his path set their clocks, thinkin' the S&P is passin' by." The only thing that Martha liked to hear him play was the train. Why? He never knew.

But most of all, Martha hated that one of her own kind, especially her brother— a good-looking Creole, with straight hair, light skin, and Catholic from birth, had the audacity, and the shamelessness, to take up with a black woman.

* * *

Martha limped in on the arm of her attendant. Her legs were swollen twice their normal size, her fingers were gnarled and knotted, the beauty had gone from her face, her uncombed hair tangled down around her shoulders in a stringy mess of black and gray, and her mismatched clothes hung loose like moss on a tree. Lightfoot was shocked to see his sister in this condition.

He moved in her direction, and she left the grip of her attendant and hobbled the rest of the way on her own. She threw her arms around his neck, slobbered kisses over his face, and said, "My baby brother, Johnny."

He returned the greeting. Although her reception was not what he expected, he figured that being in the crazy house had softened her heart. They settled at the table, facing each other, and Martha smiled, ran her hand over her hair, and smoothed it down like he remembered she used to do.

Then she asked, "Did Papa go hunting today?"

Lightfoot knew she was reliving the past, which explained her greeting. He decided to play along with her flight of fancy.

"Not today. He's going tomorrow," he replied.

"You go with him. Don't let him go with that nigger Silas."

Lightfoot was not surprised to hear that their Papa's death was still on her mind. He had felt all along that this might be what had brought her to Pineville.

He continued her illusion. "I'm going with him."

"Good. You got your harp?"

"No. I left it in the tree house."

She smiled and said, "You remember that time I came to your tree house for you to help me with that nigger gal?"

"Yeah."

31

Martha was seventeen then, and he heard her voice screaming, "Johnny, Johnny come quick."

He stuck his head through the entrance of his treehouse, where he hid away to learn his harp.

"What's wrong?" he asked

"Susie Mae's hurt."

"What happened?"

"Come on down here, quick."

Martha and John ran across the freshly plowed field and headed for the barn. She stopped at the door to catch her breath.

John came up behind. "What you doing way out here?"

"I was lookin' for you. Mama wants you to finish stackin' that wood before Papa comes home."

"Where's he at?"

"Huntin'."

"Again?"

"We ain't got time for that now. Come on," she said.

Susie Mae, a twelve-year-old black girl, was on the ground crying. Her left arm was wrapped with strips of cloth from Martha's petticoat, which formed a tourniquet.

"What happened?" John asked.

"Her Pa drove off in the wagon and left her to unhitch that mule. The mule kicked her, and she fell back on the plow. It musta cut an artery."

John and Martha put Susie Mae in the back of the buggy and took her to the hospital.

That was one of the few good things he remembered that Martha had done for somebody else, and that was a long time ago.

Martha continued, "Go get your harp from the tree house. I wanna hear you play the train."

Lightfoot was puzzled about what to do, but he didn't

want to upset Martha. Phillip had told him how unpredictable her mind was; sometimes she remembered things correctly, and sometimes they were confused. Phillip had also emphasized that the doctor said there was something she wanted to share with her brother. So Lightfoot decided to continue playing along with her imagination and said, "I'll be right back."

When Lightfoot returned with the harmonica, the attendant met him at the door. "Mr. Broussard, she waitin' for her confession."

He looked in. Martha was on her knees, leaning against the table. "Confession?" He asked.

"She think you're her priest."

Lightfoot whispered, "But, I'm not, I'm . . ."

The attendant interrupted. "Why not? Anyway, it can't do no harm. It'll keep her calmed down, and God knows she give us enough problems."

The attendant left the room and closed the door.

Martha looked up to greet Lightfoot. "Hello, Father. I'm ready."

He didn't know what to say. He slid his chair next to her kneeling position and listened.

"Bless me, Father, for I have sinned. It's been over ten months since my last confession, but I want you to know what I've done so you can pray to God to forgive my sins."

Lightfoot looked into Martha's eyes and saw the pain slowly creeping to the surface of her once beautiful but now wrinkled face. He felt he was about to look at his sister stripped naked, and he wanted to get up and run out, but he remained frozen to the spot.

She continued, "I made arrangements to take away that baby my daughter Rosa was carrying for that priest. And then I had her fixed so she wouldn't get pregnant again. And I made that sinful Father Pat suffer and die for what he did to my chile. I fed him glass that tore up his insides, and he bled to death just like that ill-conceived baby that he gave to my Rosa. And Father, I was unkind to my only brother. He's a good man when he's not drinking and playing the devil's music, so I paid BookTau to burn down the place that brought him to sin. I knew that was wrong, but he was living with that ol' black voodoo woman, who I hated. And I tried to kill that other black thing called Ruth. I hit her with my car, but she didn't die. I hated her because she let my baby boy die. I'm sorry for all I've done. I know God said, 'vengeance is mine', but I took it into my hands because He works too slow. I'm sorry for everything I've done. I'm asking His forgiveness so I can get to heaven."

There was a long silence during which Martha's water-filled eyes remained fixed on those of her confessor. Lightfoot remained frozen, afraid to say anything that might upset the delicate balance, afraid she would recognize his voice. Plus, he was still in shock from what he heard.

Finally, she spoke, and the tone of her voice remained the same as it had been during her confession. She leaned in close and whispered, "Excuse me, Father, but I've got to go pee."

Lightfoot could tell from the look of urgency on her face that she was in discomfort. He limped quickly to the door and summoned the attendant.

While they were out of the room, Lightfoot entertained thoughts of leaving, but if Martha returned and found that the priest had left before giving absolution, it would upset her. So now he had to figure out what penance he would give, perhaps two rosaries and a novena along with a litany to the Blessed Virgin. Since she had committed such serious sins, he didn't think this was excessive. He shook his head and covered his face with his hands. It was hard to believe what had just filled his ears. She was indeed crazy.

When she returned on the arm of the assistant, she greeted him with hugs and kisses, just as she had done when she first entered the room. She had forgotten he was her confessor a few minutes earlier.

Lightfoot was relieved that he did not have to pronounce a penance for her sins.

She asked, "You got your harp?"

"Right here."

"Play the train for me, but don't let Papa hear."

Lightfoot began with the musical spinning of the wheels, then a high pitched blowing of the whistle followed by the increasing tempo of a train gaining speed. Martha closed her eyes as always, and imagined that a real train was passing by. When the train faded into the distance, the attendant came in and helped Martha out.

Dr. Comeaux, who had been alerted to the goings-on, was standing outside the door. He addressed Lightfoot, "How did things go, John?"

Lightfoot thought to tell him about the confession but then decided against it. Martha had confessed to crimes that may only have been in her imagination. He needed time to sort out everything before he told anybody.

He wagged his head and said, "She told me some stuff that she imagined, and then she thought that I was somebody else, but she really wanted to hear me play the harp like I did when we were young. Our Papa didn't like to hear it, so we'd sneak off to be alone. She wanted to relive those old times hiding away from Papa."

Dr. Comeaux patted Lightfoot on the shoulder and said, "You did a fine job. The girl said you calmed her down. Thanks for coming."

* * *

As soon as Lightfoot reached the city limits of Pineville, he floored his white, fishtail Cadillac to seventy miles an hour. He wanted to put as much distance as he could between himself and Martha's confession. He needed time to think. It was difficult for him to believe what he had heard. Maybe it was all a dream. Or maybe he imagined it. He thought back over what had happened, and he was convinced it was real. There was no way he could imagine or dream up what she had said. He decided to look back over the past and try to figure what could have caused her to lose her mind.

He remembered the gentlemen callers who lined the parlor on the weekends to take the most beautiful girl in Estilette to the *fais-dodos*. She was happy and content, and there was nothing in her life as a young debutante, that he could figure, that would cause her to go crazy. Yes, she had peculiar ways, and there were lots of people and things that she didn't like, but none of that should have caused a breakdown. Maybe it was something that had happened even before Papa Broussard's death. Lightfoot's mind's eye flashed back to an earlier time with the same speed that his car was traveling.

Yes, it was a fact that Judge Kenneth Estilette had taken back most of the four thousand acres of rich bottom land developed by their great-great-grandfather, Antoine Broussard. The judge had lied and claimed that the land had been sold by mistake in 1845 and that it was illegal for a man of mixed blood to own property and slaves. Over the years, the judge had watched Antoine control flooding on the property by erecting levees and dams. And he saw how the perennial swampland that he thought worthless was turned into a gold mine. And year by year, the judge watched as the Creole's bank account multiplied and his plantation house grew to be the finest in town, containing furniture and tapestries from France. And the judge watched as Antoine's slaves increased in numbers. The judge turned green with envy. And then sadly, after the Civil War, Antoine Broussard watched as the crafty Judge Estilette took back enough property to form the basis of the town that now bears his name.

Papa Joe Broussard had also watched his father Antoine Junior struggle to keep his share of the forty acres that was left. But the best and most productive land was gone, and what was left was barely enough to sustain division among the large family that the sexual appetite of the Broussards had produced. And even though Joe worked hard to rebuild the wealth that the family once possessed, he was not able to do so. He was a proud man, and the fact that most of what was now Estilette once belonged to the Broussard family was a bitter pill to swallow. So he shot himself because he couldn't live with the shame of not being the rich man that his rightful inheritance would have made him.

Martha did not take this well. In Lightfoot's way of thinking, this could have caused his sister to be committed to the mental asylum. *She never accepted the fact that Papa killed himself. She blamed ol' Silas. Everybody knew that Silas would never hurt Papa.*

Lightfoot heard himself talking to himself. He laughed, shook his head and said, "Then there was Mama."

* * *

His mind's eye flashed back to 1914.

He was 15 at the time and had just crawled under his Mama's bed to get his ball when he heard her voice.

"Come on in here and try on this dress."

37

Martha entered and Mama Marie closed the door. From his vantage point under the bed, John saw Martha's dress fall in a circle around her feet. He decided to remain hidden to see what else he would see.

Martha slipped into the recently completed wedding dress.

"Oh, Mama, it is beautiful."

Marie stood back and looked admiringly. "I was hoping to have lots of girls for lots of big weddings."

"Mama, this is perfect. I love all the lace and the little pearls. You've been working on this a long time."

"Nothin' too good for my baby. Your sister, God rest her soul, would have worn this dress first, if she hadn't died."

"What happened, Mama?"

"Yellow fever. And the other girl died at birth when you were only eighteen months. I was angry with God for taking my babies. I wanted lots of children like the rest of them Broussards. That's why I married your papa. But that was not to be. And five years later after John was born, I stopped trying."

"Mama, I didn't know."

"I didn't say nothing all these years, but now that you're getting married, I want you to have . . . Turn around, I want to tuck it in a little over here. . . I want you to have all the girl babies I didn't have."

"That means I gotta have a big house."

"A plantation house just like your great-great-grandfather Antoine."

"Ouch!"

Marie stuck her with a pin, but she ignored Martha's complaint and went on like nothing happened, "Little by little, 'ol Judge Estilette stole it away from us. But soon as you marry this doctor, y'all will have the money to buy it all back."

"And I'll be able to have those grand balls like you talk about all the time."

"Yes. Marie Mouton was the belle of the ball, and you will be, too."

"You think Phillip'll be that rich?"

"Oh, yes. He'll be the only doctor for miles around. The colored people have to go all the way to Alexandria to get looked at. The white doctors don't treat 'em. It's just us Creoles that the doctors treat."

"I sure am glad y'all like him."

"Well, he's gonna be a doctor. Of course, he's too black for you, but your papa said we'll overlook that 'cause he gonna be rich. So you'll have servants and a big house just like the Broussards did years ago. There, now that looks better."

Martha swirled and looked at herself in the mirror. "Oh, Mama, it's beautiful."

While she was posing from one attitude to another, John got bored under the bed and watched a spider weaving a web from one spring to another.

Martha got his attention again when she asked, "What about your family, the Moutons?" Martha used the occasion of her Mama's talkative mood to probe family matters that were never discussed. Very few Creoles told their children about the past, and Martha made the most of this rare occasion. John listened.

"What do you mean?" Marie asked.

"Were they rich, too?"

"No, they were just poor ignorant trappers and fishermen. You had to have land and slaves to be rich, plus they had too many children. My papa used to ride Mama like she was an 'ole mule. Every time I turned around, Mama was having another baby. I had to get away from all those diapers and cryin' soon as I could. So I married your Papa. Then he started. After your brother was born, five years after you, I refused to let him ride me like Mama was ridden. I found out them Broussard's were just living, breathin', baby makin' machines."

Marie finished the adjustment and said, "There now, that's fine."

Martha carefully took off the wedding dress and reached down to pick up her clothes. She saw John's reflection and yelled out, "Mama, John's under the bed!"

Marie pulled up the counterpane and said, "Boy, what are you doing under there?"

"Getting my ball."

"C'mon out and get outta here."

John emerged, bouncing his ball and left the room.

Martha said, "Mama, he saw."

"Oh hush, he's just fifteen years old."

* * *

Lightfoot looked out at the rapidly passing blur of bare cypress trees and the colorless moss that waved in the breeze of that December afternoon. Both sides of the blacktop macadam road were lined with greenish bayou water that was home to moccasins, turtles, crawfish and the few alligators that sought refuge from the deeper streams and remained long enough for an easy meal, and every now and then a heron would flutter an escape from the bank and take refuge in the nearest cypress. Lightfoot admired the rugged beauty of this primeval land.

He breathed out as if talking to an unseen person in the car, "Mama put a lotta thoughts in her mind, too. I guess it was all too much. Both Mama and Papa left Martha with holes in her heart."

40

Then his eyes were drawn to the flashing lights reflected from the rearview mirror. A patrol car was trailing, and he pulled over to the shoulder. The officer from the sheriff's car strutted proudly to his prey. There were few, if any folks around these parts that drove white Cadillacs, and it caught the officer's attention when it zoomed past. It was difficult for the officer to tell whether the driver was white or colored; there were Creoles around these parts who could be either, so he adjusted his gun belt to be sure that his holster was hanging just right if it was needed.

He stood all-powerful, looking down into the opened window of the car, his hand resting lightly on the handle of his gun. For a quick moment, he surveyed the inside of the car, then his eyes settled on Lightfoot. He had long straight black hair, his facial features had the look of a white man, but his skin coloring was light brown, and he had a look of fear in his eyes. Without a shadow of a doubt, he was a nigger Creole.

The officer breathed in deeply to detect if the smell of liquor was present, and then he spit out, "Nigger, you're either runnin' from a robbery, gettin' away in a stolen car, or goin' to a fire. Now which one is it?"

Lightfoot was careful to speak as respectfully as he could, "I'm sorry, officer, I didn't realize I was goin' so fast."

"I asked you a question, boy. Now get out of the car."

Lightfoot knew he was in trouble. He was on the outskirts of Bunkie, and it was a well-known fact that if you were colored and went as much as one mile over the speed limit, you were likely to get pulled over, but he forgot. His mind had been occupied with other thoughts. Lightfoot walked to the back of the car as the officer commanded.

The sheriff continued his interrogation. "Now what is it causing you to drive so fast?"

"Nothin'."

"Is this your car?"

"Yes, sir."

"You got the registration and a license?"

"Yes sir, in the car."

Lightfoot had sense enough not to move until told to do so. The sheriff began to get impatient. He said in a louder voice, "Well, hell boy, get it and let me see it."

Lightfoot limped toward the passenger side of the car. The officer watched and concluded that the boy was crippled because he had been shot while running away from a robbery of some kind. He concluded that he should be especially careful, and he followed Lightfoot and watched as he opened his glove compartment and took out his registration. Lightfoot handed this and his driver's license to the sheriff. The officer held them in his hand as he looked past Lightfoot to the object lying on the front seat.

"What's that?

"My harp."

"Your harp? What's that for?"

Lightfoot picked it up and handed it to the officer. "I'm a blues musician."

The sheriff turned it over, looked at it, and handed it back. Then he focused his attention on the documents. He looked suspiciously at Lightfoot.

"You John Broussard?"

"Yes, sir."

"Where you get the money to buy a car like this?"

Lightfoot was the richest colored man in Estilette and had more money than the officer could ever dream of having.

42

He responded, "From my business."

"What kind of business you in?"

"I own a blues club."

"Where is this blues club?"

"In Estilette. It's called the Black Eagle." Lightfoot thought that the extra information would show that he was trying to be cooperative and maybe the officer would not be so tough on him. But he was wrong.

The sheriff came back with, "The one that created that big traffic jam for Sheriff Cat Bobineaux last year?"

"Yes, sir."

"You god-dammed niggers think that because you got money enough to buy a big car you can do anything you want. Well, not in my parish." The officer took out his book and began writing a ticket.

Lightfoot's mind flashed back to a story that Phillip had told years earlier about an ignorant white sheriff who couldn't write. He was hoping that this sheriff would ask him to write his own name and address on the ticket. The thought brought a smile to his face.

The office tore out the ticket and said, "Wipe that smile off your face. You think this is funny?"

"No, sir. I was just thinking how dumb I was to be driving so fast."

"Well, you're right about that, boy. Now you gonna have to come back to Marksville to appear in court in three weeks. If you don't, I'll have the sheriff in St. Landry parish arrest you and call me to pick up. And it won't be funny. You got that?"

"Yes, sir." I'll be back in three weeks. Right there at the court house on Main Street."

The officer handed him back his registration and license and watched him drive off. He followed at a distance for the next five miles.

Getting that ticket was a sobering experience. Now, traveling at a lower speed, his thinking was more logical. There was little doubt that what Martha had confessed really happened. He decided to tell Phillip.

* * *

The sweet aroma of pecan pralines greeted him as he ran in the door calling Phillip's name. Rosa was in the kitchen stirring a pot of boiling milk, sugar, and pecans.

"Papa's not here, Uncle Johnny."

"Where's he at?"

"Scotlandville."

"When he be back?"

"I dunno."

Lightfoot watched Rosa stir the boiling mixture. He had seen Martha do that many times and he knew that the stirring had to be constant or the stuff would boil over. On the table were two pans of cooling chocolate fudge, ready to be cut into squares, along with stacks of round pralines.

Rosa looked away from the pot for a second and nodded in the direction of the table, "There's some pralines on the plate over there."

Lightfoot headed to the table and took a seat next to the stack of sweet round candies. He asked, "Are you making these to sell for the church?"

"Yes."

"How long you been doing this?"

"Since right after Father Pat died." Rosa made the sign of the cross, then continued. "And Father O'Riley came to take his place. He needed some new vestments."

Lightfoot looked at the gentle Rosa and tried to imagine her having sex with Father Pat. He had always wondered about the loneliness priests must feel at night with no woman to comfort them, and he had heard tell that some of them liked to be with men or boys, but no doubt Father Pat liked to be with women. He wondered where sex between them took place. Did it happen in the confessional, the rectory, or on a dark bayou road? Had Father Pat come on to her, or had she flirted with him? Rosa was such a sweet, religious woman, it was a difficult thing to picture, but no doubt something had happened. Maybe she had fallen in love with him.

She asked, "What you want with Papa?"

"Got something to talk over with him."

"I'll call him this evening and tell him you want to see him."

"O.K." Lightfoot put a couple of pralines in his pocket and got up to leave. He kissed Rosa on the cheek, took out a fifty-cent piece, and put it on the table. "Here's for the candy."

"You don't have to do that, Uncle Johnny. That plate was for the family."

"That's all right. I went to see yo mama today."

Rosa's attention left the boiling pot. She asked, "How is she?"

"She seems fine."

"Did she know you?"

"Every now and then. She even asked me to play the harp. But I could tell sometimes she thought I was somebody else."

He pointed to the boiling pot. "Your candy's 'bout to boil over."

Rosa slid it off the flame and then turned back to Lightfoot. "Is that what you want to talk to papa about?"

Lightfoot could have kicked himself for bringing up the subject of Martha. He started for the door and lied. "Naw."

I wanta tell him about some blues musicians coming to the club."

Rosa followed, sliding her hands down the sides of her apron. "Oh, I thought you might want to tell him about mama. Did she say anything about me?"

"Naw, she didn't talk about nothing much, just rambled on 'bout the change in the weather and stuff like that."

Rosa reached out and caught his arm. "Y'all didn't fuss did you?

"Naw."

"I have to go and see her. Papa and I have been alternating our visits."

"Look, I gotta go. Tell yo' papa to come by and see me when he gets back."

Rosa nodded and brought her fingers up to her lips.

Lightfoot left with a heavy heart. He thought about that hypocrite who called himself a priest. This was the first time he had heard of a priest making a baby. Then he thought about what Martha had said about making arrangements to have the baby aborted, and he wondered who had helped her. He could not imagine that Dr. Rossini would do such a thing, although Martha had been his nurse for so many years that maybe she persuaded him. Everything was so hard to believe. He didn't know how his sister could even think of doing something like that. But then again, it was becoming clear that he never really knew his sister.

Chapter 4

Relief and Turmoil

The time spent with Martha required that Phillip relive and relieve his feelings of guilt.

He had not been in this quaint cottage for six weeks, and it lifted his spirits. The walls were bookshelves and those not covered with books were hung with paintings by Negro artists the likes of John Biggers, Aaron Douglas, and Lois Jones. There was also a print of Gainsborough's *The Blue Boy*, and African sculpture filled every nook and cranny. The fragrance of roses drifted through the air on swirls of incense, and the voice of Bessie Smith filled the candlelit room Phillip had a delicious meal of baked catfish and tomatoes over rice with string beans and fried eggplant. There was wine with dinner, and Phillip stretched out his feet on the hassock and relaxed. Alicia was as relaxed as he, and from time to time they spoke about Bessie Smith and talked trivia. Phillip however, made a point of not telling her his nightmares or his feelings of guilt. No matter how much he tried not to think of Martha, she was always there, but he was determined that tonight would be different.

After moments of silent contemplation, Alicia spoke.

"A penny for your thoughts."

"Just letting my mind drift like the incense smoke."

"Liar."

Phillip opened his eyes, sat up in the easy chair, and asked, "Why do you call me that?"

"Because you are. I know what you are thinking, and I know how to take care of that."

Alicia raised her skirt and straddled his legs, took off her blouse and bra and kissed him long and tender.

Phillip kissed back, followed a path to her breasts and let his tongue trace circles around her nipples until they were firm and hard--the same as his Johnson.

Alicia took away his clothes, one piece at a time, and then covered his exposed body with kisses.

In bed, she was close to the point of climax, whispering and moaning. "Yes, yes, that's the right spot...Don't stop...Faster, faster, faster. Sweet daddy, fuck me good...Yes, yes, yes. . ."

The phone rang.

Phillip flopped. He rolled off to the side.

Alicia raised her balled up fist into the air and yelled, "Shit!" Her left hand came down on the phone receiver along with the fourth ring.

She answered with a frigid voice, "Hello." She passed the phone to Phillip, "It's for you."

Phillip listened and said, "O.K., I'll take care of it tomorrow."

Alicia dropped the phone on its cradle and pleaded guilty. "I forgot to take it off the hook. Do you think it was a good idea to give out my number?"

"That was Rosa."

"I know. She sounded a bit hostile when she heard my voice."

"I'm sorry. I have to tell her where I can be found. She's by herself, and if something happens. . ."

Alicia interrupted. "I understand. It's just that her call came at a bad time."

"I'll make it up to you. But I have to go back after breakfast."

"What's wrong?"

"I don't know. Lightfoot has a problem. Something about the club."

* * *

Getting caught up on the news was Phillip's early morning thing to do; it didn't matter if he was in Estilette or Scotlandville. As Alicia warmed his cup with hot coffee, he folded down the *Times Picayune* and said, "I see here where the Senate has censured Joe McCarthy for, and I quote, "abusing his colleagues".

Alicia glanced over his shoulder. "It's about time they did something about him accusing everybody of being communist."

"Everybody but Negroes."

"He'll get around to us before long. Breakfast is almost ready."

Phillip stood, stretched, and retied his robe as he watched the woman he had grown to love fix breakfast. They had known each other since graduate school and met again 24 years later. He remembered that stormy night in '40 when her exotic body had turned him on again and they made love. Ever since that night, he had wished to be free of Martha, but that was not to be. Since Martha was confined to the asylum, any attempt to get a divorce would

49

be unthinkable.

He gazed through the lacy curtains at the house next door and wondered if the people there ever saw his comings and goings. He didn't like the clandestine nature of being with Alicia. They could not go out publicly, except maybe to a blues joint across the river where they were not known. He was still a married man, and she was a professor of Education at the university. It would be a disaster if gossip got back to university president Felton Clark that they were having an affair. It was risky enough to arrive under the cover of darkness and have to park two blocks away.

However, being with Alicia was what he needed during his time of stress, but it was taking a toll.

Phillip felt Alicia's arms circle his midsection and her breath on his neck.

She said softly, "Whatcha thinking so hard?"

"Everything and nothing."

Alicia responded, "Which means that there's a lot on your mind that you don't want to talk about."

"That's what I like about you. You know me so well . . ."

Alicia interrupted and completed his sentence, mimicking his voice, "You know what I'm thinking." She continued in her own voice, "You're right. But your thoughts are your own, and when you want to share them, you will."

The beauty of her character sparkled and brightened her brown-sugar face. She was entirely different than Martha-- kind, considerate, and thoughtful.

She said, "Now come on and eat this breakfast."

Phillip kissed her, and his hand slid down her back and cupped her ass.

Alicia reached around, took his hand, and pulled him to the table. "We don't have time for that now. It'll be waiting when you come back."

Alicia watched as Phillip poured syrup on his biscuits. There was a question on her mind that had been there for several days, and she needed an answer. Now was as good a time as any.

"What do you have planned for Christmas?"

Phillip washed down the biscuit with a sip of coffee. "A family get-together. Vel wrote that she planned to come home."

Alicia wished that she hadn't asked, because she could have figured what the answer would be. She was the outside woman, and there was no way she would be included in the family's holiday celebration.

Christmas was getting to be very difficult. Her parents had passed on, she had no siblings, no children, and her only meaningful relationship was her friendship with Leo and Catherine Roberts, and she was reluctant to burden them again with her presence.

Phillip sensed her anxiety and asked, "Why?"

"Well, it's getting close, and I just thought that if you didn't have anything else

planned we might go on a trip."

"A trip?"

"Yes, maybe Puerto Rico, Jamaica, or the West Indies, but it was just a thought. I know it's not possible." Alicia realized that she was engaged in verbalized wishful thinking, and the only purpose it served was to let Phillip know that she would be alone.

Phillip detected her sadness but didn't know what he could do about it. Not one of his children would understand or feel comfortable with her around. He said, "Well, maybe later on we can take a trip to the West Indies. I'd like to see a voodoo rite."

"You can see that in New Orleans."

"I know. I'm being selfish. When you mentioned trip, I thought about the fact that I'm sixty-five and I've never been out of the country, and that is one place I'd like to go. But why don't you decide where you would like to go, and we'll go."

Phillip drained his cup, got up from the table, kissed Alicia, and made his way to the bathroom to get dressed.

For several minutes, Alicia tried to figure what she could do for Christmas so she would not be alone.

A distant roll of thunder brought her back to the present. She looked out the window; the first few drops of rain had begun to fall.

She was clearing the table when Phillip appeared, dressed to leave. He was his usual dapper self: white shirt, blue tie, three-piece dark gray suit, watch chain laced across his vest, and highly polished black shoes--the true image of the professor, which he always maintained.

She said, "It's raining, you'd better take this."

Phillip pulled her close as she extended the umbrella.

"I know these times are rough, but I do love you. I promise to steal away during the holidays so we can spend some time together. Later in the spring, we can take that trip to wherever you decide."

At least she knew Phillip cared enough to let her know she would not be completely alone.

Alicia watched from the window as he walked to his car, hiding his face beneath the umbrella.

* * *

The late morning shower had turned into a December downpour by the time Phillip arrived in Estilette. He drove directly to Lightfoot's house and ran out of the car to the back door. He found Lightfoot sitting on the edge of the

52

bed, trying to focus his eyes to the light of day. Phillip waited in the doorway while Lightfoot slipped into his pants.

Lightfoot brushed past Phillip on his way to the kitchen, and yelled for Naomi. Getting no response, he said, "She must be at the club. You want coffee?"

"Yeah."

Lightfoot fumbled around in the pantry trying to find the coffee, while mumbling that Naomi should have already made coffee and not let him sleep most of the day away.

Meanwhile, Phillip meandered through the house, surveying once more the three bedroom brick structure that Lightfoot and his construction buddies had thrown together on weekends. Phillip admired the progress made since Lightfoot's fall from the church steeple. He remembered when Lightfoot came to him to get his share of the Broussard estate to buy Blue's Tavern. It seemed that his good fortune began rolling in from that time on. And it wasn't all luck; Lightfoot was a talented blues man, and he was a good bricklayer in spite of his bad leg. Phillip regarded Lightfoot's life as a metaphor for the blues--he had overcome his trials and tribulations and let the good times roll.

While the coffee brewed, Lightfoot settled at the table with his head in his hands, rocking from side to side.

Phillip took the chair on the opposite side of the table and asked, "Bad night?"

"Naw, bad day." Lightfoot raised his head and looked Phillip straight in the eye and said. "She killed him."

Phillip was confused and asked, "Who killed whom?"

Lightfoot placed one cup in front of Phillip and held the other with both hands wrapped around, as if to warm away the shivers that were running through his body. He began slowly.

"It was so hard for me to believe, I just sat and drank all night long. Now I'm hung over."

At that moment, Naomi ran in from the rain along with a clap of thunder. When she heard voices, she stopped in the hallway near the pantry. She waited and listened.

Phillip repeated his question with some irritation. "What are you talking about? Who killed whom?"

Lightfoot blurted out, "Martha killed Father Pat."

It was such an unbelievable statement that Phillip laughed.

Naomi's mouth dropped open, but she remained quietly hidden behind the opened pantry door.

Phillip's laughter faded into speech. "You still drunk, not only hung over."

Lightfoot got more intense, "Man, this ain't no joke." She told me. That is, she confessed it to me."

Phillip's manner now took on a serious nature. "You've been to the hospital?"

"Yeah, *yestiddy*. When I got back, I went straight to the house to tell you. Rosa said you was in Scotlandville."

"What happened?"

"Lemme tell you how it was." Lightfoot kept shaking his head in disbelief. "When they brought her in, she recognized me right off. But it was like she was seeing me from a long time ago. She called me her baby brother and started talkin' about Papa going huntin' with Silas and told me not to let him go alone. Then she said that she wanted to hear the train. I told her my harp was in the tree house. I thought maybe that would be the end of that, but she told me to go get it. So I went out to the car and got my harp. When I come back, she thought I was the priest come to hear her confession. Man, that blew my mind. There I was with Martha starin' in my face, believin' I was a priest. Her eyes were like somethin' I'd never seen before--like deep

54

pools, clear as glass. It was like I was looking into her soul and seeing her naked. It was awful."

Phillip took a deep breath and shook his head Naomi closed her eyes and remained quiet.

Lightfoot continued. "She said she fed Father Pat glass because he got Rosa pregnant. Then she said she had Rosa get an abortion, and she had her fixed so she couldn't get pregnant again. And she said, she ran over Ruth 'cause she was black and had let Bobby die. Then she paid BookTau to burn down my blues tavern 'cause she hated the music as much as she hated that black voodoo woman I had married."

Lightfoot poured it out quickly as if emptying the vessel of Martha's soul.

Phillip's face was drained of blood. He was in shock. Shivers trembled through the entire length of his body. He was dumbfounded.

Naomi walked boldly into the kitchen and yelled, "That woman needs to be charged with murder."

Lightfoot cried out, "What the hell are you doing here?"

Naomi yelled back, "I live here, remember?"

"You wasn't supposed to hear that."

"Why? You tryin' to keep it a secret?"

"It was a confession."

"A confession to murder."

Phillip blared out, "Shut up!" He hit the table, knocking over his cup of coffee. "Both of you, just quiet down!"

Lightfoot sank to his chair.

Naomi folded her arms across her chest, drew her lips into a tight knot, and leaned against the cabinet.

Phillip began slowly. "We've got to remember that Martha is out of her mind. She's crazy. We can't put too much stock in what she says."

Naomi rolled her eyes, turned three hundred and sixty

degrees, and said, "Well, now I've heard everything. That woman confessed to murder, and abortion, and you want to pretend it didn't happen?"

The moment *abortion* came out of her mouth, Naomi remembered that years back, Martha had asked the whereabouts of a midwife who could do abortions because, "One of Doc Rossini's patients wants the cure and he refuses to do it. The patient will pay fifty dollars to know how to get there." And all the while she had been talking about Rosa's condition.

What a tricky bitch Martha was. Naomi thought.

Phillip said, "We don't know for sure. There's no proof that any of this happened. It could all be her state of mind." At this point, Phillip didn't know what to believe. He was confused, uncertain. Everything was tumbling through his brain a mile a minute.

Lightfoot had figured out some things and said with confidence, "We know for a fact that she paid BookTau. She gave him that inlayed pearl harmonica and fifty dollars. He told me. And he took that stuffed alligator off the wall before he set the fire and later brought it to me to hang over the bar. Naomi was there."

Then he appealed to Phillip, "Man, if you had just seen that look in her eyes, you'd know she was telling what was in her heart. I'm sure that whipping was her punishment for all those things she did, but killing that priest was the heaviest sin. That glass musta tore up his insides."

Naomi added, "And I remember how he died. When Martha went to cook at the rectory, it wasn't long after that when Father Pat went to the hospital."

Phillip's eyes stared into space. Tears formed in the corner of his eyes and expressed themselves in his voice. "I guess you got a point there. I did have my doubts about the accident with Ruth. It just didn't seem to make much sense the way Martha told it."

Naomi took a seat at the table and faced Phillip. "Whatcha gonna do about it?"

Phillip shrugged in complete resignation and whispered, "What can I do?"

"You can tell the sheriff."

Lightfoot came back with, "Nobody's ever been convicted from a confession."

Naomi was persistent and said defiantly, "That's a confession to a *priest*. You ain't a *priest*."

"No, I'm her brother."

And with disdain in her voice, Naomi spit out, "Oh, well, I guess that means blood is thicker than water."

Phillip added with despair, "And what would telling Cat Bobineaux accomplish?"

"She'll go to jail, that's what."

Phillip said softly, "She's in jail now."

Naomi came back quickly, "Well, she'll get punished for what she did."

Lightfoot and Phillip turned and looked at Naomi at the same time.

She concluded quietly, "Yeah, I guess she's gettin' that now." She headed for the door. Phillip called out, "Naomi!"

She stopped and turned with annoyance.

Phillip continued, "There are lots of people who would be hurt if this got out. We have to think of what this would do to Rosa. And Ruth. It would be devastating for her to know that while she was picking flowers for Martha's table, she was intentionally run over. And think of all those people at church who put their trust in Father Pat, only to be told that he was having sex with a parishioner, who could have been any one of their children. God knows I've had my problems with Father Pat. I never did like him, and he was the reason that I left the church.

"If I had known what he did to Rosa, I would have killed him myself. But I don't think that letting everybody know what a hypocrite he was will accomplish anything. The three of us are the only ones who know what happened, and we have to keep this to ourselves. Now, can I have your promise to keep this secret in the family, just between us?"

Phillip looked at Lightfoot, who silently nodded his head. Then he looked at Naomi.

"Phillip, everything you said makes a lot of sense. It's all true. And that's what worries me. It's the truth, hiding what's true. I've always been of the belief that the truth will make you free. What that means is you ain't got to pretend when you do the right thing. Some people try and figure out ways to make things not be, what they really are, but in the end, shit is shit, and it stinks. I know some people like to pretend their shit don't stink, but I've always called a spade a spade. Now, as long as I've known Martha, she has been a mean and hateful woman, and keeping this shit covered up won't change that. I've always liked you, Phillip, and I'll keep the promise you ask. But you must understand that I've got my own ways and means of talking to the powers that be. And just like I've spoken to the spirits in the past, I will do it again. Who knows? That confession that she made just might have happened because of the hex I put on her."

* * *

Phillip had difficulty seeing through the rain-spattered windshield as well as his water-filled eyes. More than once, he pulled over, took off his glasses, and dried his eyes to see the road. He remembered crying over Martha once before, when he saw her scarred and bleeding from self-flagellation. But he could not understand why his tears were flowing now.

A deluge of thoughts, reasons, and excuses for the answer flooded his mind. Perhaps it was the comeuppance given to avenge Rosa's abuse. Although it wasn't clear whether Rosa was raped or was a willing partner, evidently Martha felt Father Pat was the evildoer, so she fed him glass.

Maybe he was crying because she had sacrificed so much to protect her daughter from shame. After all, this was a natural reaction for a parent; animals protected their young all the time. He had spouted off earlier that he would have done the same had he known. But he didn't really know whether he was capable of murder.

At the same time, he could not forget what Naomi had said, that Martha was "a mean and hateful woman." And he knew she had done other evil things.

It seemed God did have a way of keeping things in balance--she had broken his commandment and was paying the price.

At that moment, Phillip's mind shifted from seeking reasons for crying over Martha to remembering another broken commandment; "Thou shall not commit adultery." He had done that. Now both he and Martha had sinned. He wondered, was adultery as bad as murder? Which was the greater sin? It did not seem possible that they both could have the same degree of seriousness. To take a life was a sin and a crime. To sleep with someone else was only a sin. Maybe he was just trying to rationalize his own sin by seeing hers as more serious. Maybe he was also crying for himself because he had sinned just as she had sinned. At that moment, he found himself doing exactly what Naomi had said: "Some people try and figure out ways to make things not be what they really are, but in the end, shit is shit, and it stinks."

The rain was coming down heavily. He tried to see, but the wipers were not clearing the windshield fast enough. It was too much. He slowed down, and the car behind him had to cut around to avoid ramming into him. The tears in his eyes and the rain on the windshield obscured his vision, and although he knew the road, he was not able to make the curve.

When he realized he had run off the road, he tried to stop but slid right into a tree. For several seconds, he sat there trying to clear his head and regain composure from the whack he got hitting the steering wheel. He rubbed his forehead; a bump was beginning to swell. There was no blood, and he was not hurt, except for the embarrassment.

He opened his umbrella and got out of the car. The radiator was smashed, and water was running out as fast as the rain was coming down. He walked the last several blocks to the house.

* * *

Rosa was at the kitchen table working on a lesson plan. Christmas vacation was approaching, but still she worked out her plans, revising and keeping them fresh, even though she had been teaching for many years. When she heard the door close, she greeted her Papa.

Phillip held Rosa as if she was a lost sheep.

She pushed away and said, "Papa, you're wet."

"I smashed the car."

"Were you hurt?"

He rubbed his forehead and said, "Just this bump."

"Ohhh, let me see." Rosa examined his head. "I'll put something on it."

"Naw, don't bother. It'll be all right. I'm fine, but the

60

car isn't."

"What happened?"

"I ran into a tree."

"Where?"

"Down the street near the Duprees." Phillip made his way to his room to change.

"Did you see Uncle Johnny?"

"I had just left his house when I had the accident."

"What was he talking about?"

Phillip stopped long enough to create a lie. "He wanted to borrow some money."

"Oh, he said he wanted to talk about some blues musician coming to the club."

"Yeah, that too."

"He came by looking for you, and I thought it musta been important. He said he went to see Mama."

Phillip stopped, turned, and came back. He was worried that Rosa may have heard about the confession. "What did he say about your Mama?"

"Nothing much. She's about the same. She recognized him for a while, then didn't know him any more."

"Did he say anything else?"

"No. Can we go visit her?"

"We'll talk about it."

Phillip continued to his room. The day had been exhausting and depressing, yet there was so much more he wanted to know to which Rosa held the answers. Had Father Pat forced her to have sex or did she do so willingly? He wanted to know how she felt about losing the baby, but he would not dare breathe a word of anything that Martha had confessed.

When he returned to the kitchen, Rosa had his dinner on the table--his favorite T-bone steak, potato salad, and butterbeans. There was also a plate of pecan pralines for desert. He sat and began eating.

Rosa returned to her schoolwork.

Phillip took a long look at Rosa and it saddened him. She was thirty-six years old, kind, gentle, and unmarried. His thoughts went back to the confession. Maybe she was unmarried because she knew she could not have children. Or maybe she didn't know. It was a terrible thing that Martha had done, and he believed that it was all Martha's idea. He knew she was too proud to let the shame of Rosa having a child with a priest stain the family name. The more he thought, the more unbearable and horrible it was. He felt like throwing up. He pushed his plate away and held his head in his hands.

"What's the matter, Papa? Your steak not cooked right?"

"No. The steak is fine. I'm just not hungry."

"Must be that all that excitement you had today."

"What excitement?" A terrible thought flashed through Phillip's mind: maybe she did know about the confession. He said with impatience, "What are you talking about?"

"Your accident. Have you forgotten? Maybe that bump on the head affected you more that you thought."

"No. I'm fine. Just not hungry, that's all."

"Why were you holding your head? Do you have a headache?"

"I guess maybe I do."

The full impact of everything was taking a toll. Just sitting there looking at Rosa brought every emotion that Phillip could feel: rage at Father Pat, anger at Martha, and sorrow for Rosa. His head was bombarded, and he could feel his heart beating in his ears.

"Why don't you go to bed?"

Rosa was looking at him, and he was grateful that she did not know what was going through his brain.

"I think I'll do that." He kissed Rosa and headed to his room.

"Papa, could we go and visit Mama?"

The question brought tears to his eyes, but he was able to hold them back. "Why don't we all go and visit her for Christmas? Me, you, Vel, Lala, and the children."

Chapter 5

Christmastime

V el stepped off the train in Estilette tired, hungry, and resentful.

She watched as four white people got off the car in front of hers and headed for the *"whites only"* waiting room. She resented the fact that they seemed so relaxed and tranquil after such a long grueling trip. They had the advantage of extra space between the seats, a diner to eat prepared meals, and a club car to have cocktails.

She had to travel as a nigger and have her knees smashed against the back of the seat, little to eat, and nothing to drink. She refused to be identified as a nigger carrying a paper bag of fried chicken, and she didn't want to soil her clothes with grease. The only thing she had to eat was a ham sandwich that she rushed off to pick up when the train stopped in St.Louis.

Yes, she was resentful, and she had been that way most of her life. There was nothing left that she could do to make herself look Creole enough to pass for white. Her Mama had tried to help change her appearance, but it was not good enough, and she was still recognized as a nigger.

Although the car was jam-packed, she was the only Negro who got off. All of the other passengers in her car were headed for New Orleans.

She waited patiently until the porter unloaded the bags for the white passengers and then watched as he stacked her bags and boxes on a separate wagon. When she was sure that all of her possessions were accounted for, she followed the wagon to the side of the faded yellow building where the taxis for coloreds parked. The porter pulled the wagon to a stop, set the brake, and disappeared in the direction of the white waiting room to move luggage for passengers getting on board.

Willie stopped playing his harp to watch as Vel strolled in the direction of his taxi. As soon as he recognized the familiar face of the woman dressed in the tight-fitting, pleated red skirt, white silk blouse, and fur coat over her arm, he got out of the car to greet her.

"How do, Miss Velma? I ain't seen you in a spell."

Vel looked curiously at the jet-black man in the khaki shirt and pants and wearing a chauffeur's cap and asked with annoyance in her voice, "Do I know you?"

"Yes, ma'am. I wuz in your fifth grade class. I'm Willie."

"Willie?"

"Yes, Ma'am. Willie Johnson. I recognized you right off in them fancy clothes."

Vel did not remember the boy, now a man, named Willie Johnson, but she knew that there were no students in her fifth grade class worth remembering. So she said with some irritation, "I'm sorry, that was such a long time ago."

"Yes, Ma'am, I know. But I 'members you. You used to make me stand in the corner fer actin' up."

It all came rushing back. The troublesome boy who cried to her papa that she was treating him unfairly. It was because of him that she and her papa had that big fuss over her treatment of black-skinned students, and that was one of the reasons she had moved out and went to live at Miz Julee's.

Vel said bluntly, "Oh, yes, I remember. You driving for Mr. Richard now?"

"Yes, ma'am. Bes' job I could get after I graduated. I hear yo teachin' up north somewhere."

"Yes, in Chicago. Where is the other taxi?"

"It's on da way, but I kin take you."

"I'm going to need both taxis to carry all those things on that wagon over there."

"You ain't gotta worry none, Miss Velma. I'll git everythin' loaded soon as he git here. Just git on in my car."

Her memory of the boy returned as clear as day with every word he spoke. She remembered that he used "ain't" and "git" a lot. Willie opened the door of the taxi and she sat down.

While standing in the opened door, Willie took out his harp and said, "I plays the blues jes like yo' Uncle Lightfoot, and I goes to the Eagle Club all da time."

"Well, that's nice."

"Wanta hear me play the blues?"

"That's not necessary, Willie. When will the other taxi be here?"

"Dere he is now."

Vel looked, and sure enough, the other taxi was rounding the corner. "Well, you can start loading my things."

After everything was crammed in the two cars, they headed toward the Fergerson house.

Rosa heard the door open and ran to the parlor expecting that it might be Vel. Rosa was delighted that now she would finally get to decorate the tree. She had promised to wait until Vel arrived, and for many days, the tree had been standing bare, filling the house with the fresh pine scent of Christmastime. The boxes of lights, angel hair, icicles, and shiny balls sat stacked in the corner waiting their assigned spots.

"Girl, why didn't you call me? I would have picked you up."

"I had too many bags."

After the sisters kissed and exchanged greetings, Vel held the screen door open and the parade of packages began. "Just put the boxes on the floor over there and take the suitcases upstairs to the first room on the left," Vel ordered.

When Willie and the other driver finished, Vel gave each of them one dollar and said, "Thank y'all and have a nice Christmas." Then she took off her coat, kicked off her shoes, and plopped down on the sofa.

"Where's Papa?"

"In his room."

Vel sighed, took a deep breath, and said, "Guess I'll run back in a little while. How's Mama?"

"About the same. You never came to see her."

"Now don't you start. There wasn't much I could do from what you said about her condition. If she didn't recognize you, you know she wasn't going to recognize me."

"The least you could have done was come to see how she was."

"Girl, it's a long ways from here to Chicago, and you told me everything I needed to know every time I called. Plus, you know me and Mama wasn't on speaking terms when I left."

Rosa decided not to hash over those past unpleasant events, so she smiled, gave her another hug, and said, "Go see Papa."

"I've got to go to the bathroom first." Vel stopped, then turned back. "Have you got something to eat?"

"I'm cooking now. It'll be ready soon."

"I'm talking about something I can eat now. I haven't had anything to eat since St. Louis."

"I've got some fish from yesterday."

Vel yelled back, "That'll be fine," and continued her trip upstairs.

When she entered the kitchen, Rosa placed on the table a plate with fried catfish, potato salad, and sliced tomatoes.

"That looks good. Got any beer?"

Rosa laughed. "Girl, you haven't changed in all your 39 years."

"Now you know better than to mention my age."

Rosa playfully slapped her on the arm, and said with a laugh, "Like I said you haven't changed and just as prettily dressed as ever."

As Vel bit into the fish she said, "That boy who drove the taxi was one of my students."

"Which one?"

"The black one in the khakis."

"You remembered him?"

"No. He remembered me. And it's really strange that I would see him first thing, because he was the little nigger that Papa and I had that big fuss over."

"The one Papa said you didn't treat right?"

"That's the one."

Rosa laughed.

"What's so funny?"

"You thought it was strange. I think it's funny that the

first person you see when you get back is the one who was the cause of you leaving."

"I didn't leave because of that nigger."

"Well, that *nigger*, as you put it, was the reason you and Papa had the falling out. Now I think you ought to go in there and say hello."

"Soon as I finish."

Phillip looked up from his reading when he heard her enter the den. "Why, Vel it's good to see you."

She leaned over and gave him a peck on the cheek. "It's good to see you too, Papa."

"How was the trip?"

"Long."

There was an uncomfortable silence that signaled that there was nothing much left to say. Then Phillip took out his watch and popped it open to reveal the inscription written on the inside cover. *To Papa, Everything in its time. Remember, keep time for everything. Love, Vel - 1948.* She got a little teary eyed as she read and realized that he was still using her present, which had replaced the watch he previously used.

Phillip snapped it close and said, "It still keeps good time."

"Oh, Papa, I'm glad." Then she gave him another kiss.

Phillip took off his glasses, rubbed the bridge of his nose, and said, "A lot has happened since you've been gone."

A slight shiver went through Vel's body and she felt that he was getting ready to admonish her for not running back when her mama was committed, or worse, he would pick up where they left off about the clothes she wore to school and the way she treated the troublesome students in her class. Her desire not to revisit these unpleasant subjects

69

of the past was the main reason she was reluctant to return, and she was beginning to feel sorry that she had come back this time.

Phillip continued, "I decided to retire."

"Oh, Papa, that's great. It's about time. You've been principal as long as I can remember. Now you can take a rest and do all of the fishing that you like."

This breath of relief gave them the subject of education to talk about for the next thirty minutes until Rosa announced that dinner was on the table.

* * *

Lala arrived from her home in Frilotville with Lester Junior and Ann to decorate the tree. Vel had never seen them before and made a big to-do over how fine she thought they were. "Boy, you are going to be as big as your daddy, and Ann, you're as pretty as a picture. How old are you?"

Ann blurted out, "Nine."

Then Junior followed, saying, "Eleven."

Vel shook her head as she realized how much time had passed since she had been home.

She turned to Lala and said, "I just can't imagine you as a mother with such grown children."

"Girl, don't say that, it makes me feel old."

Ann, who was holding Vel's hand and looking at her beautifully manicured nails, asked, "Do you have a little girl too?"

"No, honey, I'm not married."

"When are you going to get married?"

Vel rolled her eyes and made a face as if to say, "What a smart-ass little brat you got."

Lala came to the rescue and said, "All right, it's time

for us to start on the tree. You can talk to Aunt Velma later."

Phillip watched as the children went about helping to decorate the tree. He remembered Bobby, Vel, Lala, and Rosa helping when they were the same age. However, this time he kept hearing, "Junior do this," and "Junior do that. Junior hang these lights over here," and "Junior put these icicles on that branch.." All of a sudden, Phillip realized his grandson would grow up being called Junior. He knew it was necessary to make a distinction between the boy and his father, but he didn't believe calling him Junior was a good idea. So he shortened Lester to "Les," and before the tree was finished, everybody was calling the boy Les.

Even Lala liked the idea and said, "Lester's gonna like this, because he's started calling him 'Little Lester' rather than Junior."

Ann was indifferent to all of the hullabaloo over her brother's new name. She only wanted to make sure she would get her heart's desire from Santa. She plopped down in Phillip's lap and said, "Grandpop, isn't the tree pretty?"

"It's the most beautiful tree I've seen."

"Do you think Santa Claus will think it's beautiful, too?"

"I think he will."

"And do you think he'll leave the bicycle that I asked for under this tree?"

"Yes, I think he might."

Not to be left out, Les yelled out excitedly, "And he'll leave mine, too?"

"And yours, too."

Phillip had now been put on notice what presents they expected. Lala could hardly contain her amusement and had to leave the room so her laughter would not spoil the myth of Santa.

Later that evening, Lester Senior, Lightfoot, and Naomi came over for eggnog. Phillip liked having the family together for Christmas, which had not happened in a long time. Vel was really feeling comfortable being back home and "saved" her wig on a form on top of the sideboard. Ann was fascinated by what she saw happen and yelled out, "Look, Mama, Aunt Velma just took off her hair."

Lala responded, "Since Vel has let down her hair, I'll play the piano."

The children sang and were joined by the grown-ups on "Silent Night." The spirit of the season had taken over, and everyone was civil, even though every now and then, Vel would steal glances at Naomi and shake her head, remembering that her Mama always said, "I don't like having that black voodoo woman in my house."

* * *

On Christmas Eve, two cars took off, headed to Pineville. Ann, Les, and Rosa rode with Phillip. Vel and Lala rode with Lightfoot, who really didn't want to see Martha again, and he told Phillip, "Nothing but disappointment gonna happen."

Phillip needed the extra car and convinced Lightfoot that this was a special time for the family to be together. There was space enough for Naomi and Lester Senior, both of whom declined the invitation, saying they had other important matters to attend.

When the group arrived at the sanitarium, the staff had arranged a special meal in a private dining room in accordance with Phillip's request.

Dr. Comeaux had done everything he could to accommodate the occasion. However, he warned, "Martha is unpredictable, and it's not always possible to tell how

72

she will react to any situation." He also insisted that Phillip cover the cost, because, as he explained, "Our budget does not provide for this sort of thing." Phillip was agreeable and everything was set up, including a small Christmas tree and decorations.

The family entered the room in silence. Vel and Lala had never visited Martha before and did not know what to expect. Their eyes wandered around the room. Lala realized her Mama's condition was more serious than she thought, since she was confined in a place with locked, screened, and barred windows. Vel was sorry she came. Now the memory of the horrible olive-green walls surrounding her proud Mama would also be in her thoughts.

Finally, the attendant rolled Martha in, accompanied by the staff nurse. The wheelchair was parked in the center of the room, and they turned to leave. Martha called out after the nurse and said, "I want my girl to stay with me." The nurse nodded and the attendant returned to her place in back of the chair.

There was silent anticipation from the family as Martha looked from one to the other. It was clear that some effort had been made to prepare Martha's appearance for the occasion. Her hair had been pulled back in a bun, and it was grayer than anyone remembered. She wore a flowered print blouse with daisy designs that did not exactly match her dark blue flannel skirt.

Martha's eyes were opened wide and her head moved in quick, bird-like gestures, dreading danger.

Rosa slowly approached and said, "Merry Christmas, Mama."

Martha looked at her for many long seconds and finally said, "Merry Christmas! You look jes like my daughter, Rosa."

That broke the silence, and there was applause and

laughter. Rosa hugged and kissed her.

Vel came over and kissed her and said, "Merry Christmas, Mama."

The children took their turns, and Ann looked at Lala and said, "Mama, she smells like pee-pee."

"Hush, child," Lala replied.

Phillip and Lightfoot were the last to wish her greetings.

Martha seemed overwhelmed with so many visitors. Then she asked, "Why y'all call me Mama?"

Vel said, "'Cause you are our Mama, that's why."

"Who are you?"

"I'm Vel, Mama. Don't you remember?"

"Who sent you?"

"Nobody. I came to see you on my own."

"Are you sure the judge didn't send you to get my grandpa's land?"

Vel turned and looked inquiringly at Phillip. "Papa, what is she talking about?"

Martha continued, "Don't be asking him nothing. He's in on it, too. They're all after my grandpa's land and his plantation and slaves. My great-great-grandfather left that property to my family and me, and they trying to steal it, saying that we ain't white, saying that Creole people ain't supposed to have that kind of money."

Rosa knelt next to Martha's chair and took her hand. "It's all right, Mama. They are gone now. They didn't take your house."

"Is it still there?"

Tears began to well up in Rosa's eyes, and she said, "Yes, it's still there."

Fear and anguish took over Martha's face, and she asked, "Did Papa go huntin'?"

"No, ma'am."

"Well, don't let him go with that nigger Silas. He's out to kill him."

Ann tugged at Lala's sleeve, and she whispered loudly to her mother, "Mama, what is grandma talking about?"

Lala did not try to explain. "Hush, child. Be quiet."

Phillip came to the rescue with the suggestion, "Why don't we have dinner?"

Rosa went over and knelt next to Martha. "Mama, are you hungry?"

"Yea, I'll eat a little something. Where's my girl?"

The attendant looked around from the back of the chair and said, "I'm right here, Miss Martha."

"Well, what are you waiting for, nigger? Push me to the table."

Martha was placed at one end of the table, Phillip went to the opposite, and the others took various seats around. Martha began looking from one to the other as if searching for someone. Then she said in a loud inquiring voice, "Is that woman here?"

Phillip dropped his head into his hands, and with his elbows planted on the table, he slowly shook from side to side.

Martha continued, "I won't have that woman eating at my table."

"What woman are you talking about Mama?" Lala asked.

"You look jus' like that woman who plays that devil's music. Are you the woman I'm talking about?"

"No, Mama, I'm not."

Martha pointed to the children and asked, "Who's them?"

Lala said, "Mama, they're your grandchildren, Ann and Lester. They brought presents." Then to the children, she said, "Go get your presents for Grandma."

The children ran to retrieve what they had brought.

Lala said in a gentle voice, "We all brought presents. We were going to wait until after dinner, but they can give theirs now."

The children put their presents in Martha's lap, and she said in a voice reminiscent of her old self, "I remember years ago my husband got two small children for a present. Now the children bring me presents."

Lala and Phillip exchanged knowing glances.

Rosa was confused, and she asked, "Mama what are you talking about?"

Vel moved in closer to Rosa and whispered, "She just talking out of her head. She doesn't even know who we are."

Phillip overheard but was not convinced that Martha did not know what she was saying or who they were. He believed she was trying to make a point, just as he believed that Martha knew who Julee was but pretended that she was talking about another friend from her past. He was sure that she still held bitter thoughts over an incident with Lala.

Phillip remembered the time he was recuperating from the beating he got when he tried to register to vote. He woke up to hear Lala's voice in the kitchen telling Martha about her walk through the fog with the children to get away from Lester's abuse. When Phillip entered the kitchen, Lala said impulsively, in an effort to cheer him up, "Papa, I've come back, and you'll have your grandchildren as a Christmas present." Martha was so filled with jealousy and rage that she slapped Lala violently across the face.

Phillip figured that Martha was now referring to that incident, and although she was supposed to be out of her mind, she was behaving very much the same as the Martha he had known most of his life. Lala's closeness to him and her youthful beauty, which even exceeded Martha's, had always incited her resentment. His tolerance for Martha's masquerade had begun to wear thin and he said, "It's time to eat. I'll bless the table."

Dinner was eaten in silence and without much ceremony. Martha had a healthy appetite and quickly ate all of her turkey, ham, sweet potatoes, string beans, macaroni, and mustard greens. Then she pushed herself away from the table and said, "Girl, I'm ready to go back."

Rosa said, "Mama, you didn't open your presents."

Martha remarked sharply, "I'll do that later when my family comes."

"Mama, we're here now. We came to see you."

"Did you bring the baby?"

Phillip and Lightfoot exchanged glances, and Phillip closed his eyes and shook his head. Rosa remained unaffected by the question and responded, "Mama, they're not babies anymore, they almost teenagers. Aren't you going to open the presents they brought?"

"They tell me my family's coming to see me today, and I got to go and fix up for 'em." She motioned to the attendant and was wheeled out of the room.

The family stacked the presents around the tree on the table and slowly filed out.

As Lightfoot limped past Phillip, he said, "I told you."

* * *

Early the next the morning, Lala, Lester Sr., and the children came over from Frilotville to open presents and find out what Santa Claus had left at Grandpop's house. All other presents paled in comparison to the bicycles, and the children could hardly wait to eat breakfast and go outside. The opening of presents was bittersweet, as each in their own way remembered what had happened with Martha on

Christmas Eve.

Before dinner, Vel helped Ann to get prettied up in her skirt and blouse Christmas present, along with make-up and painted nails. Lala was not too happy with the young lady look imposed on her nine-year-old, but she bit her tongue and enjoyed the makeover that delighted Ann to no end.

Phillip watched, his chest filled with pride, as he realized these two were the only grandchildren he was likely to have, so he made a secret resolution with himself to spend more time getting to know them.

The whole family, including Lightfoot and Naomi, gathered for Christmas dinner prepared by Rosa, Lala, and Vel. The table was covered with the traditional turkey and dressing, ham, goose, candied sweet potatoes, macaroni and cheese, dirty rice, baked eggplant, and string beans. For dessert, there was ambrosia, coconut cake, and a choice of apple or pecan pies that were made by Naomi. Food was aplenty, and everyone had seconds except Lightfoot, who had thirds.

Ann wanted another serving of dirty rice and saw the bowl sitting in front of Naomi and she said, "Miss Nigger Woman, would you please pass the dirty rice?"

The entire table went silent.

After recovering from the shock, Phillip asked, "What did you say?"

Ann responded as any child would. "I asked Miss Nigger Woman to pass the rice."

Phillip closed his eyes.

Naomi flashed hers, gritted her teeth, and took a deep breath.

Phillip said, "Ann, come here." She was out of her seat and on her grandfather's knee in a flash.

Lala and Lester exchanged glances and dropped their heads.

Phillip put his arm around Ann's shoulder and said quietly, "Now, I want you to apologize to your Aunt Naomi for calling her a nigger. We don't use that word in this house."

Ann looked up at her grandpop with terrified eyes and then at Naomi and said, "Aunt Naomi, I'm sorry."

Naomi was silent for several seconds, then she said, "I accept your apology, Ann, but that is not a nice word."

Ann said, "I didn't know. That's what Aunt Velma said when you came in."

Phillip was furious but was able to control the tone in his voice enough to inquire, "What did Aunt Velma say?"

"She said to Aunt Rosa, 'Here comes Miss Nigger Woman.' And I thought that's what I should call Aunt Naomi. I'm sorry if I said the wrong thing." Ann began crying.

Phillip consoled her and assured her that she would be forgiven.

Then he said, "We don't use that word in this house. It's not a good word. Aunt Velma just forgot."

Ann put her arms around Phillip's neck and continued to cry.

Phillip patted her back and said, "I understand . . . Don't cry . . . Aunt Naomi understands. Don't cry."

Phillip cast a disapproving look at Vel, who wiped her mouth with her napkin and left the table.

Lala said, "Anyone for coffee?" And that was the signal that everyone should return to what was going on before.

Naomi said, "I'll have my dessert with coffee."

When Lester got his coffee, he and Naomi drifted into the parlor. Amidst the disarray of boxes, presents, and wrappings, they started a conversation about how Marie Laveau used the many rituals from the Catholic church in her practice of voodoo. Lester was surprised to discover that her use of candles, images of the saints, and rituals of sacrifice to the gods had their origin in Catholicism. They were still deeply involved in discovering similarities in religious practices when there was a knock on the front door.

Lester opened the door to Stephen Estillete and his daughter, Alexandrine, who entered bearing their traditional gift: a case of wine.

Alex was thirty-two now, only two years older than the age Bobby would have been if he had lived. She was unmarried and had blossomed into an attractive young woman who was working as a journalist on the newspaper with her father.

When he heard her voice Phillip was taken back to a conversation he overheard with Bobby and his Mama.

Martha said, "Alex is a nice girl."

Bobby stopped on the stair, "Yeah, she sure is."

"Did you two see a lot of each other while she was in Nashville?"

"Some, but not much."

"You might think about going to visit her in Chicago."

"Mama, I . . ."

Martha interrupted, "Y'all been friends since you stayed over at her house. And I know y'all talked on the phone a lot before going off to school. It sure would be nice to bring our families together. I know it's kinda hard to get together around here, but up there in Chicago…"

"Mama, I got some homework to finish."

"I know. Just go on up and do your work. But don't forget what I said. And remember your grandfather was Creole, and that's just as good as white."

Phillip kept his head buried in his book and pretended not to have paid attention to the exchange between Bobby and Martha. Bobby headed on up to his room, and Martha stood at the bottom of stairs, shaking her head. Phillip knew she was disappointed because Bobby didn't seem to be too anxious about getting serious with Alex. It would have been Martha's greatest joy to have the families merged; she wanted to somehow get back title to at least some of the property taken by the Estilettes.

Phillip exchanged hugs with Stephen and kissed Alex. No one was more pleased to welcome them than Phillip. The singing of carols, and the drinking of eggnog, bourbon, and wine carried the celebration far into the evening hours.

Chapter 6

Promises Promises

955 - Ann came running into the den yelling, "Grandpop, Les is gettin' ready to jump off the top of the house!"

Phillip went outside in time to see Les fly from the porch roof, on a rope tied to a tree, screaming like an ape. At the end of his travel across the yard, he let go of the rope and dove into a mountain of hay. When he came up from his burial in straw, Phillip was waiting for him.

"Boy, have you lost your mind?" Phillip yelled.

"No, sir."

"Then what do you call yourself doing?"

"Playing Tarzan."

"Now you take all of this hay and put it back into that wagon. And when you've finished, come on in the house."

"Yes, sir."

Phillip headed to the house with Ann running to keep up. Finally, she reached and grabbed his hand while he mounted the steps. She held on tightly until he had returned to his desk. Then she settled on the floor and looked up at him.

Her silent stare was disturbing, and Phillip looked down from his book and asked, "What?"

That was the only enticement that Ann needed. She crawled into his lap, took off his glasses, and asked, "Grandpop, are you gonna whip Les?"

"Do you think I should?"

"Yes."

"Why."

"Cause he's bad."

"Was it bad for him to do what he did?"

This was a question Ann had not yet made up her mind about, but after a few seconds she said slowly, "Yeeeeea."

"I think what he did was more dangerous than bad."

"Why?"

"Because he could have fallen and hurt himself, and then we would have to take him to the hospital and get his broken leg fixed."

"Ohhhh, I didn't think about that."

"That's all right." He kissed her, lifted her down to the floor, and said, "Go tell your Aunt Rosa to make us some lunch." With a loving swat on her bottom as a send-off, she ran out, yelling for Rosa. Phillip smiled, returned his glasses to his eyes, and watched as she disappeared from the room.

Lester and Lala had agreed that the children could spend the weekends with Phillip. He was delighted, and they were relieved, because Les and Ann had reached the age when parents are driven stark raving mad by growing youngsters making their discoveries of life.

Saturdays were the start of their holiday from school time to spend with Grandpop. They got up early and rode their bicycles the five miles to Estilette. The next two days were spent doing things they liked and couldn't do at home. Phillip took them with him wherever he went, and always they would get *lagniappe,* the traditional something extra and for free; the candy and goodies that store keepers gave to the children of their customers. Every weekend brought a new trial of Phillip's patience and another challenge to his ingenuity as a teacher and a grandfather.

Ann ran back in, yelling, "Grandpop, lunch is ready!"

When Phillip entered the kitchen, Les was stuffing the last bite of his peanut butter and jelly sandwich into his mouth, and at the same time he called out, "Aunt Rosa, that was good enough for another." Then Les drained his glass of milk.

Phillip watched and called out, "Aunt Rosa, the boy needs another glass of milk." Phillip chuckled as he sat down in front of his bologna sandwich.

Ann placed herself on Grandpop's knee as she pulled her sandwich plate closer. She turned and looked directly into Phillip's face and asked, "Grandpop, are you gonna whip Les for being dangerous?"

Phillip laughed and said, "Girl, go sit over there."

As she moved with her plate to the space next to Les, he pushed her into the chair.

Phillip said, "Just settle down, Les, we'll have none of that."

Ann stuck out her tongue as she picked up her peanut butter and jelly.

Rosa approached the table with the extra sandwich and milk. Phillip shook his head and chuckled, and Rosa laughed and asked, "What's going on in here?"

Phillip answered, "Just growing up." Then he put his hand on Les' head and said, "Boy, I've got to talk to you. What do you say we go fishing after lunch?"

Les responded with a loud, "O.K."

Ann wanted to know if she could go along.

Phillip caught Rosa's eye, and she said, "I was planning to make some candy and thought you might want to help me."

Ann responded with a loud, "Yeah, that's more fun than fishing anyway."

* * *

Ann chopped the pecans, while Rosa prepared and measured the milk, sugar, and butter.

There was a knock on the door. Rosa opened it to a pleasant-looking man with a broad smile on his face and wearing the aroma of Jockey Club.

"Why, Mr. Joshua What are you doing here?"

He took off his hat and held it respectively in front of his waist with both hands. He said, "I just thought I'd stop by to see if I could buy some more of your fudge."

Rosa was flattered and embarrassed. She laughed and covered her mouth with her hand. "Now it wasn't really that good, was it?"

"Miss Rosa, that was the best fudge I've ever tasted. I said to myself, she oughta go into business selling this."

"Oh, I just do it to raise money for the church."

"Well, it's good. Real good. You might remember that I came back and bought a dollar's worth."

Smiling with appreciation, Rosa said, "I do remember. And that's how we met. I was flattered to know the name of somebody who thought my candy was that good."

Rosa felt the small fingers slip into her hand, and she looked down and said, "Oh, Mr. Joshua, er. . . I don't even know your last name..."

"Kane. But my friends call me Sugar."

Rosa laughed, embarrassed. "Oh, I'll just call you Mr.

Kane. Meet my niece, Ann. Ann this is Mr. Joshua Kane."

"How do, young lady. You sure are pretty."

Ann looked up at him and said, "And you're sweet."

Rosa and Josh laughed. Ann ran out of the room, yelling, "I've finished the pecans."

"Well, I see you're busy with other things. I apologize for bothering you, but I just stopped by to see if you had any more of that candy."

"I'm making some for my niece right now. I'll save you a taste if you'd like."

"I was looking to buy some."

"Oh, that's not necessary. I'd be happy to give you some. It won't be ready for a while. If you'd like to drop back by later on…."

"I'll be back, Miss Rosa, just say when."

"On second thought, I could bring it to church tomorrow, so you wouldn't have to come back. Are you planning to be there?"

"Come to think of it, I was. Yeah, that'll be fine. I'll see you at church." With that, Joshua put on his hat, arranged it in a stylish angle with a graceful pass of his fingers on the brim, turned and left.

Rosa closed the door and went to the window and peeped out as he got into his pink Cadillac car. He was new to Estilette. She had seen him at church a couple of times before the Sunday he bought the candy. It didn't seem he had any relatives or knew anybody because each time he was alone. He was friendly and had a good smile. He didn't dress like the other men around town. He wore a coat and a tie. And the car he drove was expensive. She thought of what his friends called him, "Sugar Kane," and she laughed out loud to herself.

"Aunt Rosa, what are you doing?"

Rosa turned loose the curtain and turned to face Ann.

"Nothing, I'm coming."

* * *

Every now and then, a slight breeze brought relief from the afternoon sun. Phillip and Les sat under the same pecan tree that had been Bobby's favorite spot to fish. This was not the first time Phillip had taken Les fishing. For him, it was like being with Bobby all over again, and this was something he looked forward to, usually after the admonition, "Boy, I've got to talk to you."

Today, there was more quiet time than talk. On other days, Phillip talked mostly about Bobby, how he became a doctor and was on the brink of a bright and wonderful future when God took him away. Sometimes, Les got the feeling that his grandfather was trying to talk him into being a doctor. But rather than saying it outright, Phillip just talked about how much he had looked forward to having a doctor in the family since he was not able to be one himself.

The other things Phillip talked about were the goings-on in the world--segregation and what white people did to keep Negroes from getting a good education and good jobs.

Phillip tied his catch to the others and dropped the full string into the water.

As he re-baited his hook, Les said, "O.K. Grandpop, tell me some more about Bessie Smith."

Phillip thought he had told him all he knew, but evidently Les wanted to hear it again. He wasn't like Bobby. Bobby would sit and listen and soak it up like a sponge, but Les was always challenging, asking questions and wanting to hear stuff over again. Phillip couldn't tell whether this was a good thing or not; maybe Les didn't learn too fast, or maybe he just liked to hear his grandfather talk. At any rate, Phillip liked his inquiring mind—that was a good thing to have as a doctor.

Phillip took off his glasses, leaned his head back against the tree and began.

"She was one of the first women blues singers, toured the back roads of Mississippi and the Delta singing in juke joints, and made a lot of records in the twenties. She learned everything she knew about singing the blues from Ma Rainey. Now if you want to know about Ma Rainey, you've got to ask Mr. BoBo. He knew her personally and heard her sing the *Black Bottom Blues.*"

"Why they call it the blues?"

"You know how you feel down sometimes, kind of sad and gloomy?"

Les knowingly nodded his head.

Phillip put back on his glasses, ran his hand over his chin and continued, "Well, that's called melancholy. Back then, that's the way Negroes felt most of the time. It came out of slavery and hard times. In the early days, the slaves sang stories from the Bible in songs they called 'spirituals.' And then they made up songs, which helped them work in a rhythm, and that made what they had to do seem less of a burden, and they called those 'work songs.' After slavery, colored people didn't have much work--no home, no job, nothing to call their own, and they worked for the white man, who gave little pay and a hard way to go. So in order to keep from feeling sad all the time, they sang away their trials and tribulations. Their sad and gloomy feelings were sung as stories about the man--stories about the good women and the evil women, stories about the good times and the bad times, stories about the dreams and wishes of their hearts. And they played the music to those stories on the guitar and the harmonica, and they called it 'the blues.' It made both the player and the listener feel better. It's impossible to listen to the blues and feel sad. It makes you feel *good*."

Les smiled and threw his line out into the water, and Phillip figured this was as good a time as any to say what he came fishing to say.

He continued, "You've got to stop pushing and punching your sister."

"Whatcha talking about, Grandpop?"

"At the table today, you pushed her down into the chair. A real man does not man-handle women."

As the words left Phillip's mouth, he remembered the time he raised his hand to Martha. He saw once again the looks on the faces of his children. It was horrifying. That was an image he did not want repeated. That was also the very first time in his life he had raised his hand to his wife, although he had wanted to several times. He knew many men did strike women, including his father and Les' father. He didn't want Les to grow up like that; he wanted him to know it was wrong.

Les said immediately, "I was just playing."

"That's fine, but mind you, don't get in the habit of hitting and pushing your sister or any other woman for that matter. Women are special. They are the ones who carry and birth the babies, and because of that, they have a very special relationship with us men. I know they can be trying sometimes, and it seems to be in their nature, but you should remember a real man does not hit a woman."

"I'll remember, Grandpop."

"And I want you to remember something else. I'm an old man, and it makes my heart skip a beat when I see you swing off the roof like that."

"You won't see me do that again, Grandpop."

With that, Phillip returned to his fishing, feeling confident that Les was open to suggestions about his behavior. If only he could be sure that the idea to be a doctor was getting through, but there was still enough time for that to happen.

* * *

As Ann tested her fourth piece, and as Rosa piled the last of the fudge on the plate, there was a knock on the door. Rosa wiped her hands on her apron as she headed out of the kitchen.

"I told that man I'd bring it to church tomorrow."

The woman standing in the opened doorway with two suitcases smiled sweetly and said, "Hi."

Rosa's mouth dropped open. She held out her arms and said, "Ruth!" Then she kissed her and said, "Girl, I haven't seen you since the accident!"

"It's been a long time," Ruth said.

"How are you?"

Before Ruth could answer, Rosa continued, "You look great! C'mon in and sit down." Rosa led the way to the parlor, hanging on to her arm as if afraid Ruth would fly away.

Ruth looked around and asked, "Where's Papa?"

"Fishing."

"I might have known."

Ann came running in, chewing a mouth full of candy.

Rosa said, "Girl, you've had enough. Come and say hello to your Aunt Ruth."

Ann stopped, took a step backwards, swallowed, and questioned, "Aunt Ruth?"

"Yeah, you were too young to remember. She was married to your Mama's brother."

Ann's eyes widened. "Uncle Bobby?"

"Yes."

"He's dead." Ann said it so matter-of-factly that it brought a new sorrow to Ruth's face.

Ruth opened her arms and said, "Yes, we know, darling. Now come give Aunt Ruth a kiss."

Ann embraced her new-found relative, sat on Ruth's lap, and began an interrogation. "Where do you live?"

"Virginia."

"Virginia is a person not a place."

"Yes, darling, I know. It's also a state that's far away from here. But soon I'll be living here in Louisiana."

Rosa dropped to the sofa, clutching her apron. "Girl, tell me what's going on."

"I've been offered a job at Southern."

Rosa burst into tears. Between sniffles and wiping her eyes with the apron, she said, "You can stay here. I know Papa is gonna love this. You gotta tell him right away."

"Is he fishing in the usual place?"

"Where else?"

"I'm gonna change and go out there."

"You can change in Bobby's room. I'll help you with your bags."

The women headed upstairs, with Rosa still giving instructions. "Be sure to wear a hat 'cause that sun will dry out your hair. After you change, come on down and taste the candy that Ann just made."

* * *

Les had taken off his high-top canvas shoes and was sliding his feet through the clover. He liked the feel of flowers breaking between his toes. He sat next to his pole, held in place by a pile of rocks, picked the flowers out of his toes, gathered them into a bunch, brought them to his nose, and then flipped them into the air, where they were caught by the breeze and scattered over the water.

Phillip watched the current carry the flowers out of sight. He looked at Les. "How old are you, boy?"

"Twelve."

"Have you decided what you are going to be when you grow up?"

"Not yet."

"What do you like to do?"

"Have fun."

"Having fun is nice, but you can't make a living doing that."

"The people in the movies do."

"Oh, that's just an illusion, plus they're white. You don't see any Negroes in the movies."

"No, but I'm gonna change that." Then Les stood up like he was on stage and began reciting:

"To Be a Leader. What is that to be?

To stand between a people and their foe and earn suspicion for gaining a recompense.

To care for men more than they care for themselves.

To keep a clear, discriminating mind between the better counsel and the best.

To be a judge of men that none may rank in estimation higher than his worth or fail of scope to prove his quality.

To search the motive that explains the act before it is accounted good or bad.

To trust a man and yet not be dismayed to find him faithless, going on to trust another.

To build up failure into the tedious structure of success.

To labor through the day and through the night.

To watch and plan and exercise by prayer the devil troop of doubt that teases the will while selfish little critic parasites heckle and plot and spread malignant lies.

To have a body that endures the strain of labor after labor, each in turn deserving more nerve than hardihood.

To walk through trouble with a heart that drips the blood of agony and yet with a face of confidence and bright encouragement.

To do and do and die to raise a tribe so robbed and bound and ignorantly weak that God himself conceals their destiny.

To be a leader? God, that is the price."

Then a voice came from behind, and said, "Leslie Pinckney Hill."

Phillip and Les were startled. They turned and saw Ruth standing next to the tree.

Phillip was up in an instant and hugged her without another word. After the embrace, he said, "You're back."

"Yes, I'm back."

"You look great. I'm so glad to see you."

Les was standing there with questioning eyes. *Who is this chocolate-colored lady that Grandpop likes so much? I wonder how she knew who wrote the poem?*

Phillip said, "This is my grandson, Les. He's Lala's boy. Les, this is your Uncle Bobby's wife, Aunt Ruth."

Les approached with his hand extended. "I'm pleased to meet ya."

Ruth returned the handshake, and said, "I just met your sister."

Phillip added, "Isn't she's something else?"

"She sure is, and so is he. He did a marvelous job in

93

reciting *To Be A Leader*." She turned to Les, "Where did you learn that?"

"In school. My teacher gave it to me to recite for assembly. How did you know who wrote it?"

"Dr. Hill is from Lynchburg, Virginia, and he's a friend of my father's. He teaches in Pennsylvania now."

Phillip said, like the educator he was, "See that boy, you just met a lady who knows the man who wrote the poem." He turned to Ruth, "He's smart, he'll make a good doctor."

There it was again, the suggestion to be a doctor. Les was now sure that Grandpop wanted him to follow in the footsteps of Uncle Bobby. Les, however, was not interested in making sick people well.

"Grandpop, I told you I'm going to be a movie actor."

Phillip smiled, and in an apologetic voice, he looked over at Ruth and said, "I'm still trying to inspire another doctor in the family."

Ruth laughed. "He's young yet. He has plenty of time to think about that."

At that moment, a stiff breeze blew off her hat and it rolled into the bayou.

Les said, "I'll get it."

As quick as lightning, he slipped out of his pants, took off his shirt on the run, threw it back over his shoulder, and dived into the muddy water.

Phillip made a lurching motion in his direction, but he stopped on the edge of the stream, remembering he couldn't swim.

Les caught up to the rapidly floating hat, put it on his head, turned around, and easily stroked back to the bank. He strolled to where Phillip and Ruth were standing, took the hat off his head, and presented it with, "It got a little wet."

Ruth planted a kiss on his cheek and said, "My, aren't you a gentleman. Thank you!"

The embarrassed Les shook the water from his arms and went to retrieve his clothes. Ruth's eyes followed admiringly. His naked body, clothed only in his underpants, glistened in the sun, and she compared him to Bobby. Les was already as well developed and as tall as she remembered Bobby was. *What a handsome man he will be,* she thought.

She turned to Phillip and said, "He's a fine boy." And in a whispered comment to Phillip, she said, "He may yet be a doctor like his uncle. Don't give up hope."

Phillip's responded, "Yes, he *is* a fine boy. Got his mother's good looks and is built like his daddy, strong and sturdy."

Then he raised his voice in Les' direction. "Boy, where did you learn to swim?"

"My daddy taught me."

"Where'd he learn?"

"Kansas City, at the YMCA."

Phillip realized how many simple pleasures of life were denied to Negroes who lived in the South. Very few men he knew could swim. There was no place for them to learn unless they threw caution to the wind and braved the snake and alligator infested bayous and streams, and only the very brave or foolhardy took that risk.

Les continued, "He taught me in that pond on our place."

Phillip went back to his spot under the pecan tree. Ruth followed and sat on the ground next to him. He looked lovingly at her, remembering all the pain and suffering she had gone through. He could not help but think about Martha's confession of trying to kill her. This was the first time he had seen Ruth since he had taken her back to

Petersburg in '52. She looked healthy and well and did not show any signs of ailment from the accident. He did not want to bring up the subject for fear that he might say something that would reveal the accident was not an accident.

He asked softly, "What brings you back to these parts?"

"Next week I have an interview with Dr. Felton Clark. I've been offered a position on the faculty."

Phillip was overcome with joy. He closed his eyes, leaned his head back against the tree, and yelled, "Glory hallelujah!"

Les turned his attention away from his fishing pole and asked, "What's wrong?"

"Nothing. Everything's right. Your Aunt Ruth is going to be teaching at Southern University."

Les added, "So, you're a teacher just like Grandpop."

"No! Better than me. She's got a PhD in Biology. Used to teach your Uncle Bobby at Fisk University." Then he turned to Ruth. "When do you start?"

"This September if all goes well."

He seriously questioned, "What do you mean, 'if all goes well'?"

"We're still negotiating a salary."

"Well, I wish you luck. Felton has to spread his budget over a lot of ground. His daddy left him a big job, and those white people on the board keep him begging for money." After that, Phillip was silent. He didn't want to bring rain to her hope.

Ruth let her hand skim along the top of the clover, and she picked a flower and twirled it between her thumb and forefinger. Her face was solemn, and her eyes were fixed in a distant gaze across Bayou Courtableau.

She asked softly, "How is Martha?"

"You've heard?"

"Yes. That was the only thing the taxi driver talked about after I told him I was going to the Fergerson house."

Phillip knew her ears had heard as much gossip as necessary to fill the time between the train depot and the house, and he felt she needed to hear some truth. "She's not too well. She's been in the asylum almost a year."

"That long?"

"Time does pass, and it doesn't seem she's made much progress. Did Rosa tell you anything?"

"I didn't ask. I figured that it would be a very emotional subject for her, so I thought I'd wait and talk to you. What happened?"

Phillip was hoping this question would not be asked. But now that it had been, what should he say? He wanted to tell the truth, but he could not say anything about Martha's confession, and he had to be careful not to give any indication that Martha's breakdown had any relation to the accident. The best that he could do was concentrate on the flagellation. He took off his glasses and rubbed his eyes, and cleared his throat. After taking a deep breath he began.

"Her mind just snapped. Why? I don't know. I do know that Martha never got over her papa's suicide, although she never allowed herself to admit the truth about how he died. And on top of that, the loss of her family estate constantly nagged her mind. Other than that I don't know why."

"How sad."

Phillip watched as Les moved to another fishing spot some distance away out of earshot of what he was about to tell Ruth. He continued.

"I came home one night to the horror of what she had done to herself. She was hanging on to the kneeler in front of her altar full of lighted candles. A buggy whip was dangling from her hand and her back and buttocks had been whipped bloody. I put her in the bed and Rosa and I treated her wounds as best we could. I called the doctor and he did a full examination. Afterwards, he said that her mind had snapped, and she would have to be institutionalized. Rosa took that hard, but after a while she calmed down."

"Ruth said quietly, I'm sorry." Then she wiped her eyes with the back of a finger, and she talked about what Bobby had told her about Martha.

"Right after he discovered how sick he really was with meningitis, he told me there were some things he wanted me to know. I'll never forget that. He was in Homer G. Phillips Hospital in Kansas City."

Phillip said, "I remember."

"I had just arrived from Nashville a few days earlier. He held my hand and told me there were some things that he wanted to say. I said, 'Don't bother with that right now. You can tell me later.'"

"He said, 'I might not have a later. So I want to say what I have to say while I can.'"

"I kissed him and said, 'Go ahead.' "

"Bobby said, 'I love my Mama very much, but she has disappointed me because she does not like people with dark skin.' "

"I said to him, 'This is a shock for me to hear, because when we went to visit after our marriage, she was very nice and I did not suspect anything of that kind.' "

"Then Bobby continued, 'I'm not surprised, because Mama has a way of concealing her true feelings. But she wanted me to marry a white girl from Estilette whose family is very rich. When I married you, she was disappointed, and she told me as much. So I want you to know this in case anything happens to me. I also want you to know that my papa is just the opposite, so I'd like it if you got to know him. He will make up for some of the feelings of love that you will not get from my mama.' "

Phillip's eyes were moist. He reached over and took her hand and kissed it. "Thank you for sharing that."

After a moment of silence, Phillip said, "The white girl Martha was hoping he'd marry is the daughter of my friend Stephen Estilette. It was Stephen's great-great-grandfather who took Martha's family estate and Martha hoped and prayed for the day when the wealth would be returned. She believed that a marriage of the families would do that."

Ruth's eyes widen and her mouth dropped open but uttered no sound.

Phillip continued, "As incredible as it sounds, Martha was obsessed with the idea."

Ruth went on to tell about the love expressed between them in the final days of Bobby's life, the moments when souls are revealed in complete nakedness, and how after his death, she wanted to live in Bobby's space to continue feeling his love and get to know his family. How she picked Martha's favorite flowers every morning hoping that the gift would express her love and joy as a new member of the family. She had no expectation that the act of gathering flowers would put her in harms way.

She said, "I wish now that I had apologized to Martha for being in the wrong place when she drove back from church. Perhaps it would have made a difference."

Ruth's eyes were now focused on the space across the bayou, but Phillip could tell from the tears in her voice that there were tears in her eyes. Although Phillip understood Ruth's good intentions, he seriously doubted if forgiveness would have made a difference to Martha. But he felt, from what she had said, that Ruth had a slight suspicion the accident may not have been an accident. He was convinced now, more than ever, that Martha's confession must remain a secret.

For a long while, neither of them said anything; they

allowed the peace of the place to bathe over them like warm sunshine.

Les yelled, "I got another one!" He pulled up a two-pound catfish, swung it over the bank, and let it flop around in the clover.

Phillip yelled back, "That'll do it for the day. We've caught enough."

After Les put his catch with the others, he stretched out on the ground at his grandfather's feet, focused his eyes on the slowly moving clouds, and listened to the small talk between Phillip and Ruth.

Ruth told about some lady named Althea Gibson who had just won a tennis game over in England at a place called Wimbledon. It seemed like a big deal because she was the first Negro to ever do something like that. They both knew a lot about a woman named Rosa Parks, who sat down in the white section on a bus and caused a lot of commotion, and about a preacher named King, who was heading up an organization to fight segregation.

A cloud formation of a large ship, followed by a flock of sheep, sailed by, and Les' eyelids began to droop. The last thing he heard before they closed shut was about a Negro band leader named Count Basie playing for the first time at a place called the Waldorf-Astoria in New York City.

* * *

In September, Ruth had finally negotiated her contract with Dr. Felton Clark by a compromise that both felt satisfied with--she would accept less salary, and the university would provide campus housing at no cost.

The renovation of her apartment would not be completed for thirty days, and in the meantime, she stayed with the Fergersons. This required a fifty-mile drive twice a day in Phillip's car, which he let her use until she could get one of her own. Phillip was thrilled to have Ruth in the house again, and without Martha around to throw a veil of secrecy over conversation, they enjoyed the exchange of ideas on just about everything.

Rosa also enjoyed Ruth's being there, especially on the weekends when the two ladies had time to visit without the expectation of having to meet schedules. Ruth soon became her confidant, a relationship that Rosa had missed since Father Pat's death. She had enjoyed revealing her soul and sharing secret thoughts with him. And now that her Mama was in the hospital, there was no one to talk intimate feelings with, so Rosa felt Ruth was a godsend.

"Girl, this man is too good to be true. He's about my age, in his late thirties, and he's from Chicago. He came here to get away from the sin of the big city, and he sells insurance for North Carolina Mutual. He dresses like a professor, wears a shirt, coat, and tie, and smells divine, and when he goes to church, he wears a suit. He's got a nice smile. He's not like any of the men around here. He's got ideas and ambitions, and he's interesting. He loves my candy, and guess what?"

Ruth was listening carefully, seeking to find the blemish in the too-good-to-be-true man that Rosa was taken with. She asked sincerely, "What?"

"He wants to sell my candy."

"You're kidding!"

"No. He loves it! He thinks it is the best he's ever eaten, and he thinks we can make lots of money."

"How does he propose to do this?"

"Well, I don't really understand all of what he says, but he plans to get some people to invest money in what he calls 'the development of the product.' Then, with that money, we'll package, advertise, and sell the candy all over."

Ruth was still trying to get the whole picture. She continued to ask questions. "And who would manage all of this?"

Rosa said without thinking, "Sugar."

"Sugar who?"

Rosa laughed, "Ohhhhh, did I say Sugar? I'm sorry, I meant to say, Joshua Kane, that's his name. I get so confused with all of this sweet stuff. The name of the candy is *Sweet Rosa's Fudge*. He thinks the fudge is better than the pralines. But I told him I like the pralines better, and he says that maybe later on we can sell both, but we should start with the fudge."

Rosa went on a mile a minute. She closed her eyes and giggled like a schoolgirl.

Ruth perceived how naive she really was. "How do you feel about this man?"

"What do you mean?"

"Do you like him?"

"I like him a lot. He's nice, and I like the way he talks, and he dresses attractively, wears his hat cocked to one side, and he's got a good smile."

Ruth continued to probe. "Do you like him as a boyfriend?"

"Oh, Ruth. I don't think of him like that. And I don't think he thinks of me like that. He wants us to go into business."

Ruth began to feel she had a pretty good picture of the situation. The man sounded like a wheeler-dealer looking for another way to make money. However, she felt Rosa would not see him the same, so she decided that she would not express an opinion.

She said, "Well this guy certainly sounds interesting."

"He is." And in a flash Rosa changed the subject. "Have you found anyone interesting since Bobby died?"

Ruth was blindsided. This question was obviously triggered by their conversation about the Kane fellow, and it was now clear to Ruth that Rosa's interest in this man went deeper than business, although Rosa tried her best to conceal her true feelings. Ruth did not want to have this conversation any longer. She yawned and pretended she was tired.

"Can we talk later? A wave of tiredness has just come over me. With this driving back and forth all week, I'm all worn out."

"Oh, I'm sorry. I'm just going on and on with all this talk. You just go on up and get some rest. When you come down, I'll have something for you to eat."

Chapter 7

Strange Bedfellows

1958 - The hoola hoop was the craze of the land. Martin Luther King had been stabbed by a crazy woman. There was scandal in the Eisenhower administration over a vicuña coat, which caused Sherman Adams, chief of staff, to resign his post. The affluent society was not as well off as it thought. Elvis Presley was inducted into the Army, and nothing was as it seemed or as one wanted it to be.

Years earlier when Martha paid BookTau to burn down Lightfoot's tavern, incensed because he had allowed Lala to play the devil's music in what she considered a "den of sin," she unknowingly laid the foundation for a bigger and better blues joint.

Out of the ashes, Lightfoot built the Black Eagle. The stage was elevated in the center of the back wall, and it didn't matter where anyone sat or stood; all could see the musicians. A large dance floor was in front of the stage, and tables were arranged on three sides, with a railing separating the dancers from the table area, so everyone was happy and comfortable in their own space. The toilets were inside, a great improvement over the outhouses of '44. And Naomi now had a kitchen where she could fix fried catfish, shrimp, chicken, potato salad, hush puppies, and cole slaw. In the shadow of the old tavern was the shining light of the blue's whirl, and Phillip had his own special table, honored by the waiters, whenever he attended.

The Black Eagle attracted blues lovers from most nearby cities: Opelousas, Lafayette, Crowley, Alexandria, Baton Rouge, and even New Orleans. It was the crownpiece for any blues musician worth his salt. The blues singer Otis Hicks, who took the name Lightnin' Slim, was the regular musician for the quiet country church suppers in Crowley, but when Lightfoot made the offer for a weekend gig playing for a let-the-good-times-roll audience at the Black Eagle, he jumped at the chance.

Phillip suggested to Alicia that they attend the Lightnin' Slim opening.

Alicia had been secluded as the other woman so long she had begun to take on the characteristics of a she-wolf, and when Phillip had his fill of bitchiness, he would take her out to a late-night movie or to a quiet dinner in an out-of-the-way all-night chicken shack. Now, all of a sudden, he didn't care if they were seen together in public. Alicia was delighted to get out of the house for some fun and thankful that Phillip's feelings of guilt seemed to be fading away. However, she hadn't heard the gossip on the lips of the people in Estilette: "Since Martha is in the crazy house, it's all right for Phillip to have his woman, since his wife can no longer be a wife" And after Martha had insulted Julee, and confessed her criminal activity, Phillip had lost all hope that Martha would ever recover.

From the moment they settled at his table, Phillip's friends came over and one by one, introduced themselves and made Alicia feel welcome. Phillip smiled. He and Alicia let the good times roll. They danced the belly rub, yelled and cheered, clapped their hands, and popped their fingers. The townspeople were amazed and delighted to see "the professor" get down.

The joint was jumping, and Lightnin' Slim was in a groove and on cloud nine because he had gotten away from the straight-laced church supper crowd for the weekend.

At intermission, while waiting for the waiter to bring their order, Alicia noticed a smiling man going from table to table. She took a sip of gin and tonic, leaned over close to Phillip's face, and said, "He's headed this way."

"Who?"

"That man."

"What man?"

Phillip turned to look, and through clinched teeth Alicia said, "Don't look now, he's right here."

Joshua Kane approached their table. "Good evening, folks. Can I have a word with you?" He was moving to sit before Alicia could make a response. She did anyway. "Have a seat."

He extended his hand, first to Alicia and then to Phillip, "My name is Joshua Kane, and I have a proposition that I think you will find irresistible."

Alicia placed her elbows on the table and leaned toward the man, *"Irresistible? Proposition?"*

"Yes, ma'am. But before I tell you what I'm talking about, how did you folks like Lightnin' Slim?"

Phillip was already getting annoyed by the intrusion and said, "He's O.K., now what do you have to say?"

Joshua put a piece of fudge wrapped in waxed paper on the table and said, "Taste that and tell me how you like it."

Alicia unwrapped the candy, "O.K., I'll try it." She took a bite and then placed it in Phillip's mouth and said, "You try it."

Phillip said, "It's good."

And before Joshua could say another word. Alicia remarked, "So you've got a good piece of candy, so what?"

"I know it's good, too. How would you like to make money selling it?"

Phillip was getting impatient. "Look Mister. . . what's your name?"

Alicia interrupted, "Mr. Kane."

Joshua said, "Just call me Joshua."

Phillip continued, "Well Joshua, what do you have in mind?"

"Marketing this candy all over." Joshua leaned in closer. "My associate and I need some capital so we can produce, package, and put this candy in stores all over Louisiana. All you have to do is invest $100 dollars, and you'll get back 15 cents for every dollar."

Phillip's patience was wearing thin. "Now let me get this straight. You want $100 dollars so you and whomever can make and sell this candy and I'm going to get back one hundred fifteen dollars? That's fifteen percent profit."

"You got that right."

"Who's going to make this candy?"

"The best candy maker in Estilette. Rosa Fergerson!"

Phillip's eyes widened and his lips tightened. Alicia kicked him under the table and quickly said, "Well, Joshua, we'll think about it. How do we get in touch?"

Joshua handed her a card. "You can reach me at this number."

"If we decide, we will. Thank you."

Joshua got up, took another piece of fudge out of his coat pocket, and said, "Have another piece on me. It was nice talking to you folks."

Phillip watched him move on to another table then

shifted his eyes to Alicia and said, "What the hell is going on here?"

"I don't know. That's why I kicked you. If you want to find out, you can't let him know who you are."

"I've never seen that man before. He must be new in town."

The waiter brought their order. "Here you are, 'fessor. Sorry it took so long, but Naomi's gone, and we kinda short handed in the kitchen."

Phillip flipped his thumb in the direction that Joshua had gone. "Who's that man?"

The waiter looked, "Don't know. Never seem him before."

"Tell Lightfoot to come here."

The waiter left and Alicia said as she peeled a shrimp, "What are you planning?"

"I'm going to find out who he is and what he's up to."

"Why don't you ask Rosa?"

"I plan to do that, too."

Phillip had just bitten into an ear of corn when Lightfoot sat at the table. "What's up?"

"See that man over there?" Phillip turned in the direction that Joshua went. He scanned the area, but the man was nowhere to be seen. "He was right over there a minute ago. Anyway, he came over here with a piece of Rosa's candy and wanted me to invest money so he could sell it."

"Well, I'll be damned. Did he know who you are?"

"No, and I don't know what he's up to, but I'm going to find out. His name is Joshua Kane."

Lightfoot said, "I'll check him out. Slick Waters knows every dude who comes to town."

Then Lightfoot asked, "How do y'all like Slim?"

Alicia answered, "He's all right. Knows how to get

down. I just love his *Lonesome Cabin* and the *Voodoo Blues*. His style kinda reminds me of Lightnin' Hopkins."

"That's true, and I think Otis Hicks kinda borrowed Lightnin's name, too." Lightfoot chuckled as he got up to leave.

Phillip asked, "Where's Naomi? Bud says she took the night off."

Lightfoot dropped back into his seat with a frown on his face. "Yeah, that pissed me off. She's back at that voodoo shit again. Said she's got a powerful hex to fix and it's a full moon. She left me shorthanded, and everything's backing up. I gotta go. It's intermission, and I gotta play."

* * *

The Teche thicket was located on the edge of a bayou, several miles away from Estilette, down a narrow winding road surrounded by a heavy growth of trees and brush. The road ended in a clearing large enough for a sagging shack that was the home for chickens, pigs, dogs, and cows. It was the same place that Martha had taken Rosa for the abortion--the home of Tante.

The old woman with a withered face and primeval bony hands sat on the porch in the dark. The flickering light from the fire danced on the walls of her cabin, casting weird images of the voodoo dancers. She took long, slow drags from her corncob pipe and listened to the heart-beat sounds of the drum. She knew about casting spells and voodoo and all, so when Naomi said she wanted to have a wanga on her place she had some doubts. A wanga was terrible. It was the strongest voodoo hex--black magic against an enemy. She had heard tell that Marie Laveau could call down the spirits to avenge a debt or right a wrong, so she figured that maybe Naomi could do the same thing. At least she was persuasive enough to overcome the doubts that Tante had in the beginning.

Tante thought back over what had transpired after Naomi got out of the truck and sashayed up to the porch.

Naomi said, "There're people who need my spirit-force to solve their problems, and your Teche thicket, is the perfect place."

Tante replied, "I nevah believed in your hocus-pocus stuff myself. All I do out here is my midwifery thing. I just heps out the women folks who don't wanna keep the fruits of their frolic."

"It don't matter to me what you believe about what I do, old lady, but it might be worth your while to change your mind."

Tante looked past Naomi at the truck in the clearing, turned her face away and spit out tobacco juice. "How many peoples you got wid you?"

Naomi was getting a bit impatient. She took a deep breath, and said, "Two girls and a drummer."

"Lemme think on it." Tante walked away, stooped down on her haunches, closed her eyes and after a few minutes, returned to complete negotiations.

Now, as the smoke from her pipe commingled with the smoke from the fire, she chuckled, and said to herself, "It don't pay to be too easy, you gotta be tough." She smiled as she slipped the roll of money that Naomi had paid to use her place, into her bra.

At first, the drumming from SipZu was constant and unchanging. Now the beat got faster and stirred Tante's curiosity. Tante had seen him before, hanging out around the Sugar Patch pool hall whenever she went into Estilette.

He was a strange one, a big fellow, black as tar, with a strong muscular body that moved like an eagle gliding through the air. He worked at the King Cotton Hotel as a bus boy during the day and at night danced and played drums for any voodoo rite that wanted him. All anybody ever called him was SipZu, and nobody knew where he or the name came from.

Tante left the porch drawn by the sound of the drumbeat. A full moon lit her path through the briars and cocklebur. When she reached the clearing where the fire raged, she stopped behind an ancient oak and watched the carryings-on from the concealment of the hanging moss that blended her body with the night darkness.

Naomi was buck-naked. She grabbed a chicken by the head and swung it around and around until the head was the only thing that remained in her hand. The body of the chicken quivered on the ground. Then Naomi threw the head in the fire, picked up the pulsating body, and sprinkled the spewing blood over the candle-covered altar. After that, she took a long stick and spelled out a word on the ground. Tante spelled it out in her own mind as each of the large letters were formed in the dirt. "M-A-R-T-H-A." When that was done, Naomi and the two girls danced over the writing on the ground--their movements got faster and faster and more and more frantic and continued on and on in time to the drum beat. It lasted so long that Tante got tired of watching and decided that she would go back to her porch.

As she turned to leave, the drumming stopped. When she turned back, she saw Naomi stretched out on the ground, body quivering and vibrating as if scuffling and doing battle with an unseen force. At that moment, SipZu jumped away from his silent drum, stripped off his clothes, and fell on top of Naomi, thrusting his stiff dick, the size of a boudin sausage, between her legs. The two girls writhed and moaned and echoed every twist, turn, and sound that came from Naomi. When the energy was drained from their bodies, they collapsed dog-tired on their backs, arms extended, legs spread apart and facing up at the full moon. Tante had seen enough. She headed back to her cabin as the flickering flames faded and the sounds of the night took back their rightful place.

* * *

Miles away in Pineville, Martha sat up in bed with a jerk. Her face raised upward, her body quivered, and she said, "Yes, Lord, I'll do that." Then she fell back into a deep sleep.

The next morning, the phone rang in the Fergerson house. Rosa answered.

"Papa, its Dr. Comeaux for you."

Phillip put down his paper and carried his coffee to the phone. He said, "Dr. Comeaux, this is Phillip."

"Good morning, Phillip. A situation has occurred that I think you should know about. A nurse called me first thing this morning and told me to come over right away. I found Martha dressed and sitting on the porch with her bag packed, waiting for a taxicab."

"Is she ready to leave?"

"By heavens, no! But she thinks she is. I asked why she was sitting out on the gallery dressed to leave, and she said that God had spoken to her last night and told her He had forgiven her sins and that she should go home to her children."

"Well, can you beat that? Is she getting better?"

"After a full examination, I'd say she is about the same, if not worse. Now she has this obsession about leaving and believes that since her sins were confessed and have been forgiven there is no reason to be here. I was hoping that maybe you could shed some light on what she's talking about."

112

Phillip found himself between a rock and a hard place. He had made Lightfoot and Naomi promise not to reveal what Martha had confessed. He could not find it in his heart to tell the doctor what he knew, plus the fact Rosa was standing there listening.

"I'm sorry, I can't help you with that doctor."

"I was hoping that you could. At any rate, we plan to watch her more carefully now that she has this notion about leaving. If she gets out, she could be a danger to herself or someone else. I'll keep in touch."

Rosa was overflowing with questions, and Phillip filled her in on what the doctor reported.

"Papa, what does this mean?"

"Can't rightly say. And the doctor doesn't know either."

He knew that when Martha got her mind fixed on something she would not let go, and he hoped and prayed to God that they would watch her closely. There was nothing more he could discuss with Rosa. He took a long sip of coffee and watched the tears grow in her eyes. He wanted to ask about the man who was trying to sell her candy but decided this was not the right time.

* * *

Later that week Lightfoot entered the Sugar Shack Pool Hall. Walter Waters, nicknamed Slick, the thirty-two year-old numbers runner, son of the owner of the Sugar Shack, was sitting on his stool at the bar. From this perch, he could keep his eye on everyone who entered to buy carry-out liquor as well as everything that went on at the pool tables. He wore his trademarks: a skinny brimmed hat and a colorful Bellefonte styled shirt, opened down front to reveal his golden chains.

113

Lightfoot limped in and headed in his direction.

Slick said, "Well, I ain't seen you in a month of Sundays. What bring you over here?"

"Had some extra time and thought I'd shoot a game or two for old time's sake."

Slick reached up and took the cigarette from behind his ear, stuck it between his lips, struck a match, and said, "Put yo' money on the table. I'm always glad to take it from ma friends."

"I know, that's why you ain't seen me in a month of Sundays."

Slick laughed his lusty chuckle as he slapped a pack of Camels against his knuckle, took out a cigarette, and replaced the spare that was behind his ear. He yelled out, "Rack 'em up."

SipZu appeared from out of nowhere and began gathering the scattered balls left by the men walking out.

Lightfoot followed Slick to the table in the corner near the door that led to the back room--the place where Slick was king of the poker table, the place where the hard earned money of the day laborers, construction workers, and the yard men was lost in hopes of making more. It was also the place where Lightfoot learned how *Slick* came to be Walter's moniker.

Lightfoot selected his stick from the wall rack, and Slick picked up his from its fancy case sitting on the window sill.

SipZu silently retreated to his bench in the dark on the back wall where he rested between chores of racking balls and sweeping up.

During the course of the game, Lightfoot casually asked, "What you know 'bout that Kane fella just come to town?"

"The one drive that pink Caddy?"

Lightfoot didn't know what he drove, but there were not too many other people in town, who could fit that description, so he said, "Yeah, that's him."

"Ohhh, man. That cat's somethin' else. I don't play no poker wid him. I watched him the other night clean out them fellas work for Scott Construction."

"What else he do around here?"

"Sell insurance. Been here a while. He's a hustler, and he's sharp. Always wear a coat and tie and got a courteous manner, especially wid the womenfolk."

Lightfoot looked up from his lined-up shot and questioned, "Where's he from?"

"Chicago."

"What he do there?"

Slick stopped shooting and rested his hand on his pool cue. "Man, I called up my man in Chi town and asked the same thing, especially after the way I seen him deal them cards."

Slick took a step closer to Lightfoot, and emphasized each word. "Man, the dude is a first-class con-artist. My man say he sold a repossessed Caddy three times. Don't know how he did it, but he did. Then he had to leave town 'cause the law was lookin' for him, not to mention the pissed off cat that he sold it to the second time. And I'll bet you anything that's the same car he driving now. He's smooth. Better'n me. He got what they call style. I kinda like him, but I keeps an eye on him."

Lightfoot missed his shot to sink the eight ball.

Slick said, "Too bad. You fucked now." The eight ball rattled in the pocket and Slick picked up the two crumpled ten-dollar bills from the table's edge, then crushed out his cigarette with his foot. "Wanna play another?

Lightfoot hung up his stick. "Naw, gotta go."

"Why you wanna know about Sugar?"

"Is that what they call him?"

Slick chuckled and said, "Yeah. Sugar Kane."

Lightfoot's laughter merged with Slick's on the wordplay of the name. Then he said, "He's been hanging out at my place a lot. I was curious."

"Just don't do no biddness wid him, know what I mean?"

"Yeah, I know. I ain't got to worry 'bout that."

Slick unscrewed his stick and put it back in the case. "What else can I do for you?"

"I'll let you know."

"C'mon back and join the game sometimes. I'd like to take some mo' of yo' money."

"I know you would. See you, Slick, and thanks."

"Anytime a'tall. You're my blood."

He put his arm around Lightfoot's shoulder and walked with him to the door. While he stood there watching Lightfoot drive off, he took the spare cigarette from behind his ear and lit up.

SipZu walked up next to Slick and asked, "Who is that man?"

"Lightfoot Broussard, the owner of the Black Eagle."

"That ol' cripple man?"

Slick looked at him, blew smoke in his direction, and said, "He's the richest nigger in town."

* * *

The next week, Naomi was cleaning house and was startled by a knock on the door. Most people she knew walked in announcing themselves. She opened the door, and SipZu was standing there smiling with his hands behind his back.

"Well, what are you doing here?"

"I just dropped by to give you this." He revealed a

branch of beautiful azalea flowers.

"And I see you just dropped by Miss Ann's garden. Well, that's mighty thoughtful of you. Wanna come in and sit a spell?"

"If'n you ain't too busy and ain't got company."

"Naw, I'm just cleaning up a bit, then I gotta go to the club and help Lightfoot, but I got a few minutes. C'mon in."

SipZu followed Naomi into the kitchen and she lit the fire under the coffee pot and said, "What you been doing wid yourself since I last seen ya?"

"Bussing dishes at the King Cotton and helping out at the pool hall, but I'm looking to make some changes in my life."

Naomi turned and looked at him. "What kind of changes you talking about?"

SipZu was up like a flash and grabbed Naomi and kissed her.

She was so surprised she just stood there, limp. But as his tongue stroked and aroused her lips, she surrendered and wrapped her arms around his muscular body.

"Man, you don't waste time on words, do you?"

SipZu laughed. "After that night in the thicket, I couldn't get you off my mind."

"I'm a married woman."

"I know. But I could be your backdoor man."

"What makes you think I need a backdoor man or was looking for one?"

"I felt it the other night. You was hungry for a good fuck, and it was so good I couldn't get you offa my mind."

"It was a surprise to have you jump me while I was feeling the spirit. For a minute I thought you was the spirit. And you're right about one thing."

"What's that?"

117

"It did feel good. Now sit down and drink this coffee." Naomi poured two cups and sat across the table, sipping and looking into SipZu's eyes.

He returned the admiring glances and said, "I hear tell your ol' man is jus' that, a old man. Must be over sixty."

"So?"

"You need a strong young man to satisfy your soul."

Naomi's thoughts came alive. He was right again. There was a twenty-year age difference between her and Lightfoot, and their sexual visits were getting less and less frequent. With the club and all, there wasn't as much time for frolic as there used to be. And she could do with a little more excitement in her life, especially when she was aroused by a Voodoo session. After a pensive few seconds she said, "So you think you're the one?"

SipZu said as seductively as he could, "Judgin' from the way you got into it the other night, I'd say you feel the same as me."

Trying not to sound as eager as she felt, Naomi said, "Maybe and maybe not."

"I'd be willing to go with that."

SipZu drained his cup, placed it in her hands, squeezed both for a second, and then stood up to leave. "You kin look for me any evening after the sun go down. Now, you'd better put them flowers in water 'fore they whither."

"Go on away from here, man." Naomi gave him a goodbye kiss and the arrangement was made.

Chapter 8

Love Story

1959 - In four months Joshua had taken in over $500.

On his weekly collection rounds for the North Carolina Mutual Insurance Company, he would put a piece of candy in front of his client and say, "lagniappe." On the next visit, he would say, "Now, my lovely lady, I know you enjoyed that tasty candy I gave you the last time I was here. Now I'm gonna tell you how you can become an investor in the makin' and the sellin' of that candy. All I'm asking is a small investment so that my partner and me can do some research and development that'll help us put it in grocery stores and restaurants all over Louisiana. That's the way the white folks do it. Know what I mean? Now, let's say you invest twenty-five dollars. You get back twenty-eight dollars and seventy-five cents. That's three dollars and seventy-five cents for doing nothing, and you don't have to die to get it back. This is as good as insurance, and you can't lose. And don't forget, I am the messenger. I've been sent by the Lord to help you provide for your earthly resting place and to bring you the sweetness of life. Now, when I come back next week, I'll pick up your investment so you can be a stockholder for Sweet Rosa's Candies. Now, don't that sound good to you? Think on it. I'll see you next week."

Except for slight variations, his spiel was the same when he talked to the men who hung out at the pool hall or in front of the liquor store. He even allowed his clients to pay their investments on the installment plan just like they paid their insurance premium.

Joshua sat waiting in the last pew of the church after school on Friday. He watched as Rosa knelt at the altar rail in front of the Blessed Virgin. When she completed her novena, she genuflected, crossed herself and headed out. Her eyes fell on Joshua waiting for her at the door.

"Why, Joshua, what are you doing here?"

"Waiting for you."

"Waiting for me?"

He extended a small bunch of daffodils that he had picked up from the graveyard on his way to the church. "For the sweet Rosa."

She took the flowers and brought them to her nose, breathing in the fragrance. "How thoughtful, but how did you know I would be here."

"You make your novena every Friday after school."

Rosa sheepishly let out a schoolgirl giggle and said, "Aren't you the sly one? You know my every move."

"Like the good Lord up above, I am watching over and watching out for you. Know what I mean? And I came by to give you your share of our partnership and take you out to dinner."

He put two fifty-dollar bills in her hand.

"Oh, my goodness! Where did this come from?"

"Our investors. It's the money to make, package, and

put your candy in the shops and stores. Check it out!"

Rosa was too overcome to say anything. She began walking towards her car. Joshua walked beside her. She turned to face him and asked, "What happens now?"

"We'll have dinner and celebrate."

"No, I mean with the candy."

"You make it. I'll take care of the rest. And the money will start rolling in. Know what I mean?"

Her smile quickly faded into worry. Nothing like this had ever happened to her before, and she was not quite sure what to make of it.

Joshua could tell that concern was on her mind, and he came to the rescue. "Now don't you worry about a thing. Tonight I'm gonna take you out to dinner."

"Where?"

"Lena's Place. They have the best Creole cooking in the area."

"Where's that?"

"Lafayette."

"Oh, that's kinda far."

"It's only twenty miles, and you'll be back before you know it."

And before she knew it, she had agreed. Joshua followed in his car to her house so she could change into something more suitable, and they were off.

The trip to Lena's was filled with small talk about humorous encounters with insurance clients and lesson plans and inattentive young boys passing notes to the girls.

At dinner, the talk was mostly about the candy-making business and how and where Joshua would do the marketing. He took a small cellophane bag out of his pocket and slid it across the table. Printed in the middle was a beautiful rose, and written in a semi-circle above were the words *Sweet Rosa's Fudge*. Rosa held it in her hand and

121

smiled. She was impressed. Joshua had thought of everything. She got more and more excited about this business venture, and she was getting more and more impressed with him.

After dinner, they drove back to Estilette and stopped under a moss dripping oak on the lane next to the graveyard.

Rosa turned and looked around and asked with widening eyes, "Why are we stopping here?"

It was dark and lonely, and a full moon gave off a silver shimmering glow, highlighting the limbs and leaves of the trees. The night creatures played their symphony of sounds, and it was peaceful and soothing.

Joshua said, "Thought you might want to end your evening near the church where it started. Know what I mean?"

This man was indeed a very thoughtful person. Rosa had never been in the company of anyone like him before. She felt warm and safe. Joshua took her hand and stroked it gently with his index finger and continued up her arm and onto her face, lightly tracing her features. She relaxed and leaned her head back against the car seat headrest.

The moonlight bathed her face, and Joshua whispered, "You look just like a Madonna in that light."

His lips slowly moved towards hers. It was a leisurely advance that allowed time for her to reject the onward travel if she so desired, but she held her face constant and his lips found hers open and willing. That one kiss was all that Joshua attempted. He started the car and headed in the direction of the Fergerson house. The silence was welcomed by both. There was nothing more that she could say, and there was nothing more that he wanted to say.

He walked her to the door where Rosa extended her hand and said, "I've had a lovely evening. Thank you." She disappeared into the house.

*   *   *

In the next three months, Rosa's life got too complicated for her to handle.

She stood on the porch of Ruth's duplex on the campus at Southern University. She raised her hand to knock and realized that she should have called first. She didn't really know how to tell Ruth that she had come because she needed her advice. Her trip was an impulse; she left a note on her Papa's desk, got in her car, and drove to Scotlandville. It never occurred to her that Ruth may have left town, may have had something else to do for the weekend, or may have company. Nothing mattered to Rosa except that she had to talk.

Ruth was delighted to see Rosa. She felt flattered that Rosa thought of her as family so completely that it was unnecessary to call in advance.

Rosa began, "Girl, I just had to talk," and she went on from there. She related how Joshua had been gradually making their business relationship more and more personal, how he had taken her out to dinner several times and afterwards parked and exchanged kisses, and how he had arranged an elegant dinner at his house with food catered from a restaurant that turned into an intimate romantic evening complete with candles. "Girl, I felt like I was in church."

Ruth laughed. Then she said, "I'm sorry. I'm laughing, but it's not funny. You are the only person that I know who would compare a candle-lit dinner with being in church."

"Well, it wasn't the same. That's why I'm here. He wanted me to go to bed with him." Rosa was serious and frightened.

Ruth abruptly ended her response of humor. She asked

bluntly, "Are you still a virgin?"

The question brought uneasiness to Rosa's eyes, and Ruth was sorry that she had been so direct. She tried to soften her inquiry. "I mean, have you ever been intimate with a man?"

Rosa was silent.

Ruth realized that she was traipsing on forbidden ground.

Rosa began slowly. "Yes. Many years ago, I was in love with a man with whom I shared the secrets of my heart and soul. It was more of a spiritual than a physical thing. You understand?"

Ruth nodded.

Rosa continued. "Well, this went on for a long time, like maybe a couple of years. And one day, I accidentally spilled a cup of coffee on his pants and I wiped them dry. I guess all that rubbing on his leg started up his manhood, and the next thing I knew he was kissing me. From that time on, we made love often."

Rosa began to cry. Ruth did not know what to say. She realized that Rosa had opened her own Pandora's Box, and she didn't want to tip the balance. She waited quietly.

After a minute or two, Rosa dried her tears, smiled and said, "I guess you think I'm behaving like a child."

"No. Not at all. Evidently it was a very upsetting experience."

"It was also very distressing, and I've never told anyone about this before."

Ruth was about to say, "And you don't have to tell about it now," but she held her tongue. She suspected that Rosa needed and wanted to get it out, and she did not wish to say anything that would interrupt her release.

Rosa continued, "Well, after a while I got pregnant."

Ruth had not anticipated hearing this. She was shocked

but tried hard not to show her response. She waited. Rosa was silent. When it was clear that Rosa was not going to say more, Ruth asked, "Where is the baby?"

Rosa said very softly, "The baby died." Then she got up from the tufted Victorian sofa and moved slowly around the room.

Ruth watched her every move. Apparently, this distressing experience had been a dark secret for a long time. She knew how hard it must have been for Rosa to bring this out into the light. There were many questions that she wanted to ask, but she felt that Rosa needed a breathing spell.

Ruth asked, "Would you like something to eat? I have some left-over chicken, and I think there's enough potato salad left for a meal."

Rosa smiled and welcomed the suggestion. "That would be nice."

In no time at all, between idle chatter about settling into her new home, Ruth had placed an appetizing snack on the table. But she wanted to get back to their earlier conversation. She asked, "When were you married?"

"I wasn't."

Ruth's hands went to her mouth along with a slight gasp. She reached across the table and held Rosa's hand with loving compassion. She knew without further comment the pain that came with this admission.

Rosa continued, "That's why I came to talk. Joshua wants to make love. And I don't want to until I get married. And I don't know if I want to marry him. But I should get married to someone."

Everything on Rosa's mind and in her heart came gushing out in a flood of emotion. Ruth detected the anxiety and urgency that floated along on the sound of

Rosa's voice. However, what was most troubling was the statement, "But I should get married to someone." Ruth wanted to ask, "Is that what people in Estilette expect you to do?" But she remained silent. Ruth wanted to help, and the best way that she could do that was to listen.

Rosa continued, "Joshua is a nice man. He's kind and thoughtful. He has good ideas, and he talks well, but his skin is the color of burnt toast."

Ruth said, "Oh, then he's about the same color as me."

Rosa immediately became defensive, "Ohhhhh, Ruth, I didn't mean to give the impression that you're too dark. I was thinking about children and marrying a man darker than me. Mama just couldn't stand it if I had a dark-skinned baby."

Ruth was speechless. The attitude that Creole's had about skin color had to be dealt with, but Ruth wasn't concerned about that right now. It was more important that Rosa stay on the path of dealing with her feelings about Joshua.

Ruth tenderly asked, "Do you love him?"

"I don't know. And I don't know whether or not it's because he's dark. I get that from Mama, and I don't want to feel that way. I like Joshua, but this skin color thing keeps getting in the way."

"Well, if you like him enough, why don't you sleep with him to find out if you can love him, no matter what his color. But be careful that you don't get pregnant again."

"Yeah, I couldn't stand to have another abortion."

The word cut like a knife. Ruth went numb. Dumbstruck. When she recovered, she repeated, "Abortion? You had an abortion?"

For Rosa to hear the word from someone else's lips made it sound revolting and ugly. Rosa wished that she had not shared this with Ruth, but it was too late. The secret that had plagued her so long was now released. The memory brought back the pain.

Rosa cried. "Yes. I had an abortion."

"Why didn't you marry the father?"

"Because he was . . ." After a moment she continued, "My priest."

Ruth took a deep breath and closed her eyes. She walked slowly around the table with her arms locked tightly across her chest, rocking her body back and forth. Then she broke down and cried, collapsing across Rosa's back. The flood of tears from the two women washed away the pain of their hearts.

* * *

Early the next morning, they walked silently around the campus and finally settled on a bench overlooking the Mississippi River. The moss-covered oaks and gentle breeze created a feeling of peace and contentment that belied the turmoil in Rosa's heart. They sat in silence and looked out over the mighty river bearing the barges and the boats.

Then Rosa picked up where she had left off last night. She said, "Mama made me have that abortion."

Ruth closed her eyes.

Rosa felt relieved and lightened.

Ruth looked deeply into Rosa's eyes. She echoed Rosa's statement as a question, "Your Mama made you have the abortion?"

"I was twenty-six and in love with my priest, and Mama thought it best."

"What did he say about it?"

"Oh, he denied that anything had happened between us. He said it was not his child and that I had been with someone else. And then a strange thing happened. A few months, later he got sick and died. It was almost like God had taken him away for breaking his vow of celibacy. I was crushed. He was the only man I ever loved."

Ruth could not even begin to imagine what turmoil had rocked the soul of this woman all these years. The price of unrequited love, the deception by a trusted man of the cloth, the decision to terminate life urged by a mother who had given life, the years of guilt knowing the wrongness of it all, the years of struggle to justify the rightness of it all--it was a cross too heavy for anyone to bear. Some small measure of happiness for this troubled woman was long overdue.

Ruth remembered how a visit to Memphis had brought her and Bobby to a resolution about their student-teacher relationship. Maybe a trip to a different city could do the same for Rosa.

"Why don't you and Joshua go to New Orleans for a weekend?"

"You are right. I have to find out how I feel about him, and a trip to New Orleans might just do that, because that evening at his house did not."

"What happened?"

"Well, in one way he was nice, and in another way he was disgusting."

"What do you mean?"

"He invited me to dinner at his house. He rents one of those shotgun houses that has been fixed up, over where Uncle Johnny used to live."

Rosa told what she remembered:

"When Joshua opened the door he had a surprised look on his face, and I said, You look surprised to see me."

He said, 'I expected you at five o'clock.'

I looked at my watch, and said, 'Oh, it's only four-

128

thirty. I forgot. I set my watch ahead so I will not be late for Mass.' Then I laughed. I thought it was funny but he was serious.

He said, 'Well, I'm not done cooking yet. Know what I mean?'

Then I offered to help, but he insisted he wanted to do it himself. So I said, 'I'll be back.' "

Ruth said, "Now wait a minute. Yesterday you said he had an elegant dinner catered."

"Yes. He did. But he had told me before that he was going to cook a meal that I wouldn't forget. I could tell he was annoyed when I came early, so I left. And I parked in the next block. About five minutes later I saw the truck from the *Cajun Palace Restaurant* drive up to his house. That's the best restaurant in town and colored people can't eat there, so I don't know how he arranged to have the food sent out, but he did."

She continued.

"I went back exactly at five o'clock. I looked in the window and everything was arranged--the food was on the table and the candles were lit. He was sitting at the table picking his nose. He dug around and pulled out a big booger and flicked it at the window and it stuck to the glass. I was mortified and I wanted to get back in my car and drive off. But I knocked on the door. He opened the door wide and gave me a kiss. He was the most gracious person I had every met. He told me how lovely I looked and admired my new dress, and pulled out my chair and unfolded my napkin, put it on my lap and said the blessing. The dinner was great."

Ruth could not resist. "I think you have here a great pretender. He's really an unpolished street dude, but he tries to be everything that he thinks you want. That explains the elegant dinner that he could not cook and his crude manners. I think you should be flattered, because it seems that he is trying to be what he thinks you want a man to be. You just happened to see his true nature when he picked his nose. That was not meant for you to see. Most people express their true character when they think no one is looking, and that's what he did."

"You really think so?"

"Yes. And I think that the crudeness you resent in his character gets expressed in your reservations about his color."

"You are so smart."

"So what happened after dinner?"

"We danced to Nat King Cole records, and he started kissing and feeling all over me. I told him to stop, that it was making me uncomfortable. Then he said he didn't want to force me to do anything I didn't want to do, but he was ready to make love. That ended the evening because I told him no and I left."

"If that's all you resent, I don't think you have too much to worry about. He didn't force you to do anything you didn't want to do, and it seems to me that he really likes you. I think the New Orleans trip would be helpful."

* * *

When Rosa got home, Phillip was waiting. He was in a quarrelsome mood.

She was feeling relieved and unburdened and entered with a light and jovial manner. "Hi, Papa, what did you do today?"

"Worry about you."

"Worry about me? Why?"

"You were gone overnight."

"I left a note telling you where I was."

Phillip slammed his book shut and flipped it further down the sofa where he was sitting. "I think you ought to stop seeing that Joshua fellow."

Rosa put down her overnight bag and sat in the chair opposite Phillip. "Papa, I wasn't with Joshua, I was at Ruth's. I left you a note. Incidentally, she sends her love."

Phillip tried to rein in his attack, realizing it was too abrupt. "I'm sorry. I didn't mean that you lied about where you were last night. I just feel that you should stop your association with Joshua, whatever his name is."

Rosa was now beginning to get annoyed. "Now what brought this on?"

"I just have my reasons why you should stop seeing him."

"I don't believe this. You were the one who told me to meet some nice man, and I've done that."

"He's not a nice man."

"How do you know? You don't even know his name." Rosa got up and moved in the direction of her bag.

"I know enough to know he's not nice. He's not even honest. All this stuff about selling your candy is all a sham."

Rosa turned and looked back. "Papa, is that what this is about?"

"He's just setting you up to make money off your candy."

"Is that what you're so upset about? Him selling my candy? Well, that's a business deal. I want you to know he's already given me a hundred dollars."

Phillip got up and moved to face Rosa. "That's just to bait you in. You'll be doing all the work, and he'll take all the money."

"How do you know?'

"I know!"

"How?"

131

"Lightfoot told me . . ."

Before he could finish, Rosa interrupted. They were now face to face, yelling at each other. "Uncle Johnny! Uncle Johnny doesn't even know Joshua."

"He talked to Slick Waters."

"Oh, Papa. You gonna listen to what Slick Waters says? You know his reputation. He's a numbers runner and a pool hall thug, and you gonna take his word for things?"

"He says Joshua is wanted by the law in Chicago."

"He doesn't even know Joshua, and Joshua doesn't go in places like that."

"Slick told Lightfoot that this man hustles people, and he's what they call a con man."

"I'm surprised that you even listen to gossip like that. And I'm surprised at Uncle Johnny."

"Nobody even knows why he suddenly shows up here selling insurance."

"Papa, he works for a respectable insurance company and he dresses and looks respectable."

"All that may be, but he's not good enough for you to be seen out in public with."

"Papa, I'm a grown woman and I'll go out with him if I want to, and there's nothing you can do about that." Rosa picked up her bag and started heading out of the den.

"That may be, but I'm just trying to protect you from another heartbreak that's all." As soon as it was out of his mouth, Phillip realized he had made a mistake.

Rosa turned and came back to face her father. She did not believe there was any way he could know about Father Pat, but it certainly sounded like he did.

"What do you mean *another* heartbreak?" Rosa emphasized the word "another" to find out exactly what her papa was talking about.

"I'm sorry. I misspoke. As far I know you haven't been

serious with anyone before."

"That's right. I haven't been serious before." With that settled, she believed her secret was safe and she headed out again.

Phillip's voice stopped her. "Are you serious about him?"

"I don't know yet, but I could be. You were the one who wanted me to go out and meet somebody, and he's the most interesting, intelligent, and church-going man around here. I'm sorry you don't approve, but I intend to keep on seeing him."

"You got your reputation to think about."

"And what about you? You're a married man, or have you forgotten that Mama's still alive?" With that, Rosa walked down the hall to her room. That was the hardest thing Rosa had ever said to her papa.

* * *

The next day, Rosa went to see Martha. The attendant wheeled her in, parked the chair, and left. Martha looked at Rosa and then around the room with short, staccato, bird-like movements of her head.

Rosa went over and knelt next to her chair. "How are you, Mama?"

"I'm fine. And you?"

Rosa looked at the disarray of Martha's hair and decided it needed combing. She wheeled her toward the table where her purse rested, saying, "Not too good today. I want to talk with you."

"About what?"

"Things. Like we used to talk before you got sick." Rosa began combing her hair.

Martha looked around at her and asked, "What you doing?"

"Fixing your hair."

"Do I know you?"

"I'm Rosa. Your daughter."

"Oh, yes. I remember you. You're the one who goes to church."

Rosa smiled and felt comfortable that Martha knew who she was. "That's right. Do you remember how we used to talk about things?"

"I sure do. We talked when you got into trouble one time."

"I'm in trouble now."

"You still seeing that wolf in sheep's clothing?"

"No, Mama, he's dead."

"He is? Oh, yeah, that's right. I confessed that already."

"Why would you confess about Father Pat's death?"

" 'Cause I sent him to hell."

Rosa was curling Martha's hair into the bun that she liked, then turned her face so she could look into her mama's eyes. "Oh, Mama, you shouldn't say things like that."

"I know, it don't sound too good. You sure do look pretty. You married yet?"

"Not yet. That's what I came to talk about. There's a nice man that's interested in me, and I'm interested in him."

Martha asked, "Is he Creole?"

"No."

"Does he like that devil's music?"

"I don't know. He's never said."

"If he likes the devil's music, he ain't no good. Stay away from him."

Martha was beginning to sound more and more like her old self, and Rosa felt they would be able to talk like they once did. She said, "Papa doesn't like him."

"Why?"

"He says he's wanted by the law."

"Is he?"

"No."

"Then you can't put too much faith in what your Papa says."

"Anyway I wanted to find out what you had to say about me going to New Orleans with him."

"With who, your Papa?"

"No with Joshua."

"Who's Joshua?"

"The man I was telling you about."

"Oh, the wolf in sheep's clothing!"

"No, Mama, the man I want to go to New Orleans with."

"Don't you go to New Orleans with your papa, and don't let my papa go hunting with Silas. He's a sheep in wolf's clothing, just like that other one."

Now Martha was talking in circles again. For a brief moment, it was all too good to be true. Rosa thought that her mama was well enough to have an understandable conversation, but that didn't last very long. It was time for her to bring her visit to an end.

"Well, it sure is good to see you again," Rosa said gently.

"You too. And when you see my daughter Rosa, be sure to tell her that I love her best of all. She's gonna be just like me when she grows up."

Rosa went to the door and summoned the attendant.

Martha continued, "She's not the prettiest one, but she's the most religious. I got another one who's prettier and likes that devil's music, and that ugly one likes men, lots of men. They're both just as bad. Lord, if I was still able to walk, I'd go where she is and slap her face good."

135

The attendant entered and stood behind the chair waiting for Martha to finish.

Rosa kissed her good-bye, but Martha paid no mind and kept on talking.

"But I don't know where she is anymore. Just run off to Chicago, I think, and never thinks of calling or writing. And that other wolf in sheep's clothing that used to be married to me is running around with that woman."

Martha took the pins out of her hair, dropped them on the floor, shook out the bun, then roughed up her hair and made it look like it did when she came in.

Rosa motioned to the attendant to take her out.

Martha kept on talking. "I think I met her once, and then I shoulda poisoned her food like I did for that wolf in sheep's clothing. All of them, all those sinners deserve to die."

Rosa picked up the pins from the floor and put them back in her pocketbook. She sat at the table and cried. Both of her parents had brought tears to her eyes in as many days. She decided right then and there that she would go to New Orleans with Joshua Kane.

Chapter 9

Spitting in the Wind

1962 - "What you sow you shall reap" was a biblical phrase to which Phillip would get an unexpected masterpiece. After instructing Les on the importance of respecting women, Phillip was amazed by the direction in which it drove his grandson's behavior.

Holy Ghost School decided to present *Medea*, and the drama director cast Les as Jason. It was well known that Les had a flare for dramatics, and when he recited poetry, the assembly was held spellbound, so casting Les in the lead was a foregone conclusion. He was excellent. He was the talk of the town, and this induced Les to wear his newfound image like an elegant suit of new clothes. Girls were at his beck and call, and he had been more of a hero on stage than on the basketball court.

Because of feeling like a celebrity, he no longer wanted to do chores around the farm or practice piano, which was now thought of as "sissy stuff." All he wanted to do was party and have a good time with his admiring supporters.

While leaving the Black Eagle, late one evening, Les and Dora, his female-companion, approached the door as two of the town rowdies were entering.

As Tim and Parker entered, Les and Dora stepped aside. When Dora tried to exit, the door was slammed shut in her face.

Les considered this an insult and said, "Hey, man, you let the door slam in my girl's face."

Dora said, "That's all right, Les."

Les responded with a mannish, "Naw, it's not all right. They gotta apologize." Les caught up with Tim, who was the last to enter, tapped him on the shoulder, and said, "Hey, man, maybe you didn't hear me. I said you let the door slam in my girl's face."

Tim's response was, "So, who gives a fuck?" Then he turned to Parker, waving his thumb in the direction of Les, and said, "He's the fairy who was in that play."

Parker wagged his head up and down, and responded, "Yeah, I know. He eats with the white kids."

Tim said, "He might think he's white, but he ain't."

The boys laughed.

Les said, "I'm not kidding. Are you going to apologize?"

Tim gave his answer. "Mutherfucker, you can kiss my ass."

Les fired back, "I rather *kick* your ass."

Tim growled, "Don't nobody talk to me thata way." He charged Les, who side-stepped his path and pushed him headfirst into the wall. Before Tim could recover, Les landed a right cross to his jaw, and Tim fell to the floor.

Parker attacked. He and Les circled and exchanged blows. Dora screamed.

Lightfoot was alerted and came over. He stepped between the shufflers and yelled, "Break it up!"

Parker yelled back, "He started it!"

"I don't give a damn who started it, get the hell out!"

Tim, wiping his bloodied mouth with the back of his hand, replied sharply, "He think he's hot shit 'cause he look white."

Parker screamed as he backed out of the door, "We'll fix your ass at school!"

Lightfoot said, "And if you touch him, you'll have to deal with me." Lightfoot watched the boys leave, turned to Les, and asked, "Are you all right boy?"

While opening and closing his hand, Les said, "I'm fine."

Lightfoot gave him a close inspection and asked, "What happened?"

Les began, but Dora intervened and told her version of the incident.

Lightfoot was impressed to hear that his nephew was fighting because the boys had insulted Dora. Then he advised, "You watch out for them boys. They live over by the cotton mill, and they like to make trouble."

Dora added, "Sister is always putting them out for fighting, and I heard they are frequently in trouble with the law for one thing or another."

Les pleaded, "Uncle Johnny, please don't tell Mom about this. She's got enough to worry about."

Lightfoot made no promises, and not only did he tell Lala, but Phillip as well.

In the weeks after, the gossip around town reported, "Les is more than you wanna mess with. He's a no-nonsense, kick-ass kind of guy."

Phillip decided it was time for them to go fishing. He explained that although Les' motives were honorable, his actions were hotheaded and irresponsible.

"You should not be so quick to fight."

"Grandpop, those guys let the door slam in Dora's face."

"I know. Lightfoot told me."

"And didn't you tell me that women should be respected?"

"Yes, I did, but I did not mean that you should fight at the drop of a hat."

Les continued baiting his hook with the foul smelling concoction of rotten meat that he prepared especially for catfish and said proudly, "Well, I just was doing what you said I should."

Phillip did not know what else to say after that. Les was developing the kind of character that he had encouraged. However, Phillip was disturbed about the racial undercurrent that Lightfoot had noticed, and he felt a need to address that.

"Did you have any trouble with those boys at school?"

"No, sir. I don't even know their names, but I've seen them standing by the fountain. They have something smart to say whenever anybody takes a drink."

After a moment, Phillip thoughtfully replied, "Over the years I've taught a number of students from that section of town, and most of them seem to have troublesome attitudes."

Les cast out a few feet from Phillip's line. "Those boys made a remark about me thinking I was white."

"Yeah, I know. Lightfoot told me."

"But that's not true. I don't know why they feel that way."

Phillip realized this was difficult to answer. How could he explain the years of conflict between the field niggers and the house niggers, between the haves and the have-nots, the widening gulf between the educated Negroes and the laboring class? He decided to rely on history and hoped Les would get the picture. He said, "It seems they left us with one hellava problem."

"Who did?"

"Our Founding Fathers."

"Our Founding Fathers? What do they have to do with this?"

Les pulled in a nice sized fish and put it on the string.

Phillip continued, "Our Founding Fathers brought us here and worked us as slaves to plant and build this land into the richest country in the world. And all the while they satisfied their sexual appetites and created a skin color problem that we've never gotten over."

"I understand that, but what does that have to do with those boys thinking, I think I'm white?"

Phillip knew that the attitude of the boys had come from years of injustice and mistreatment, and the best he could do was hope that Les was able to understand what he was going to say.

"You criticized their behavior, and when you insisted they apologize, they felt you were also giving them the message that you felt you were better than they were, and that's the same message they get from white people."

Les asked, "Are Creoles white?"

Phillip pulled in his line and found a small fish, which he unhooked and released. He said, "Yes and no. They are a mixture, like gumbo."

Les laughed. "Come on Grandpop, you're joking."

"No, I'm not. They're all mixed up."

"Where did Creoles come from?"

"Many years ago, some people from France settled in Arcadia, which is what we now know as Nova Scotia. At that time, the French and the English were at war, and the English Governor of Arcadia insisted that the Frenchmen swear an oath of allegiance to the King of England. But being good Frenchmen they said, 'No way will we leave our Catholic faith and take up arms against our own countrymen.' So the Governor of Arcadia said, 'O.K., have it your way, but you have to leave Arcadia.' Most of them came to the Louisiana territory, which at that time was owned by France. And over the years, they married up with the Spanish, Indians, and the freed blacks." Phillip had not counted on giving a history lesson, but he was glad to find that Les was interested in knowing about his roots.

Les pulled in a fish much larger than the one Phillip had released and looked at Phillip. Phillip nodded his head, "Yes," and Les took it off the hook and put it on the string. As he re-baited his hook, Les asked, "What's it mean?"

"What does what mean?"

"The word *Creole.*"

"It's from a Spanish word *criollo,* which means 'sprung from.' The French pronounced it *Creole*, and they built a whole language and lifestyle around the word."

"Yeah, I know. They were proud people, like grandma."

Phillip agreed with him about that but felt that Martha had carried the pride thing a bit too far. He imagined that she would have been delighted to know that Les had taught those "nigger boys" a lesson, and he was glad that she was not around to confuse the grandchildren about skin color.

Since he felt it was his responsibility to keep Les on the right track, he said, "I notice that you're not doing your chores around the farm like you used to."

"I've been too busy with my school activities."

"Now don't let the success in that play go to your head and make you forget about your other responsibilities." Phillip could tell by the look on his face that Les was not too happy about the turn of direction that the conversation had taken.

Les was silent for a long while and then said, "Don't you think we have enough fish?" Although there were only two on the string, Phillip agreed that they had done enough fishing.

* * *

Things were never right with Lala and Lester Martel Senior. It was one of those relationships in which verbal expressions of love were freely exchanged, but actions did not support the feelings expressed.

Before they were married, Lala was adored by most of the Creole men of the area, but it was Lester she loved. He was hard-working with a rugged body and a good-looking face. He was a man's man. And like most men at that time, he believed that women had to be kept in place; if they acted up or got out of line, they had to be slapped around.

This was ironic because when Martha slapped Lala for playing blues in the tavern, Lester was compassionate. He would not leave Lala's side. And when they made love that night, Lester felt that the right thing to do was to get married. He had been raised in the church to believe that nice girls should hold their virginity until marriage, so it came as a given that, by taking her innocence, they were married by the deed. He was a tender and loving person until he had too much to drink, and then the man's man image became a monster.

After a hard day of work on the farm, and an all-night drinking binge, Lester came home early one morning.

Lala was making biscuits. As soon as the door opened she questioned, "Where have you been all night?"

"Out with my friends."

"You mean out drinking."

"No. Out with my friends. Why the hell do you care?"

"You said you were going to stop this."

"I don't feel like hearing this shit right now."

"Well, I feel we need to talk about all this drinking that you're doing."

"You just keep on making the damn biscuits. I'm gonna lie down."

Lala decided to stand in his path as he tried to leave the kitchen.

Lester yelled, "Get out of my way!" and he swung out his arm to clear his path.

Lala grabbed his arm and yelled back, "Lester, we have to talk about this." She was determined.

"Let go my arm."

She hung on.

Lester slapped her.

Lala hit back.

The more she hit back, the madder he got.

Les and Ann heard the commotion and came down from their rooms. They stood in the doorway and watched their parents trade blows and yell insults. It was more than Les could stand, he remembered what his Grandpop had said, and he picked up the rolling pin and whacked his father in the head.

Lester fell bleeding to the floor.

Les was so upset that his father had struck his mother he didn't give a damn whether Lester got to the hospital or not.

Lala stood next to the hospital bed with Ann by her side. They listened as the doctor said that Lester had a slight concussion. His head was shaved so that the wound could be stitched, treated, and bandaged, and he would have to remain in bed for a few days.

Although he had regained consciousness, he was still

groggy and hung-over. He looked around the room and he said, "Where is that asshole who hit me?"

At this point, Lala made the decision she felt she had to do. She swore silently, "I'll never live with that man again."

Lala moved out the same day. She and the children went to her father's house. There was not too much that Phillip could or would say. He knew the history of their violence and would not suggest that Lala try again to make her marriage work. Rather, he accepted them with open arms. In one respect, he was happy that his grandchildren would be close; in another respect, he was displeased because he would not be able to spend as much time with Alicia.

Phillip felt that Les needed some work responsibilities, and he talked Lightfoot into giving him a job. Les was now the new stock boy and assistant to BookTau, who was delighted to have the extra hands for cleaning. BookTau taught Les everything he knew about mopping floors and about alligators as well.

When it was time for sugar cane harvesting, Les took his place alongside the hired cane cutters. He had done this since he was fifteen, the same age his father was when he began swinging the large sharp knife with the hook on the top. And like all of the other heirs to sugar cane farming, Les was expected to learn from the bottom up. He had cut cane for the last two years, and he felt that he had an obligation to do it again this year. It didn't matter to him that his mother and father had parted ways--his father was still his father.

When Les appeared in the field, Moses, the rhythm-man, greeted him with their personalized hand jive ritual that Moses had taught him. His nickname "the rhythm-man" was given to him because he sang the cadence to the cutting process, so the work went fast and was less tedious. Moses was in his late forties and had been around cane cutting all of his life. He was more than a hired hand to Les; Moses had taught him how to shoot marbles and how to roll a cigarette from Bull Durham tobacco. Sometimes Moses would even let him take a draw, but always with the admonition, "Smoking will stunt your growth."

The cane cutters came, one by one, and smiled their welcome-back greetings with backslaps and handshakes. The gossip had made the rounds-- and filtered down to the workers and the sharecroppers alike--that Mrs. Martel had left the farm and took the children. None of them expected to see Les swinging his knife in the harvest, so his appearance brought jubilation that things had returned to what they had been.

Les took up his position and looked to Moses.

Moses stood ready to begin the call. He swung his knife at the stalk of cane as low to the ground as possible. That marked the first guttural, *"Huh"*. Before the stalk hit the ground it was caught and turned so that the next backhanded swing of the knife cut off the spray of leaves on the top. That was followed by "*Hummm*". And in one motion, the knife was rotated so that the hook slid down the shaft of the stalk and cleared away the foliage. That was in two beats, *"Hah, Hah!."* Then the cleaned stalk of cane was tossed into the valley of a designated row for a pickup. That was the final beat, *"Hump."* And all in unison they sounded: "*Huh, Hummm, Hah, Hah, Hump.*" The process was repeated over and over--*"Huh, Hummm, Hah, Hah, Hump; Huh, Hummm, Hah, Hah, Hump!"* The human voices along with the swish of ten vibrating knives, striking the stalks at the same time, created a cane field symphony that joined nature's crickets and echoed down the long rows of the thickly growing foliage. This brought to mind what Phillip had told Les about the origin of work songs.

If one were not careful, at the end of the day, he would find his arms and hands filled with bloodied cuts. The wise wore long sleeves. The rough he-men prided themselves on the toughness of their skin and the knowledge of the years to avoid the swipes of the foliage. Les wore long sleeves and gloves.

Lester Senior drove the pick-up wagon because he could keep better track of the number of loads delivered to the sugar refinery in Abbeville. He kept one wagonload to be made into syrup for the family. This year was no different, even though the family had split up. Lester had not given up hope that Lala would be back. She had left before, so he expected she would be coming back, and he continued to plan and work just as if nothing had happened. When he saw his son cutting cane, he knew it would not be long before the family was back together.

Lester got down from the driver's seat and greeted Les with a hug. The only words he spoke were, "See you up at the house for dinner."

That evening, it was only the two of them at the dinner table. There was a cool silence because neither knew what to say to the other. Les felt intimidated because he knew, man to man, he was no match for his father, and he realized that the only reason he had succeeded in hitting him was because his father's back was turned, so there was nothing that he wanted to talk to his father about.

The only sound was the scraping of forks against the plates. Les stole a glance at his father, and he remembered an incident his mother had told him:

"Your daddy's a good man. One time, before we got married, he was on his way back from Baton Rouge. There had been an accident on the Mississippi River Bridge, and a long line of cars had been stopped. He got out of his truck and walked to the scene of the accident. The cab of an oil tanker was hanging over the side of the bridge, and the only thing keeping it from falling into the river was the weight of oil in the truck tank. The injured driver was still bleeding and trapped in the cab, and the police did not know how to help. Your daddy climbed out onto the cab of that truck hanging over the water and pulled that driver to safety. He risked his own life to save that man, because that's the kind of man he is."

That story echoed in Les' memory. He was as proud of his daddy as his mother was when she told him the story. However, he still could not understand why he would hit her.

Lester Senior pushed a large cut of steak into his mouth and chewed. He ran his hand over his shaved head. His drinking buddies still teased him about getting hit in the head with a rolling pin, and he was still pissed off about that, but at the same time he was glad to know his son had balls enough to do it. He had seen him on stage doing that sissy play, and he was afraid that he might be a punk. Nothing in the world would have distressed him more than to have a son who was not a man. So he was proud of the stud sitting across the table who had courage enough to face him and come back for the harvest. However, he was not able to tell him that, so he had to find a way to let him know that he was delighted that he was man enough to face him down.

Neither of them said a word during the entire meal, but just about the time both plates were empty, Lester Senior said, "I plan to start grinding cane for syrup tomorrow. If you'd rather do that than go into the hot fields, it's O.K. with me."

Les said, "Yeah, I'll do that."

Lester knew that making syrup was less grueling than

cane cutting, and he wanted his son to feel that he had his best interest at heart. And Lester also wanted Les to get the message of his appreciation by assigning the one person he liked most. "Moses will help out with that and I'll get Frankie to keep the rhythm."

"Thanks, Dad." Les put his plate in the sink and went up to bed. Cutting cane was hard, hot work, and he was tired. Sleep was a far more attractive proposition than trying to make conversation with his father.

Les was up with the crowing of the rooster. He had a hearty breakfast, put on the table by Miz Noonie, who had prepared dinner the night before. When he got to the syrup barn, Moses had already hitched up the mule to a pole that extended twelve feet out from a grinding wheel. The mule walked in a circle, pulling the pole that turned the gears that caused the grinding wheel to crush the stalks and squeeze out the juice. The juice ran into a barrel, and the flattened stalks of cane passed through and fell out on the other side. When the pile of baggase, flattened cane stalks, reached a certain height, Moses hauled it away.

Les transferred the sweet juice from the barrel to a large tank inside the barn, where a roaring fire heated the juice to the boiling point. The cooking process continued until the desired thickness of the syrup was achieved, which could take all day and sometimes far into the night.

In the morning, when Lala realized that Les had not come home, she got worried. After breakfast and before going to school, she drove out to the farm.

Les and Moses had been working for a couple of hours, and Les had just emptied the barrel of juice into the tank, and was stoking the fire in the barn. Moses was feeding cane into the grinding jaws of the wheel. Lala drove down the road, saw Moses, and tooted the horn to ask the where abouts of Les. Moses turned toward the sound, and his hand was pulled into the grinding jaws, along with a stalk of cane.

He yelled out in pain.

Les ran out of the barn, stopped the mule, and reversed the turn of the gears. Moses' mangled, bleeding hand was removed from the grinder. He was in great pain.

Lala and Les took him to the emergency room.

At the emergency room, Les and Lala were waiting for the report from the doctor, when Lester entered. He glared at Lala, and his eyes said what his mouth did not: "How is he?"

After giving what information she could, Lala figured that she knew what was on his mind, and before Lester could say anything else she explained, "I was worried. I just came out to see if Les was all right."

Lester's mouth tightened and he shot back, "Why wouldn't he be?"

"He was gone all yesterday and last night."

"So what? He was at home." Lester's voice now carried his anger. "Noonie said she went to the window when she heard all that racket of horn blowing, and now I've lost a good man because of you." Lester saw the anxiety in his son's eyes and decided to temper his accusation. His voice grew softer, and he sat down next to Lala and began to explain, "They were making syrup."

"I know."

"Yesterday he was cutting, and I thought making syrup was easier."

Lala didn't say anything.

Lester continued, "I put Moses in to help him."

After a few moments of silence she said, "He likes Moses."

"How bad is his hand?" Lester asked.

"I don't know. The doctor is treating him now. Why do

you have to make more syrup? There's some left from last year," Lala said.

"I was hoping, that's all."

Lala knew that Lester blamed her for what had happened, and she was trying desperately to spread the blame equally. She addressed Lester's hope. "I'm not coming back, Lester, and you're not going to have a family to feed, so you didn't have to make more syrup."

Lester was silent. Slowly it began to dawn that Lala might not come back this time, but he was not going to give up hope so easily. Maybe this was not the time or place to get into this discussion. They sat for several minutes until Lala went to find a phone to call the school to tell them that she would be late.

The doctor appeared. Lester stood immediately and asked, "How is he doctor?"

The doctor rubbed his chin and said slowly, "He'll be all right, but—"

Lester interrupted, "But what?"

Lala said, "Let the man finish."

The doctor nodded his head. "Thanks. I know this is going to be difficult for you. The fourth and fifth fingers of his left hand were so mangled that they had to be amputated."

Lester shook his head and turned away.

Lala wanted to embrace him, but she was not sure how he would receive such a moment of compassion, so she said softly, "I'm sorry."

A quiver went through Les' body. He took several short intakes of air, bit his bottom lip, and tried to choke back the tears. He was not successful.

The doctor continued, "He will have full use of the rest of his hand, but he'll have to stay in the hospital until I am sure there is no infection."

Lala said, "I'm glad it was not any worse."

Lester looked at Lala with scorn then back at the doctor and said, "I'll take care of the medical expenses, so don't spare any care."

The doctor shook his hand and said, "Stop by the office and make the arrangements before you leave. You can go in to see him now."

The three walked into Moses' room. There were several IV bottles hanging next to the bed, and Moses' face was turned away. When he heard them enter, he turned toward the door and managed a smile. He lifted his good hand, waved, and said, "I'll do fine with the other."

With tear tracks showing on his soot-covered face, Les leaned in close and whispered, "Looks like we gonna have to make up a new hand jive."

Chapter 10

Shadows of the Blues

One Saturday, Phillip said to Les, "Come on, boy, let's take a ride.

Les was curious as they drove out of the yard. He knew they were not going fishing again because they didn't have fishing gear, and he could not figure out the destination from the direction they were headed.

After a few blocks of silence, he asked, "Where're we going, Grandpop?"

Phillip smiled and cast his eyes in Les' direction so he could register his reaction, and he said, "To learn some history."

"Grandpop, today is Saturday. We don't have school on Saturdays."

"Every day is school day for history."

"O.K., Grandpop. What's up?"

"I want you to learn some Negro history that they don't teach in school."

Les didn't say another word.

153

Phillip had made it sound like a chore, but that is not how he wanted Les to think of this trip. He wanted him to be aware that the story of the Negro people was told every time a blues song was sung, and he didn't want it to sound high-faluting or teachy. Usually, he just took Les along and let him gather whatever he could from what he saw and heard. But he wanted today's venture to be different. Phillip remembered that his own awareness of this came late in his life, and he wanted to make sure that the same mistake was not duplicated in the boy's life. He especially did not want Les to grow up with the same attitude of the blues that was held by Martha--that it was low-down nigger music, without any substance or reason for being.

When they arrived at BoBo's house, he was on the porch in his rocking chair with a pint of Early Times at his feet. It was apparent that Mr. BoBo was drinking more than he had in the past. However, he was getting on in age, and at seventy-five, Phillip didn't worry too much that BoBo might become an alcoholic. After all, he had spent his entire life doing the equivalent of "hard time," and he was long overdue for the peace and relaxation that a drink or two provided.

BoBo was born twenty-four years after the end of slavery. His papa had been a slave, but he never knew his name or saw his face. His mama called him "my lil BoBo," and the name stuck throughout his life. Leadbelly was only two years old when BoBo was born, and the same conditions of hard work in the fields tempered the lives of both. Leadbelly went from place to place playing his music, trying, when he could, to escape work in the fields. But BoBo didn't have an escape, so he went from place to place chopping and picking cotton. Wherever there was work, there was BoBo. He never settled down in one place long enough to have a family, but always he would come back to

Estilette, the place of his birth.

He knew the land and everything that it produced--the crops, the chickens, the horses, the cows, and the hogs--and as time passed, he took to sharecropping. He and Phillip had discovered their need for each other.

BoBo drew the back of his hand across his mouth as he watched them approach the porch. "Good day, 'fessor, what brings you out back?"

"I want my grandson to get to know you."

"Who's his mama?"

"Lala."

"Oh, the pretty one."

"Well, that's what some people call her."

"Oh, but they right. She's what you call beau-ti-ful. Come here, boy, lemme get a good look at ya."

Les walked up the steps and stood next to Mr. BoBo, who gave him the once over and nodded his head. "Yep. He's got his mama's mark on him all right. And he's big like his daddy. Dat be's that Martel fella, right?"

Phillip said, "Yes, that's right. Lester Martel."

"His papa left him that big sugar cane plantation over dere in Frilotville."

Phillip studied the map of life etched in BoBo's face, which was framed by small snow-white coils of hair that covered his head and continued down and around his mouth. Phillip nodded. "You do know what you're talking about."

"I ain't got too many peoples to talk to anymore. It's just me and Him." He pointed to the sky. "When I talks to Him, the peoples down here listen.'Fessor, you want a drink?"

Before Phillip could answer, BoBo continued, "I know you don't care much for dis kinda whisky, but I got some cherry bounce that I know you like."

Phillip didn't really want anything to drink this early in the day, but he did not want to refuse and run the risk of BoBo thinking he was being uppity. "Yes, that'll be nice."

"I ain't gonna offer dis boy a drink of whisky. He's too young. How old you, boy?"

Les felt that he would be more comfortable on the steps, and said as he crossed the porch, "I'm seventeen."

"Don't sit down. Go on in da house an look in da icebox. I got a Nehi drink in dere jus' for you. And look under the sink, dere's a jug. Bring dat and a glass for your grandpa."

Les cut his eyes at Phillip, who nodded, then he pulled on the screen door. It swung out on the one hinge holding it in place, and he disappeared into the darkness of the house.

Mr. BoBo turned the bottle up to his lips and after a swallow said, "Like I was saying, it gets lonely out here all by myself . . . just me and Him and my Early Times. I guess I done did my living and jes' waiting in line for dying."

Phillip was comfortably seated with his back propped against the post, one foot rested on the ground, and the other leg was stretched out on the floor. He studied BoBo's face again, admiring and appreciating the years of history that his eyes had seen.

He asked, "Mr. BoBo do you remember that time you told me about Ma Rainey?"

"I sho do."

"Well, I'd like for you to tell Les about some of the early blues singers you remember."

Mr. BoBo laughed. "'Fessor, you somethin' else, you know that? You 'members how I likes to tell them stories."

"I want Les to hear them from you."

Les emerged from the house with the items he was sent to get. He put them on the floor to clear his hands while he carefully swung the broken screen door shut. He brought the jug and glass to Phillip and said, "You want me to hear what?"

Mr. BoBo put forth, " 'Bout Ma Rainey. But I ain't gonna tell 'bout her. I'm gonna tell 'bout the greatest bluesman that ebber lived. 'Course he didn't live long."

Phillip was confused and a frown took over his face. "Are you talking about Leadbelly?"

"Naw, 'fore him. I talking 'bout the rambling man." He pointed to the sky. "He know I'm talkin' 'bout Robert Johnson. Now his friend, Son House, say he made him a deal with the devil to play like he played. And das funny 'cause it was Son House that swayed him to play the guitar in the first place. Son House was a powerful blues man in his own right. And he showed Robert Johnson the first thing he knowed about playing the guitar. But RJ didn't learn fast enough for Son House, and he used to say, 'Yo' drive peoples nuts. You can't play nothin.' Then Robert Johnson left and went rambling and when he come back to Robinsonville, Son House heard him play and got jealous and he say, 'Yo' musta sold yo' soul to da devil to be able to play like dat.'"

Phillip had gotten more that he bargained for. He hadn't heard about Robert Johnson before. Les was swallowing each and every word along with his Nehi drink. He asked, "Was Robinsonville where Robert Johnson was born?"

"Naw. He was born in Hazlehurst. 'Course Robinsonville wasn't dat far away and das where Son House lived, 'cause there was four or five juke joints dere. In those days it was the depression, and da WPA was building highways all thru dat country, and da work was hard. And the mens from da road gangs and da lumber camps would go to da juke joint on Friday night and stay 'till early Sunday morning. And Robert Johnson and Son

House would play the blues for 'em. Johnson learned early in his life dat playing music was easier than sharecropping or roadwork, so he just went from place to place and played the blues all the time. On top of dat, he wern't no rough and tumble guy. Robert Johnson were a small man, but he was a good looker and da ladies liked him. He learned early in his life how to be kept by womens. Soon as he hit town, he'd look for the ugliest woman there. He was smart. He knew dat she probably didn't have no man, so it was not likely dat anyone would git upset. And he knew dat givin' jus a little attention to an ugly woman would get him everythin' dat he wanted. And das what killed him."

Les asked, "An ugly woman?"

"Naw, a ugly woman's man. He made a mistake. He was playin' a juke joint in Three Forks, a little ways from Greenwood, Mississippi, and he took up wid the houseman's ugly woman. And da houseman didn't like dat a bit, and he sent him over a bottle of his favorite whisky dat had strychnine in it. And right dere in the middle of his next number, Robert Johnson jus' up and died. Poisoned to death chasin' pussy." Mr. BoBo laughed.

Phillip felt it was a little callous of him to be laughing and asked, "What's so funny?"

"It ain't. I'm laughtin' to keep from cryin'. Dat man died when he was only twenty-seven years old. Only ten years older den dis boy here. And jus' think what music he coulda made if he had lived. He plowed the ground for a lot of blues mens dat come after. All them records dat he made was made jus' two years before he died. I hear tell dat even dat Elvis fella listened to his records and tried to sound like him."

Les said, "Wow! You talking about Elvis Presley?"

"If das the one who sing about dat Hound Dog, das the fella. He white, and I hear tell he studied Robert Johnson all the time."

"Man, that is something."

"Sho is. And I'm gonna tell you somethin' else." Mr. BoBo cocked his head to one side, rolled his eyes, and said, "I think, if I 'members right, it was in '53, and I was over at the pool hall and dat's da first time I heard dat Hound Dog song. Course at dat time, Big Mama Thornton was singing it, Slick played it, and he say she had jus' put it on the wax. But a few years later dis white fella started singing it like that dog belonged to him."

Les said, "Wow! that's something."

"Sho is. And I'm gonna tell you somethin' else." He pointed to the sky and looked at Phillip. "He know dis already, but you listen. You know Leadbelly dat you ask 'bout before?"

Phillip nodded his head and looked at Les to make sure he was listening.

BoBo continued, "Leadbelly wasn't nothing like Robert Johnson. Now don't get me wrong. He did his thang too, but it wasn't like RJ. Dey were jus' as different as night and day. Leadbelly was big, ugly, and tough with a gravely voice, and RJ was itty-bitty, good looking, and had a high-pitched sissy voice. But on the other hand, dey had a lotta likeness. Dey were both hard living, hard drinking, pussy chasin' mens. And dey rambled all da time. Das da way it was if you was colored and ain't had much hope for a better tomorrow. Dey was trying to hurry da sun down, hopin' da next day might come up better. And if'n it didn't, dey would get mad and ornery and dey might kill somebody, like Leadbelly done a couple of times. It wasn't much fun being a nigger in dem days, so dey just wanted to sing da blues and forget about dey troubles. Some white people don't understand dat, and summa our light skinned Negroes don't neither."

Les asked, "Why don't they like the blues?"

"It's da music of da skin color black. And dey don't like to be associated wid dat. Plus, da fact dat most of da blues men was has-been prison people and da juke joints is considered low class by da high-yellas." BoBo pointed to the sky with his bottle and then brought it to his lips. "He know what I'm talkin 'bout. And He also know what we's hearin' now is jus da shadows of da blues."

Phillip was inquisitive. "What do you mean, shadows of the blues?"

"It means dat da peoples who really know da blues is goin' home. Dey is dying out. And da peoples singing da blues now nebber knew what it was really like back yonder. Da blues tells a story 'bout pain and suffering under da white man, 'bout lost love, runnin away, da chain gangs, and such as dat. And dem bluesmens, and the womens, too, was singing 'bout things dey knew was happenin' then. Now we got peoples singing 'bout what dey heard tell 'bout. Dey ain't nebber experienced dem things. Dey singin' 'bout the shadows. Now, I ain't saying dat is wrong, I'm jus saying das how it is. Dey got peoples singin' da blues nowdays dat ain't nebber been to jail and nebber been hungry without a job. Dey even got white folks singin' da blues, like dat boy dat sing 'bout dat hound dog. And all of 'em try and sound like dey know what it feel like to have da blues."

Mr. BoBo took a deep swallow from his bottle, dropped his head, and closed his eyes.

Phillip felt BoBo was all talked and liquored out. He motioned to Les that they should leave.

When they reached the car, Mr. BoBo yelled out, "Y'all come back anytime."

Chapter 11

Homecoming

I t was a rainy morning in February, 1962. Martha limped past the recreation room without being seen. Everyone, including the bread deliveryman, was watching television, waiting for the lift-off of Friendship Seven. John Glen would soon be shot into space to orbit the earth.

Martha made her way outside and hid in the bread truck in the back behind the boxes. It was cold and damp, and she was dressed in her robe over a beige cotton skirt and a short-sleeved floral print blouse. Her head was covered, primarily as an attempt to hide her face, with a shawl made by Julee. Since hearing the voice of the angel, Martha had combed her hair every day, and she had doused on *Evening in Paris*. She wanted to look presentable for her return home.

She curled up on the floor of the cold truck and waited, frequently blowing breath on her hands to keep warm. She was in no condition to undertake such a trip, but the voice of God had told her it was time to leave. She first heard the voice in the middle of a dream, and for Martha, this was like the Virgin Mary being told by the angel Gabriel that she was to be the mother of Jesus.

Martha was a faded image, of the beautiful woman she had been. She had deep set gray eyes, set in a delicate creamy-colored face, which was framed by gossamer black hair. She was, as Phillip used to say, "As pretty as a picture." Now, her eyes no longer sparkled, but were clouded with suspicion and skepticism, her graying hair was stringy, and knotted, and resembled moss, more than gossamer. Her face, etched with wrinkles, had the appearance of crumpled paper and more closely reflected the inner person she had become, than it did the process of aging.

Martha had no idea how she would get home, but she was confident that God would show her the way; after all, He had brought her this far, and it was because of Him that she had watched the bread truck back up to the kitchen door several times in the past. Finally, God's voice had whispered, "Get in that truck and get away from this place."

She had left early before taking her medicine and before eating breakfast. She was hungry, and her stomach was making rumbling noises, so she ripped open a loaf of bread and stuffed several slices into her mouth. In anticipation of the early morning arrival of the truck, she had not gotten much sleep, and she began to feel drowsy. She closed her eyes.

Thoughts of her homecoming filled her dreams. The culmination of years of imagination about what it would be like to live on the Broussard plantation became real: Chamber musicians played Tchaikovsky's Serenade in C. Beautiful Creole couples whirled around the ballroom. Hanging high above the foyer, decorated with huge potted palms and flowers, was a banner announcing: **Welcome Home Martha.** Velma, Rosa, Lillian, and Robert, beautifully adorned in the latest fashions, stood on the curved stairway like marble statues with frozen smiles. Ladies in silk gowns, holding fluttering fans, danced and whispered words of praise about the soiree. Uniformed black servants wove intertwining paths among the guests, passing out Champagne and hors d'oeuvres. Dr. Phillip Fergerson, with soft wavy hair, held out his arm, and Martha's fingers rested lightly in the palm of his hand as she sashayed around the room, greeting her guests. As she passed the floor-to-ceiling window, she glanced out to see John and Naomi standing in the shadows of the moonlight. Her homecoming was perfect.

The sound of the truck starting up woke Martha from sleep. After bouncing her around for a half hour, the truck came to a stop. Martha waited. She heard the driver's door slam shut, and then she saw a flood of light. She was blinded, and she remained quiet and still. The man took a box of bread and shut the door. With the return of the darkness, Martha figured it was time that she got out of the truck. When she got to the door it was locked. There was no handle on the inside, and after pushing a couple of times, she couldn't figure out how to get the door open. She decided that she would stand next to the door and wait until it was opened again.

The bread deliveryman made his way into the restaurant. He ordered a cup of coffee and glued his eyes to the television along with the breakfast eaters. The progress of Friendship Seven was being tracked, and he didn't want to miss any part of it. President Kennedy was talking to John Glen from the White House, so within the next half hour the breadman had finished his coffee and was ready to resume his rounds.

When the truck started up again, Martha, who was still standing, was thrown around so violently that she decided it best to sit on the floor to survive. After several minutes, the truck stopped again. As soon as the flood of light came, she jumped out of the truck, knocked the breadman to the ground, and ran as fast as her rheumatoid legs would carry her.

By the time the man recovered, stood up, and tried to figure out what had hit him, there was only the lingering smell of perfume.

Martha found a hiding place among the abandoned cars behind a service garage. She rested. Her legs were hurting. It had been a long time since she had moved so fast. When she was able to breathe easily, she found her way to Main Street. There were shops and stores on both sides, and she had no idea where she was. It was cold and raining. She looked first in one direction and then in the other. She didn't know which way to go. She was lost. She was confused. She was hungry. Then she saw a lady open the door to a shop with the sign: *Clothing Bought and Sold.* She headed in that direction and entered the store.

"Good morning. Can I help you with something?" the lady asked.

"You got any coffee?"

The lady was surprised by the abrupt request, without even a "good morning." But she was kind, and figured that Martha was in desperate need of something hot to drink, considering how she was dressed and the nature of the weather.

"Why, yes, I just made a pot. I'll get you some."

Martha took a seat in the chair behind the desk. The lady came back with a cup of coffee. "Here you are. I drink it black, but if you'd like cream and sugar, I'll get you some."

"Naw, this is fine."

The lady looked Martha over and was puzzled by the odd mixture of clothing. She could tell that Martha didn't have time to put on makeup and surmised that she had doused on perfume instead of taking a bath. The reeking aroma prompted the lady to say, "You must have left home in a hurry to be still wearing your robe."

"I got to see my children."

"Oh, are they close by?"

"No, they're in Estilette."

"That's a long ways from here. Do you have a ride to get there?"

"He told me somebody would pick me up."

The lady looked puzzled but didn't ask any more questions. She decided to be helpful and said, "That robe you're wearing does not look very warm. If you'd like to trade, I'll give you a warmer coat, and I could sell your robe in exchange."

Martha looked at the lady and then at the robe. She took it off and gave it to her.

The lady found a coat her size, handed it to Martha, and said, "My name is Angela, what's yours?"

She blurted out, "Martha!" After a few seconds she continued, "Your name sounds like Angel. My daughter saw an angel once. She was standing on the front porch talking out into the fog, and I asked, 'Who are you talking to?' And she said, 'An angel.' At first I didn't believe her, but now I believe, because an angel talked to me the other night."

Angela thought that was the most endearing story she had ever heard. She said, "Oh, my. What happened?"

"I was asleep, and the angel whispered in my ear and told me that I should go home to see my children, and then I woke up."

"Where were you staying while you were away from

your children?"

Martha's eyes blazed and she asked, "Why you want to know that?"

Angela immediately apologized. "I'm sorry. I didn't mean to pry."

Martha took the coat lying across her lap and put it on. Then she walked several feet away, stopping in front of the full-length mirror. She slowly lowered the shawl from her head and let it drop to the floor. Then she smoothed down her hair and turned from side to side as if modeling the coat.

Angela watched curiously.

By this time, the consequence of Martha's failure to take her medication was becoming crystal clear. Martha said, while admiring the coat, "Oh Mama, it's the most beautiful dress I've ever seen! Don't you think I'll make a pretty bride?"

Angela inhaled with a slight sound and she covered her mouth with her hand as she realized that Martha must have just escaped from the hospital at Pineville. She didn't know what to do. Her first impulse was to call the authorities. Then she thought better. She decided to try and find out what Martha planned to do.

She asked softly, "Where did he say you'd get picked up?"

"Who?"

"The man."

"What man?"

"The man who told you somebody would pick you up."

"Oh, you are talking about Jesus." She started laughing and continued, "He was the one who told me that." Then Martha turned serious. "But how did you know?"

Angela asked, "Would you like me to help you get to where you are going?"

Martha said in an angry voice. "No, that's not necessary." Martha looked outside through the display window and pointed. "There He is."

Angela looked in the same direction but saw no one. She approached Martha slowly. "Let me help you. I'll take you to him." She reached out to take her by the arm.

Martha jerked away and said, "Don't touch me! You're trying to get my Papa's land too. Don't touch me!" Then she turned and ran, limping out of the store and yelling, "He's right there, across the street. He's waiting for me!"

Angela ran behind her.

Martha ran right into the path of the bread truck.

The driver got out of the truck and looked down at Martha. He turned her over. She was not breathing. Raindrops rolled off her face like many tears.

Angela was horrified. She said softly, "Looks like she was once a beautiful lady."

The driver looked up pleadingly at Angela. "She ran right in front of the truck."

"I saw it."

The driver was a basket case. He turned in circles, rubbing his hands and shaking his head. He began to make excuses to Angela. "I was late on my run and going too fast. The road was slippery, and I couldn't stop in time."

"It's not your fault. She ran out of my store like she was crazy. She was trying to catch up to a man who wasn't there. I think she just left Pineville."

By this time, a crowd began to gather. A colored woman pushed her head in between shoulders to see what had happened. She turned to the man next to her, "That was a white lady hit by that truck."

The man said as they walked away, "Good thing the driver was also white."

* * *

Martha had finally gotten home.

Phillip arranged to hold the wake in the parlor of the Fergerson house. All of the furniture was rearranged, and the casket was put against the wall that the piano usually occupied. The room was filled with flowers, even more than there were during Phillip's recovery from the beating he got when he tried to vote. Rosa arranged the flower overflow on the front porch.

Every person in Estilette that had known the family, or heard tell of Martha, came by to pay respects. Even Silas came hobbling on his stick. He looked down at Martha, shook his head and mumbled to the corpse, "I know you nebber liked me or understood what happened to Mr. Joe. But I didn't kill him. He shot hisself. I'm here to say goodbye." Then he went back to the kitchen and Lilly Ellis fixed him a plate.

"Death is the great leveler" was a saying that could be traced back over centuries. To some, this was an expression of a circumstance that was hard to imagine--a paradox; but in Estilette, it was put into practice. It mattered little what connection the visitor had with the deceased. All came to pay their respects--the rich, the poor, the white, the colored, the childhood-friends, the holders of grudges, and the gossip mongers. Sheriff Cat Bobineaux came and laid his pistol belt and cap on a chair while he viewed the body. The teachers and the school board came, as well as the hogbutchers and store keepers. Some stayed a few minutes and some stayed for hours, but most, if not all, had something to eat and drink.

Phillip greeted people that he had not seen in years. He even shook the hand of that fellow he had seen with Rosa's candy at the Black Eagle. That was when Joshua Kane realized he had just met Rosa's father for the second time. Phillip had many question for the man but this was not the time or place, so he was cordial and brief.

Ann and Les never left the side of their Grandpop, and without fully knowing what was happening, they got an early taste of death making everyone equal. They met people they had never seen or knew were relatives, and the biggest surprise was Grandpop's brother, Luther, who was forbidden to cross the threshold of the house while Martha was alive.

Ann pulled on Phillip's hand. He leaned over to hear her whisper. "Grandpop, where has your brother been all of my life?"

Phillip smiled, patted her head and said, "We'll talk about that later."

"O.K." Ann was satisfied because she knew that she could count on her Grandpop. She believed that she was his favorite, because as much as he took Les fishing, he spent more time answering all of her questions. She was the shadow of his life—following him every place he went. The perfect young lady to whom Phillip told stories about important Negro people. So Phillip, accustomed to having her by his side, knew she would be there during the wake, because of the many questions she had about Grandma, whom she did not know very well.

Vel had made her first three-hour plane trip from Chicago, and it took almost the same amount of time to travel from New Orleans to Estilette by bus. During the trip, she had plenty of time to think, and now, as she viewed the body of her mama, all of the memories which began on her trip came rushing back. She remembered the many hours spent over the kitchen stove straightening her hair. She could still hear her mama's voice: "You gotta get your hair straight like Lala's." And following that was the memory of the Presto bleaching cream that covered her face each and every night, which only happened because Martha insisted that she, "At least try and look Creole." She also remembered the good times that were few and far between, especially during her visit from Chicago when Vel wore her wigs and expensive clothes. It was a thrill for Vel to go to church and watch her mama's face light up when people said, "Vel sure is pretty. You oughta be quite proud." And Martha was.

For Lala, Martha's death was bittersweet. The sting of slaps could still be felt but she never understood why they came. She did not suspect that Martha's striking out was out of jealousy. As she grew into womanhood, Lala reflected the beauty that was fading from Martha's face, and this was a reality that Martha did not want to admit, and the more Phillip admired the café au lait beauty of Lala, the more Martha would strike out. Lurking beneath this jealousy was pride. Although Lala never knew that jealousy was the reason for her mama's abuse, she knew about her pride--the pride that Martha wore like a badge of Creole heritage. Lala believed that her mama would rather be dead than to live in the asylum, and she was haunted by the likelihood that her mama had run out in front of that bread truck on purpose.

For Rosa, the loss was greatest. Had it not been for her mama, she would be raising the child of a priest and condemned to a life of scorn, and although she felt that the sin of abortion was great, her mama made it seem less so by making the decision seem so right. Of all the children, Rosa would miss her most. In the many months Martha was in the hospital, Rosa was alone and spent more and more time in prayer and church-going. While her mama was alive, there was hope she would return, but now not even hope was possible. Rosa would mourn her loss as long as she had life.

For Lightfoot, who knew her longest, her death was like a part of him dying. He knew that his sister detested everything he did, stood for, and loved, especially the blues. This he would never forget or forgive. However, he did remember the years of care that Martha gave to nurse him back to health, and this took the sting out of the mean and evil thoughts that he knew she nurtured. He would never forget her confession, and he believed that Martha would suffer in hell for all she had done. But in spite of all the stormy memories, he realized that the same blood ran through their veins and bonded them as one. In spite of all, she was his sister and he loved her, and this was a feeling that he could not fully understand.

Although not related by blood, Naomi's life was also strongly affected by Martha's passing. However, in a much different way--relief and satisfaction. Relief, that she no longer had to, "put up with Martha's shit," and satisfaction that her hexes had worked. She had a measure of sympathy for the family's loss, but deep down, she was glad Martha was gone.

All memories of Martha were distressing to her family because her role in their lives brought contradictions to their love. No one remembered love being returned.

The wake lasted all day and far into the night. After saying the rosary, led by Father O'Riley, many people left, but most of the long-time-family friends stayed all night taking turns to sit with the body, so Martha would not be alone.

Naomi went home to get some rest, saying, "I'll be back for my turn later tonight." She had been the perfect helpmate in the kitchen during the wake. Preparing the plates, serving drinks and washing the dishes; all done with a slight smile that could only be understood by the voodoo spirits.

Julee volunteered to be the first to sit, because as she said, "I have some unfinished business with my friend." And indeed she did. When she was sure that the air in the room was not disturbed by any breathing or movement other than her own, she waved her cane around until it encountered the coffin in the spot where the piano usually sat. Her hands found the top of Martha's head, and she lightly touched her face one last time. Every now and then, a tear fell from her membrane covered eyes and disappeared into the lovely white lace dress with the crocheted collar.

Julee breathed out, "I see you're wearing the dress with my handiwork. I know Rose picked it out because that was the one you liked best."

Julee finished her perusal and stood facing downward as if viewing Martha through seeing eyes. She continued. "Girl, the last time I saw you I was angry with you. . . but I guess what happened was not your fault. You were out of your mind, and silly ol' me thought that I could snap you back into thinking straight. I'm really sorry about that, and I ask forgiveness for what I said that upset you."

Julee reached into her pocket for the lace handkerchief she always carried and gently dabbed away her tears. " I don't know why, for the life of me, you had to kill yourself in such a shameful way . . . Either you were really crazy or, like your papa, you had your pride . . . Too proud to live in that horrible place any longer . . . I don't know which it was that caused you to do what you did, but I'm gonna miss our times together . . . drinking tea on the porch . . . gossiping about the goings-on around town . . . and all of the special things we did when we were young. I especially remember that time we went to the picture show to see Shirley Temple in *The Little Colonel*. All those white people were staring at you leading a blind colored lady through the main entrance of the Dixie Theatre. I guess we showed them a thing or two."

Julee chuckled to herself on the way back to the sofa and said, "We've had some golden times together."

She sat and remembered long into the night, until Rosa came to take her home.

Then Phillip took his turn to sit with Martha. The quiet of the room, the dancing shadows from the flickering candles, and the smell of wax all combined to carry his mind's eye back to the night of Martha's flagellation.

"I stood there in the door of the bedroom trying to catch my breath as I looked at your naked back, crisscrossed with cuts oozing blood. I cried. *Oh, my God, Martha what have you done?* I did not want to believe what I was seeing. When I laid you on the bed, and pried that whip out of your hand, you whispered 'God will forgive me now!' I never told this to anyone, not even Rosa. Ah, Rosa. Poor Rosa, she thought I had done that to you. She entered the bedroom while I was wiping the blood from your back, and she yelled, 'Papa, what have you done?' I guess she had every right to think that; we were constantly fussing and fighting. We had a stormy marriage, especially after I left the church in '37."

Now it was clear:--the flagellation had been her attempt to atone for the sins Phillip knew she was guilty of, the sins she had confessed. Although one should not presume to know the secrets of another's heart, Phillip felt that he knew Martha's heart and soul. She did not conceal hatreds very well.

And what pains had Phillip caused her to feel? Perhaps they were the same as the disappointments in his life. He stared down at her face for a long time and tried to recall what had attracted him forty-seven years earlier. He looked past the wrinkles back to the time when he first laid his eyes on her face. He remembered that she was the most beautiful Creole he had ever seen. To marry a woman so lovely was the ultimate prize of every man he knew. And what had he given up? His dream? His career as a doctor? Was it worth it? Those were questions that he could not answer. Although he knew what life with her had been, he did not know what life would have been without her.

Inside Martha was as evil as she was beautiful. She had given him four beautiful children, and each in their own way had proven more joy than the cost in pain and suffering that Martha had brought.

Yes, God had given him a challenge. The love in their marriage had died long ago, but Martha would not let him go, and his resentment increased. Now that death had released him, he was free to have an open life with Alicia. But he had to be careful that his delight for freedom not be mistaken for joy that she was gone. Of all the things that he learned to dislike most about Martha, it was the pleasure she got out of keeping him tied to an empty marriage. Yet, he had feelings for her in death. Exactly what, he did not know, but there was something there. It was hard to live with someone as long as he had lived with Martha without feeling *something*. He knew he did not feel anger. Perhaps it was sorrow because she had lived without ever knowing a true feeling of love.

While these thoughts flashed through his mind, he felt the tender pressure of Lala's arm around his waist. She said softly, "She made our lives a hell on earth, but she was our mama and your wife. Now it's time for you to get some rest."

It was now time for Naomi to sit. It was late--the time of night for the Voodoo spirits to come alive. After Lightfoot had fallen asleep, Naomi got up, got dressed, and stopped by her storage shed to pick up a few items before going over to the Fergerson house.

The full moon had just begun to wane. It was a good time for a final spell.

The parlor was empty. The candles continued to give off the same waxy smell and eerie dance that glowed while Phillip was there.

Naomi looked down at Martha's cold lifeless face staring up at her. A slight smile played at the corners of Naomi's lips. It was not a smile of pleasure; it was a smile of victory. She had won. Naomi believed that her *gris-gris* had worked. The spirits had finally prevailed. All of the hatred of blackness, all of the bad things said about niggers, all of the pain and suffering brought to her life with Lightfoot, all of the evil thoughts that she knew existed in Martha's Creole mind, all of the sins that Lightfoot had heard confessed---all was now avenged. Now Naomi claimed victory. The years of *hexes* and *wangas* had paid off, and now there was only one thing left: the send-off. Naomi believed, as did the Egyptian Pharaohs, that there was life after death, and she wanted Martha to take some earthly possessions with her in her journey to the next world.

All was peaceful and quiet. Naomi looked around in the fluttering light of the candle-lit room to be sure she was alone. She opened the flour sack at her feet and took out the gift for Martha's trip. It was a small black gutbucket filled with chitterlings. Inside was also a black snake with food enough to keep it alive until Martha's body joined her spirit.

Naomi reached into the coffin and raised the hem of Martha's white lace dress. She placed the bucket containing Martha's voyage-food between her legs. Then she smoothed down and arranged the clothes and the body as if nothing unusual had taken place, and all appeared as it

175

should. She stood silent for a moment and then softly sang incantations to the spirits while her arms and body moved in rhythm to the spell being cast. This she continued until she was exhausted and fell into a deep sleep on the sofa.

A gentle shake on the shoulder opened Naomi's eyes, and she looked up at Rosa, who said, "Thanks for sitting with Mama. I just made a pot of coffee."

* * *

Early in the morning, the undertaker came to prepare the body for the trip to the church. The funeral was held at Holy Ghost, and the mourners over filled the church and spilled into the chairs set up outside.

Father O'Riley gave the eulogy. He began with his strong Irish voice. "Do not let ye hearts be troubled. Trust in God, trust also in me. In my Fathers house, there are many rooms. If it were not so, would I have told ye. I am going there to prepare a place for ye. And if I go and prepare a place for ye, I will come back and take ye to be with me that ye may also be where I am.' Those be the words from John fourteen, verse one through three and these words are most appropriate today for the dearly departed Martha Broussard Fergerson. I am sure, as I stand here before ye, that Jesus has prepared a place for Martha in his Father's house. Martha was a good, God-fearing woman. I knew Martha for fifteen years, and in all that time, I never failed to see that beautiful face at mass every morning. She sat right over there. And every Sunday morning she sat right over there in the same pew on the right hand side of God's altar. For the last few years, Martha suffered in the hospital and was not able to come to church, but ye should know the lassie was here in spirit. The good Lord brought to her life trials, and tribulations to test her spirit. He afflicted her mind to test her love for Him, and I know that her spirit and her soul are right here in God's house, in a room he has prepared for her. This was her home. She was baptized in this church. She was confirmed in this church. She was married in this church, and all of her children were raised in this church. She was a good Christian in every way ye can imagine. I remember the good works that Martha performed. And before I came, she was a regular volunteer at the rectory. She spent many hours preparing the meals and helping any way that she could, and she was a great comfort to Father Patrick O'Neill, my predecessor."

Phillip shifted in his seat, and he tried hard to reconcile the picture of Martha that Father O'Riley was painting. What a hypocrite he was. He never once drove to Pineville to visit her in the hospital, and if he had, he would have heard her confession and would have known the true nature of her soul.

But what else does one say in a eulogy? Martha's whole life was a mystery, an enigma. She never was as she appeared. But what does one say at a time like this? What would *he* say if he had to deliver her eulogy? These questions buzzed through his mind like bees. The only words that came to Phillip's mind were those that he had once read by Albert Schweitzer: "The tragedy of a life is what dies in a person while they lived." He closed his eyes as a tear slowly crept down his face. Lala's hand slid over his as if she was reading what was on his mind.

Father O' Riley continued his eulogy for the next ten minutes and Phillip's mind fell asleep through the absurdity of it all.

At the end, Lightfoot played a musical selection on his harp in memory of his sister. It began with her favorite train that segued into a blues version of *Amazing Grace*. It was not exactly the type of music that was usually heard in the Catholic church but Phillip thought it was appropriate for the occasion.

After living her entire life as a Creole who believed she was white, Martha was put to rest behind the crucifix in the area called the colored section.

Throughout the service, the eyes of Phillip and Alicia, met in a silent exchange of affection. It was not possible or appropriate for anything more than a friendly display of sympathy be shown by Alicia for the family loss. It was difficult for both. Alicia wanted to comfort Phillip, and he needed to be comforted by her. Somehow, they were able to conceal their true feelings for each other.

After the burial, most of the people, including Alicia, left and went on about their personal affairs, but some went to the Fergerson house for a few hours of memories, food, and drink. Later, the furniture was put back in place, and the remaining flowers were passed out as tokens of appreciation. The family was then left alone.

* * *

Vel got up from the family group sitting around the kitchen table and went to answer the knock on the door. She immediately came running back, yelling and screaming, "Lord, have mercy, Mama's at the door!"

Lala laughed and said, "Girl, that's not funny."

Phillip closed his eyes and took a deep breath, remembering that Vel was always the one to do something inappropriate.

Rosa looked at Vel's trembling body and said, "I'll go." She entered the parlor and saw a stately woman dressed in an elegant dark blue business suit, staring at the large painting of Joseph Broussard.

178

In response to Rosa's "hello," the woman turned.

Rosa screamed, "Mama!" Then she crumpled to the floor.

The others ran into the room and stopped in shock when they saw the woman kneeling next to the unconscious Rosa, gently patting her cheek.

Phillip demanded, "What's going on here?"

The woman looked up.

Phillip could not believe his eyes. The woman looked exactly like a younger version of Martha. Phillip said, "I'm sorry for the commotion, but you look like my wife who was just buried."

The lady stood up and said, "I'm her sister."

Phillip closed his eyes and shook his head.

Lala, who was attending Rosa, looked up.

Vel sank into the wing chair.

Lightfoot took a step toward the lady and said, "I never had no other sister but Martha." Then the lady pointed to the picture of Joseph Broussard, "Well, he's my father."

"And who was your mother?" Phillip demanded.

The woman said, "Look, I know this comes as a shock. My name is Elvina Bergman, and I've come a long way. If I could have a little something to eat, I'll be happy to tell you everything."

Elvina was settled and made comfortable at the kitchen table. Vel put a plate of fried chicken, ham, and potato salad along with a cup of coffee in front of her. The others sat and looked at this unbelievable reincarnation of Martha. The same pride and dignity. The same deep set gray eyes, the same beautiful face framed by gossamer black hair that cascaded down to her shoulders. Around her neck was a single strand of pearls that complimented her delicate creamy Creole skin.

Elvina unfolded her past. "My mother was Clara

Broussard. She was a fourth cousin to Joe Broussard."

Lightfoot interrupted with an abrupt question, "My father, Joseph Antoine Broussard?"

"Yes. He and my mother were cousins, but they loved each other. And when my mother's father found out she was pregnant, he made her marry Paul Lamoreau, one of her admirers."

There was silence around the table.

Elvina continued, "You see, Joseph Broussard was already married, and. . ."

Lightfoot's mind began working. He held up his hand to stop Elvina. "Just wait a minute. How old are you?"

"I'm fifty-eight."

Lightfoot took a moment to figure and then said, "And Martha was sixty-eight. That means you was born when she was ten years old. Now hold on just a minute. I'm remembering somethin'." Lightfoot told what he overheard while hiding under the bed during the time his mother was fitting Martha's wedding dress.

"Mama's maiden name was Marie Mouton. And Martha asked her about her family. She said, 'every time I turned around my mama was having another baby.' She went on to say, 'I had to get away from all those diapers, so I married your Papa. Then he started.' And Mama told her a lot of stuff. But I'll never forget this, she said, 'After your brother was born, five years after you, I refused to let your Papa ride me like Mama was ridden. I found out them Broussards were just living, breathin' baby makin' machines.' "

Elvina continued, "She was right, they were. My grandfather had nine children, counting my mother. And his father had ten. The Broussards, were a big family and they're all related. Mother's father knew he couldn't marry Joseph because he was already married. It didn't matter that they were cousins."

Phillip's mind wondered about the possibility of an ulterior motive. He asked, "Why did you come here?"

"I was curious. I read in the paper. . ." I read in the paper. . ." Then she smiled slightly and diverted from her story. "I get the *Estillette Chronicle*. I kept the subscription after Mother died. Well, when I read that Martha Broussard Fergerson had died, and her father was Joseph Antoine Broussard, I figured she might be my half-sister. I was curious. My mother Clara had told me everything on her deathbed. But she never told Paul Lamoreau that I was not really his child. She said it was very likely that I had some sisters and brothers in Estilette. She used to say, ' All Broussards are kin under the skin.' I grew up believing that. Since I was an only child, I wanted to get to know my sister's family. When I saw my real father's picture in there," she said pointed to the parlor, "I knew I was in the right place. Mother kept a picture of him in her prayer book." She opened her pocketbook and slid the picture across the table to Phillip. Each in turn looked at it and quietly nodded their heads.

Lightfoot said, "Man, this is some shit." Then he quickly apologized, "I'm sorry."

Elvina said, "You're right, this is a lot of shit. But it's all I have to live with."

The family laughed, and that seemed to break the ice.

Vel figured she could now ask the many questions that rolled around in her mind. "Where are you from?"

"Birmingham."

"Do you have a family?"

"No. My husband died four years ago. I'm alone, which is the reason I'm looking for my family."

Phillip looked into her face, remembering Martha's. It was eerie to see Martha's face on a stranger who sounded so different but looked the same. He wanted to find out more about her family. He said, "Now, your mother's name was Clara, right?"

"Yes."

"Does she still have relatives living here?"

"I'm sure she does, but over the years I've lost touch. After Mother left, the family wouldn't have anything to do with her. They didn't like it at all that she got pregnant by a man who was married."

"Is the Lamoreau family still here?"

"No. What was left of Paul's family eventually died out."

Elvina continued telling them about meeting and marrying her husband David, who was Jewish, and how he started his law firm and made enough money to leave her a rich independent woman. Early in their marriage, she was pregnant twice and lost both babies. Then she stopped trying. The only semblance of family that she had was her half-sister Martha, who "died before we could get to know each other."

Lightfoot reminded her that she also had a half-brother who was a colored Creole.

This did not faze Elvina. "It doesn't matter to me what color you are. I'm just glad to find out from whence I came. Some people live their entire lives without knowing, and others spend their entire lives denying."

The more she spoke, the more the Fergersons liked Elvina. She seemed to be a kinder, more tolerant version of Martha. She was not hoity-toity, and she insisted that the family allow her to pay for the grave marker.

"I'm sorry I didn't make it here in time for the funeral."

They talked and exchanged family stories for the rest of the evening. Lightfoot offered to put Elvina up for the night, and he called Naomi and told her to fix up the guest room.

182

"My sister is going to spend the night."

Needless to say, Naomi was confused and said to herself, *His sister dead. That man has lost what was left of his mind.*

Chapter 12

True Nature Will Out

Elvina Bergman extended her visit. She was a welcomed guest in the home of her brother as long as she wanted to stay. Needless to say, this did not sit well with Naomi, and no matter what she said or how much she protested, Lightfoot's response was, "But she's my sister."

Martha had just left Naomi's life, and now this Martha look-alike was a guest of the family living in her house. It was as if the spirit of Martha had taken up residence to torment her. It seemed that no matter what Naomi did—and over that last fifteen years she had called forth all of her power as a priestess—Martha would not leave her alone. And, like the twist of a knife, Elvina was all of the things that Martha was not—kind, considerate, and helpful.

Elvina helped with the cooking and the cleaning. She made up her bed and scrubbed the bathroom and then asked if there was anything else that she could do. She even engaged Naomi in long conversations about her life in Birmingham and how she was forced to go out of her way to avoid the racial prejudices of the neighborhood where she lived and shopped.

She confided to Naomi, "Since my husband died, there is nothing to tie me to that god-awful city. It is the most segregated place on earth, and I hate to live there. As soon as I can, I plan to move away."

Naomi wanted to ask, "Where do you plan to go?" But she was afraid that the answer might be Estilette, and that was more than she wanted to hear.

To add insult to injury, Elvina asked Naomi to drive her to New Orleans to do some shopping. "I'll pay your gas and buy you some clothes." Elvina explained that because her stay was longer than she had originally planned, she was running out of things to wear and, "I've always wanted to do some shopping at Maison Blanche."

So the two ladies got in the white Cadillac and headed to the city.

At the store, Elvina was treated with the respect due a rich white woman with a colored maid for whom she was buying a few nice things. Naomi was quick to take stock of the situation and said nothing to correct the impression that was assumed. After all, she was getting the dresses, shoes, and undies that she had only dreamed of wearing, and she had the good sense to keep her mouth shut, smile graciously, and accept the gifts of her choosing.

* * *

A few days later in the office of the Black Eagle, Lightfoot hung up the phone with a smile on his face and said, "Hot damn, I did it."

Naomi saw the joy on his face and asked, "Did what?"

"You remember when we opened up the club in '44. There was a young accordion player from Opelousas who

185

was just starting out."

Naomi thought for a moment and said, "Had a singer who played a washboard?"

"Yeah, that's him. Clifton Chenier. He's big shit now, and that was him on the phone. I just booked him to play in two weeks."

"Is that gonna give you enough time to advertise?"

"I ain't got no choice. He's on tour between here and Texas and he had an opening, so I took it. I don't think I'll have any problem. His zydeco stuff is sweeping the delta."

"What's zydeco?"

"I don't know exactly. I think it's some kind of jazzy blues, but by the time he gets here, I'll know." Lightfoot took down his calendar and marked down the dates.

Naomi continued compiling lists of supplies that were needed for the kitchen.

Lightfoot rehung the calendar and headed out of the office, asking as he passed,

"Is Elvina at home?"

"Yeah, why?"

"I wanna tell her about Clifton Chenier."

"Why?"

"So she'll be here for the gig." Lightfoot continued on his way.

Naomi stopped him at the bar, and turned him around. "Two more weeks?"

"Two more weeks what?"

"She's gonna be here for two more weeks?"

"Yeah. She wanna hear some blues. What's the big deal?"

Naomi was silent for a few moments. Then she said, "I can't take this shit no more." Then she walked away.

Lightfoot caught up. "Wait a minute. What's going on?"

"I'll be at the old place 'til she leaves." She started out of the door, then stopped, turned and blared back, "Get somebody else to run the kitchen while I'm away." She slammed the door, got into her car, and drove off.

Lightfoot stood looking after the car as it disappeared in the distance.

* * *

The musty smell of stale air hit him in the face as Lightfoot walked into the shotgun shack that had been closed up for years. The place was in disarray: cases of cold drinks and beer as well as boxes of toilet paper and supplies were piled high in the living room, and the kitchen was stuffed with stacks of extra tables and chairs for the club. Lightfoot opened a window to let in light and air.

Naomi was lying on a threadbare mattress staring up at the ceiling.

He sat on the edge of the bed, looked at the dried tear tracks on Naomi's ebony face and asked, "What's the matter, baby?"

"I dunno. I can't tell what it is, but she makes me feel uncomfortable."

"But she's my sister."

"I know."

"She's not like Martha. She really likes you. She bought you all of them nice things."

"I know. I just can't figure it, that's all. Look I'll just stay here 'til she goes, O.K.?"

"What'll I say?"

"Just tell her anything you want. Tell her I left town, went to visit my family."

"You ain't got no family."

"She don't know that. Tell her what you want. Now

187

leave me be."

Lightfoot didn't know what else to do or say. He kissed her on the forehead and left.

There was no way that Naomi could explain to Lightfoot what she could not explain to herself—how Elvina's kindness made her feel guilty about the way she felt about Martha, how Elvina's presence in the form and likeness of the woman who hated niggers became a growing intimidation, how the memory of Martha's high and mighty ways came alive every time she looked into Elvina's face. It was as if Martha had been reborn to haunt her for all of the hexes over all of the years. And Elvina's sweetness made it all seem like a dream. It was driving Naomi nuts, and she just wanted to get away, be alone. She had to put her mind on other things and other people.

She got up from the bare mattress and went to the closet that still held clothes worn in the early days. She wrapped her head in a tignon, put on her snakeskin cape, trimmed with raccoon tails and duck feathers, and headed to the Sugar Patch to find SipZu.

*   *   *

The traffic was as snarled as it was when B.B. King played the Black Eagle in '53. Clifton Chenier appealed to all, and a great number of Cajuns came to mingle with the Creoles and colored people. Sheriff Bobineaux had to bring on extra deputies to direct parking and keep the cars moving at even a snail's pace. Bobineaux realized that it helped racial relations to have this kind of attraction, so he didn't mind spending the money for the extra help. It was a lot better than having the tension between the races, like when a colored boy was lynched years earlier.

Elvina joined Phillip and Alicia at his special table.

188

Lala, Vitalee, and a couple of local musicians entertained while the crowd got settled. Lightfoot did not have enough time to plan and get things set up. He had not expected such an onrush of so many people from so many backgrounds, all wanting special tables pushed together to accommodate their parties along with setups for drinks with lots of food. There were not enough waiters to fill the orders. The new cooks had only been there for one week and were not accustomed to filling such heavy demands for shrimp, crawfish, and fried chicken in such a short time. In addition, BookTau and his helpers, including Les, were trucking in extra tables and chairs from the old house. It was madness, bedlam. But Lightfoot loved it because he was making money.

And just as Lightfoot had promised Naomi, he found out what zydeco was. He sat in the extra chair at Phillip's table and explained, "The word zydeco comes from a song about snap beans, and somehow the original French word got changed to, the Creole word, and the name zydeco stuck. Clifton comes from Opelousas, just a few miles from here, and he took some Cajun music and mixed it up with rhythm and blues, and the people loved it."

Elvina asked, "Is that zydeco that lady's singing now?"

Lightfoot's expression was like taste buds to a lemon. "Naw. that's the pure blues, called, *My lover Man Was Mean and Evil, Now He's Dead and Gone.* Vitalee wrote that a long time ago."

Elvina was delighted. She had an insatiable appetite for all she had missed but felt in her bones. "I like that . . . it seems so real."

Lightfoot laughed. "It is. She wrote that about a cracker."

"Ahhhh, come on."

"I wouldn't lie to ya."

"What happened?"

Lightfoot felt trapped. He looked over at Phillip.

Phillip shrugged and smiled. "Well, you started this. I'd like to see how you finish."

Elvina bounced around in her seat like a teenager. "Tell, tell! I'd like to know."

"O.K. But then I gotta go."

Lightfoot started. "This is how it was. One night in 1940, Vitalee had finished her gig and gone home to be with her true lover-man. I was sitting at the bar of Blue's Tavern, and Frank Miller come in and looked around trying to see through the dim smoked-filled light.

"Bill Blue said to me, 'That horny bastard is looking for Vitalee.'

"Not seeing Vitalee's smiling black face, Frank headed for the bar. He yells at Bill, 'Hey, boy gimme a beer.'

"Bill got a bottle of Jax and slammed it down in front of Frank with just the right amount of force not to break. Frank threw a quarter on the bar and spit out, 'Where's Vitalee?'

"'She ain't here.'

"'I can see that. Where she at?'

"'I ain't her keeper,' Bill said.

"'Boy, you getting smart with me?'

"I knew that this second 'boy' was not going to set too well with Bill. Bill Blue was six four and 230 pounds of pure muscle. He was afraid of nothing, not to mention a 160 pound cracker who had to carry a gun to get a feeling of power.

"By this time you could hear a rat piss on cotton.

"Bill said, 'This is my place and I don't have to answer to the likes of you 'bout nothin'.'

"'Nigger, I'll close this goddamn place down.'

"'Finish your beer and get your ass out.'

"'You wanna put me out?' Frank challenged.

"That was a question that Bill Blue wouldn't leave unanswered. He came from behind that bar like a clap of thunder before a sudden storm. He headed directly toward Frank. Frank pulled his gun and screamed as he backed away from that big black storm headed his way.

"'Stop, nigger. You're under arrest.'

"Bill kept on bearin' down as Frank backed into tables, stumbled over chairs, and pushed people out of his path, while still screamin','Nigger, I told you to stop!'

"Bill wasn't afraid of a gun and would not be intimated by a white face in his own place, and he did not believe Frank was brave enough to shoot him.

"Frank's ass was on the line. He had to save face in front of a bar full of niggers, so he pulled the trigger and pumped three bullets into Bill's chest.

"Vitalee continued singing after I bought the tavern, and Frank continued fucking her. But every touch from Frank turned to hate. And Frank was too dumb to realize that she could have any feeling at all about the fact that he had killed a man she liked. Deep down inside, she was trying to figure out how she could be free of this cracker's desire for her body.

"A few weeks later, Frank passed on peacefully in his sleep.

"Sheriff Bobineaux could not understand why Frank died so young. The coroner ruled that his death resulted from heart failure. There was nothin' to suggest anything other than a congenital heart condition that no one knew about. The one thing that the sheriff was sure 'bout was that Frank died on a full stomach. Sittin' on the floor next to his bed, along with a pile of chicken bones and six empty Jax beer bottles, was an empty pie pan. Frank loved Vitalee's potato pie. The house was a mess. The sheriff came down

191

to the tavern and got Frank's nigger gal to clean up the place so it would be presentable for the wake. And that is exactly what Vitalee did.

"After his funeral Vitalee said to me, 'Now I'll get some peace for a change.'

"Right then and there, I knew. I didn't know how, but I knew she had. So I asked, 'Did you fuck him to death?'

"'Lord, no!'

"'What killed him, then?'

"There was a long silence and a devil smile took over her face.

"I said, 'Arsenic!'

"'Lord, no. His mean ol' heart just stopped beating.'

"I just had to satisfy my suspicions. I knew how much hate she had for Frank over the murder of Bill Blue. Me and Vitalee been friends from way back. And she thought for a while and said, 'Remember when my daddy come back from Alaska?'

"'Yeah, just in time to get lynched. He'd a done better staying there with his gold money.'

"'He was tired of freezing his ass in them gold fields, so he come back home. But up there, he had gotten used to bein' treated like man. He brought back with him a little jar of crystals. He told me he was saving it for the first white man who didn't show him respect. He never got the chance to use 'em.'

"Then I remembered what they use in the gold fields. Cyanide.

"She never denied or admitted what happened, but from that time on I figured I knew."

Lightfoot looked around at the people pouring in. "Look I gotta go."

Amazement filled Elvina's eyes and her lips parted to give out, "Wow!"

Alicia shook her head and said, "That is something else."

Phillip had heard it all before. There were not too many things that he and Lightfoot did not share.

Elvina was back in her questioning mood. She was really trying hard to understand. "So what's the difference between the blues that Vitalee sings and this zydeco stuff?"

Phillip chimed in, "As your sister would say, the blues is nigger, gut-bucket music, played mostly in juke joints by low-class black people."

Alicia fell out laughing at Phillip's sarcastic truth in Martha talk. Then she added,

"And zydeco is really fun-and-dance music that came from Cajun traditions, with some rhythm and blues thrown in. It's impossible to sit and listen. You've got to get up and shake your booty."

Phillip cautioned, "Now watch your talk."

Alicia said with a laugh "I know Elvina Broussard knows what the booty is. Don't you Miz Creole?"

At this invitation Elvina stood up and shook her ass in time to what was being played by Lala's group. Phillip and Alicia laughed.

Alicia said, widening her eyes in a making fun manner, "Are you sure you and Martha are from the same papa?"

Phillip reached out and touched the passing waiter on the arm. "Bring another round of what we're drinking."

Elvina interrupted, "No more bourbon for me. Do you have any wine?"

Before the waiter could answer, Phillip said, "The only wine they've got is Gallo. I'll get you some good wine." Then he said to the waiter. "Send Les over here."

When Les came Phillip instructed him to take his car and go to Stephen Estilette's house and get a couple bottles of wine. "I'll call and tell him you're coming."

Clifton Chenier and his group came on and began to set up.

Lala and Vitalee disappeared into the small room behind the stage where the musicians could change into their performance paraphernalia and relax. Lala felt that she could return to playing piano in the public once again, since her mama was gone. She had not played the blues since Martha slapped her in the crowed tavern, the year she ran off and got married.

The ladies began to towel off the sweat from the heat of the stage, and they were both in their bras as they talked. Lala thought of Vitalee as a professional singer. She had been singing since the early days of Blue's Tavern and was now a local favorite at The Black Eagle. Lala asked in a direct, straightforward manner, "What do you expect to get from the piano player?"

Without hesitation, Vitalee said, "The rhythm and the beat. I hate it when they fuck up the beat. Although I do have a tendency to change the beat sometimes."

"So I've noticed."

Vitalee laughed and said, "I hope you're not too pissed."

"No. I just follow where you lead."

"Honey, don't mind me. I just do what I do and sing what I sing."

Lala added, "And I'll just continue to follow where you lead."

At that moment, the door opened. Lala grabbed her blouse and covered up. Vitalee took a long drag from her cigarette, turned in the direction of the opened door and asked, "What the fuck you want?"

Lester said, "Lala."

The sound of his voice caused Lala to turn toward the door. She said, "Lester! What are you doing here?"

"I come to talk."

Vitalee asked, "You know this guy?"

"Yes. He's my husband."

"Didn't yo mama teach you to knock on a closed door?"

Lester had had a few drinks but he was a long ways from being drunk, and he was quick to respond, "I'm sorry, but I saw Lala come in here and I didn't know she was with anybody."

"Well, she is."

There was a pause as if Vitalee expected him to leave, and he expected her to leave. Finally, he said, "I just come to talk."

Vitalee breathed out, "Well, talk on, honey." She began to fix her makeup, and Lester got the message that she was not about to leave. The fact that she was in her bra did not disturb her in the least, but Lala seemed a bit ill at ease and so did Lester.

He looked from one to the other and then he asked, "Would you excuse us?"

Vitalee turned, her cigarette dangled from her lips, and she elegantly brought up her hand, gently took the cigarette between her first and second fingers and said, "You're excused. Say what you come to say. But if you think I'm gonna leave before I've finished dressing, you've got another think coming."

Lester didn't have a choice. It was now or never. He had made up his mind that he was going to talk with Lala tonight. He looked at Lala then turned back and looked at Vitalee. She seemed occupied with what she was doing, so maybe they could talk softly. He moved closer to Lala and whispered, "Baby, please."

Lala clinched her teeth and said, without opening her mouth, "No, Lester! I've told you. I've had it. I'm not coming back."

Lester didn't know what else to say, or do. He took Lala in his arms and kissed her. She was so shocked she went limp. As the kiss began to stimulate her, it brought back memories, and for a brief moment she received his tongue and kissed back. Then she realized what was happening. She was always vulnerable to his passion, and he knew it. She had to resist. She could not allow herself to fall back into his lovemaking seduction. She braced her hands against his chest and gave a push, but she was no match for his ruggedness and stumbled backwards, fell over the chair, and ended up on the floor.

The commotion stirred Vitalee to action. She was up like a flash. She planted herself between Lester and Lala and flipped open her switchblade.

"Alright, mutherfucker, you wanna hit somebody, hit me."

It had happened so fast, Lester didn't know what to do. He shrugged his shoulders, turned and left the room without a word.

Vitalee had some parting words for him. "That's right, you bastard, slam the door when you leave." Then she turned her attention to Lala. She uprighted the chair and gave Lala a helping hand.

Lala collapsed with her head on the dressing table and cried. She wanted to tell Vitalee that Lester had not hit her, that she had fallen and it was all her fault. But she could not. All she could do was cry.

Vitalee stroked her soft, silky hair and spoke comforting words. "Don't you fret none, hon. All them bastards alike. They slap us around 'cause they think we're the weaker sex, and that's why I carry my protection. You got to stand up for yourself and let 'em know you got some feeling, too."

Lala was grateful for the kindness, and she raised her head, dried her tears and said with a smile, "Thank you. I'm all right now. I'll be fine."

Vitalee said, "I know you will be." Then she completed her makeup, put on her blouse, and left.

Lala looked at her reflection in the mirror. She didn't know if she was all right or not. Her marriage was split apart. This was the first time in her memory that any Broussard had separated. There were many wives she knew who had difficulties, but because they had married for "better or worse," they stuck it out. She didn't know whether that phrase included being slapped around or not, but no Catholic she knew had ever gotten divorced. At this point, she hadn't made up her mind about that. She just wanted to be away from Lester and his drinking. First her mama died in that horrible way, and now this. It seemed as if her whole life was falling apart, but she was determined that this was not going to get her down. She dried her eyes, fixed her face, and prepared to join Phillip and the others.

Elvina's face was a sea of wonderment and delight. She had never before heard anyone like Clifton Chenier. In Birmingham, her husband had exposed her to operas and symphonies. But this music awakened her true, dormant, Creole nature. Her husband's taste in music had come from his German Jewish heritage and, although foreign to her feelings, she enjoyed and appreciated it. But she felt the zydeco in her bones and couldn't sit still. She extended her hand to Phillip, and they went to the dance floor. Elvina could not understand the Creole words to the songs, but she picked up the rhythm of the music without hesitation.

She yelled to be heard above the singing, "What's he saying?"

"Allons a Grand Coteau." Then Phillip interpreted, "Let's go to Grand Coteau. It's a small town not far from

here. But that's all I know. I don't speak too much Creole."

They danced on and enjoyed the music.

Lightfoot collapsed in the chair across from Alicia, watched the action on the dance floor, and said, "Elvina seems to be having a good time."

Alicia laughed and said, "She's discovering who she really is. How are things going for you?"

"I miss Naomi in the kitchen, but everything else is jumpin." He noticed the bottles of wine and read the label. "Where y'all get this Bordeaux from? I know it ain't mine."

"From Stephen. Phillip sent Les to get it for Elvina."

"Ma sister sure is making some changes around here. Got y'all drinking fancy wine now!" Lightfoot thought of the change with Naomi because of Elvina. He liked having Elvina around, but he was missing Naomi and he wondered where she was and what she was doing. His thoughts were short-lived because the dance ended and Elvina and Phillip collapsed exhausted into their chairs.

Alicia extended the crawfish that she had just peeled, and Lightfoot handed Elvina a glass of wine and said, "Chase it down with this."

Lala approached the table, finger popping and moving her body in time with the music, *Les Bon Ton Roulet*. She threw her hands in the air and shouted out, "He is indeed the king of zydeco." Then she plopped into a chair. She was determined to have a good time for the rest of the night. All of the unpleasantness had been put behind, and she wanted to forget. She reached across, grabbed a crawfish, shook it at Elvina, and said, "It's all Louisiana gumbo. The Creoles, the music, the food, and the fun."

Chapter 13

Holding up the Mirror

March, 1962 - A full moon was high in the sky. The cricket and bullfrog choirs sang songs of enchantment. The magnolia scented air was warm and sensual, and the leaves and Spanish moss provided a bed for the lovers.

Naomi knew she was playing with fire, but she didn't care. It was the best way she could exorcise the spirit of Martha's ghost from her mind. Her memory of that night at Tante's place had lured her back, and she brought SipZu with her. The musky, sweaty aroma of his muscular body was the aphrodisiac that induced the bloody fingernails tracks across his back. Naomi's backdoor man was spent. He pushed his body up and away from hers, and for several moments, he looked down into her dreamy eyes. Then he rolled over, exhausted.

They lay side by side looking up at the moon sailing across the starry sky. A waterfall of thoughts swirled through Naomi's mind. Except for that time at the end of

199

her frenzied dance, this was the first time she had made love with anyone except Lightfoot. She wanted to think of this waywardness as "making love." She wanted to think of this as more than just a fuck, but whatever it was called, she was still an unfaithful wife. But somehow it did what she needed it to do—chase Martha's image out of her thoughts.

Thoughts of Lightfoot, however, continued to float in her mind. She could see him limping from place to place, trying to balance all of everything that was happening at the Chenier gig. Guilt came along with his image, but she didn't care. She had done what she did because she had to, and that was that. And then her body trembled with the thought of what Lightfoot might do if he found out. She could not let that happen.

In the shadows, her eyes turned to the dead-tired body beside her. She rose up on an elbow, traced the line of SipZu's mouth with her index finger, and kissed his lips. She said softly, "Thank you."

"For what?"

"Being here when I needed you."

SipZu didn't understand the deeper implications of her words, but he said, "Yeah, that's all right. What're we gonna do now?"

"Nothing. Just be."

Again, SipZu didn't know what was being spoken. He blurted out, "Woman, what is you talking?"

"Just be still." Then she fell back and focused on the stars.

* * *

Spring was approaching.

Elvina had been in Estilette over two months and decided that it was time to return to Birmingham. She had made a lot of progress in establishing a family relationship with everyone except Naomi. She felt it strange that Naomi had suddenly disappeared to visit her family without saying goodbye, but after a few days, she did not think about it anymore. She had made a decision. She would be back. She liked Louisiana, especially New Orleans. She also liked Phillip. Maybe, just maybe, after the proper grieving time, the subject of her growing affection could be approached gracefully.

Phillip listened to the Longine Symphony on the radio. It was relaxing. He closed his eyes and stretched out on the leather horsehair sofa in his den. He was soon asleep.

He dreamed of Martha in the good old days when they were very much in love. They were alone on a picnic. They sat on a quilt, on the grass, under an oak near the bayou. They laughed, talked trivia, and enjoyed each other. Martha leaned over and kissed him on the lips. It felt so real that he opened his eyes. Her face moved away slowly. She was standing next to the sofa, looking down at him. Martha was alive!

A voice spoke, "I let myself in, and followed the music. I hope you don't mind"

Phillip, still in a shadowy state of delusion, rubbed his eyes.

The voice continued, "I've come to say goodbye. Well, not really goodbye, just so long for a little while."

Phillip sat up. He was back in reality. He said, "Elvina! For a moment there, I thought you were Martha."

"I know how much you miss her. No doubt she was in your dreams, if you were dreaming."

"I was, and I opened my eyes to see you."

"I hope you were not disappointed."

"Not in the least. You look so much alike." Then he changed the subject, "What does 'so long' mean?"

Elvina explained that she had decided to return to Birmingham, sell her property, settle her business, and then move to New Orleans. She went on to say she hated Birmingham and did not know why she had stayed on after her husband died, that the trip to Estilette had opened up possibilities for a new lease on life, and she wanted Phillip to know that she was in love with her new-found family.

Phillip's thoughts ran amuck. She looked so much like Martha; it was hard to imagine that she was not. And that was the irony. Everything Martha was, thought, and felt, Elvina was not, did not think, and did not feel. For a brief moment, wishful thoughts flashed through Phillip's mind. And then he thought of Alicia, cleared his head, and refocused his attention on the soft music.

* * *

Phillip went to visit Luther. It had been a long time since he had been to his brother's house. Martha had driven a wedge between them, and he had gone along with her insistence that Luther not darken their door. Yes, Luther drank, he gambled, and he lived with a woman that he was not married to. But he was still Phillip's brother, and except for chance occurrences of passing him on the street, Phillip had not seen him in twenty years, until the funeral. He didn't know why he had let that happen, maybe only to keep peace in the family. But he regretted that he had not made more of an effort to see his brother.

When he drove into the yard, he could see that the house was in need of repair and paint. He looked out over the yard filled with rusty abandoned farm machinery, cars, and trucks. Phillip could not stand to have junk-cluttered surroundings, but it did not seem to bother Luther. They were as different as night and day.

Several minutes after he had knocked, there was still no response. Phillip knew he was there; his car was in the yard. Maybe Luther had seen him drive up and didn't want to open the door. Or maybe he was sick or dead. Phillip decided that he would sound the horn, and he had started in the direction of his car when the door opened.

Luther was surprised to see him. "What are you doing here?"

"I came by to see how you were."

"Since that witch is gone, you can be your own man again."

Phillip knew he was referring to the time Martha had put him out, and Phillip made no protest.

Martha had said, "Your drinking, gambling, womanizing, and killing is the gossip of the town, and I'll not have you dirty up my house."

Luther responded, before slamming the door, "At lease I'm my own man."

Phillip decided not to take issue with Luther's remark. He went on, "We didn't get a chance to talk at the funeral, and I thought we might be able to catch up on old times."

"Well, that's very brotherly of you after all these years."

The sarcastic remark made Phillip realize how much damage had been done. But it was his failure for not speaking up at the time, so he said, "I'm sorry for that. I should have known better than to listen to Martha. But you know what a compelling woman she was."

"You can say that again." Luther walked over to Phillip and gave him a hug. Then he said, "Welcome back, brother."

This was a shock. Phillip didn't know what to say. He had not expected Luther to forgive his disloyalty so quickly. He was lost for words. He backed out of the embrace and looked toward the opened door.

"Where's . . . er. . . what's her name?"

"Barbara Ann. Ahhh, she's long gone. Went on to a younger man. I'm all by myself now. Don't have much drive anymore. Just sleep all the time."

"I know how it is. I fall asleep every time I read the paper."

"It's called getting old. When I get up in the morning, I got to clear all the passages, fart, cough, spit, and blow out my nose. And my dick leaks all day long, and it don't get hard too often anymore, so I know what you going through,"Luther said.

The brothers laughed, backslapped, and shared the common ailments of time. Although two years younger, Luther looked older. Phillip felt it might be because of the gray beard or because of stress. Luther's life had been one turmoil after the other. His wife died while giving birth to their third child, and Luther raised the children alone and along with one woman after the other. As soon as the children reached adulthood, they left. It was after the last boy was gone that Barbara Ann came into his life, and she was just about the same age as his oldest daughter. Phillip realized how different their lives had been.

Luther went in and brought out a jug of cherry bounce and two glasses and put them on the cypress tree-stump table that sat near the porch swing.

Phillip looked at the swing that had seen better days and said, "You think it'll hold both of us?"

"Yeah. It's stronger than it looks. Now sit your ass down and have a drink."

The brothers reminisced about yesteryear and the good times they had growing up. As Luther poured a second round, he said, "When you said you were going to medical school, Papa sent me to Leland College to be a teacher."

"Is that right? I didn't know that."

"And when you got married and started teaching, I decided to keep on farming, so I didn't finish."

"I wondered why you dropped out."

"I didn't want you to think I was copying you by teaching school and settling down with a pretty woman, so I married an ugly woman and became a farmer."

"Ah, come on. Helen was not a bad looker."

"But she wasn't high yella. And at that time, Papa had us dead right. He said, 'Your brother likes his gals from high yella to white, and you'll take anything from light brown to black.' "

Phillip came back, "Oh, come on. Papa didn't say that."

"I wouldn't lie to ya. It's the truth. And time has borne him out. You never did fool around with anyone darker than milk."

"What about Gertrude?"

"Gertrude Perkins?"

"Yeah."

"Oh, you fucked her that one time and then took off to school. Later she asked me why you didn't write."

"I was getting into my studies by then," Phillip said.

"And you was driving Dr. Clark all over the country, but you wasn't too busy to drive over here on the weekends to see Martha."

"We were in love."

"And she was Creole. Gertrude was a nice girl, but she was too dark for you."

"I told her I was engaged to Martha."

"I often wondered why they let you into that family. You was the color of a paper bag. "

"Marrying Martha was the dream of my life."

"And it kept you from going to medical school. That was the biggest mistake of your life," Luther said.

"Talking about mistakes, yours was gambling."

"Naw! You got that wrong. My biggest mistake was decency. That's what caused me to kill that bastard who beat up Barbara Ann. After that happened, Barbara Ann come by and wanted to be my woman 'cause as she said in that sweet voice of hers, 'You're a righteous and decent man.' And then all of those legal troubles fell on my head and ruined me. And if I remember correctly, that's about the time that woman of yours began condemning me, even though the killing was ruled self-defense."

Phillip's mind's eye went back to the night that Martha had damned Luther, and he had threatened her in defense of his brother. He wondered how decent it was of him to raise his hand to his wife when his brother's decency had prompted him to kill a man for striking a woman. Phillip realized then that, Martha had no right to judge his brother twenty years earlier.

He decided to change the subject and let Luther know that all beautiful women were not like Martha. He said, "Martha's sister showed up after the funeral."

"Didn't know she had a sister."

"She was Joe Broussard's outside child."

"You're kidding."

"Naw, it's the truth. She just left. Spent two months here with Lightfoot."

"What she want?"

"Nothing. Just wanted to get to know her family."

"Is that right?"

"And believe it or not, she looks *just* like Martha."

That was too funny for words, and Luther could not speak for laughing.

Phillip asked, "What's so funny?"

"The bitch of all bitches just died and her sister look-alike comes to take her place. Does she sound like Martha too?"

Phillip took a long drink and let it slowly trickle down. He didn't want to get into an altercation, so he said with a friendly tone, "No! She's very different. Kind, considerate, loving, and generous. She took Naomi to Maison Blanche and bought her a whole new wardrobe."

"Well, I'll be damned. You lucky bastard. Now you got a righteous sister-in-law to take the place of the wicked wife."

Phillip corrected him immediately. "No! It's not like that at all."

"Who you shitting? I know you like a book. You love Creole women, and that's been your downfall."

"I've got a woman."

"Who?"

"Alicia Wallace."

"That professor up at Southern?" Man, you can't shit me. You don't see beyond skin, and she ain't Creole. It won't be long before you have another Martha in your bed." Luther laughed and took a drink.

Phillip emptied his glass and placed it on the table as he stood. It was time to leave. His visit had accomplished more than he intended. In some respects, Luther had not changed. He was as feisty and outspoken as ever. It was the same nature that induced him to challenge the gambling man who beat Barbara Ann black and blue. And he was compassionate. Phillip never expected that Luther would embrace him as he had. It was a good visit, even though Luther had planted thoughts of unfaithfulness in his mind-- the same thoughts that Elvina had left him with.

As he drove out of the yard, Phillip realized that his brother had held up the mirror, and he had taken a long hard look.

* * *

207

It was after school on Friday and Joshua sat at the base of the crucifix in the center of the Graveyard, smoking a cigarette. He held a dozen roses that he had gotten from Ernie's Florist. He waited patiently.

After a while, Rosa appeared, headed in his direction. He crushed the cigarette under his foot and stood. When she saw him, she stopped and, with a surprised look, said, "Why Joshua, what are you doing here?"

"Waiting for you."

"Waiting for me?"

He extended the bouquet with a gracious smile. "For my sweet Rosa."

She took the flowers and brought them to her nose. "How thoughtful, but how did you know I would be here?"

"You visit your mama's grave every Friday after your novena. And I wanted to give you this." He removed a small box from his pocket. "I want you to be my wife."

Rosa was overcome. She slipped the ring on her finger and covered her eyes with her hands; tears rolled down through her fingers. After a few moments, she said, "Yes. I'd like that."

"Well, what are we waiting for?"

"What do you mean?"

"Let's get married."

"When?"

"Right now."

"Where?"

"New Orleans. Where else? We'll have our honeymoon at the Dew Drop Inn where we stayed before."

Rosa brought her fingers to her lips as she remembered that week-end in New Orleans. They had a boat ride on the Mississippi, walked the streets of the French Quarter, enjoyed a delicious dinner at the Dooky Chase restaurant, and had beignets and café au lait at Café du Monde. When they returned to the Dew Drop Inn Joshua made gentle love to her. Just like Ruth had predicted, being out of town with him had made a difference. Most of her anxieties and fears had disappeared, and she was able to overcome her mama's implanted feelings about skin color.

"Ohhhh Joshua, I don't know what to say."

"Just say yes, and it's a done deal. Know what I mean?"

"Yes!"

Joshua and Rosa kissed right there beneath the crucifix in the graveyard. After picking up a few things from the house, they headed for New Orleans, without Phillip's knowledge or blessings.

Chapter 14

Chickens Come Home to Roost

April, 1962 - Naomi had not yet returned.

Elvina had been gone for a week, and Lightfoot could not understand why Naomi did not know. In a town the size of Estilette, if someone farted on one side of town, it was smelled on the other side.

He decided to go to the old house to find out why she had not come back. When he drove up, he saw her car parked in front and he also saw a bicycle leaning against the porch. He was curious. He crept along the side of the house to the bedroom window. The shade was pulled down, but the window was cracked about six inches to let in air. He peeped in and saw two naked people fucking. One was Naomi. He did not know the man. Lightfoot sank to the ground. For several minutes he just sat there not knowing what to do.

Finally, he made up his mind. He limped to his truck, got his .38 revolver and entered the bedroom. The surprised lovers turned and looked before the shots rang out. Stunned momentarily by the suddenness of the intrusion, they realized that they had not been hit. SipZu jumped up and ran out the back door. Lightfoot aimed above his head and discharged several shots with his exit.

SipZu hightailed it down the road, leaving his clothes on the floor and his bicycle leaning against the porch.

Naomi huddled in the corner, waiting for the inevitable.

Lightfoot aimed the pistol at her trembling body, but after a few seconds, he lowered his arm, turned around, and straggled out of the house. Back in his truck, he dropped his head to the steering wheel, the empty revolver dangled from his hand, and tears puddled the dust on top of his foot.

Phillip looked up from work at his desk when Lightfoot walked into the den. "What's wrong?"

Lightfoot collapsed on the sofa, his elbows propped on his knees with his head cradled in his hands. He cried, "I caught somebody dipping in my sugar bowl."

Phillip could not understand what he meant, "What was that?"

"I came close to killing Naomi."

Phillip's eyes widened. "What are you talking about?"

"I almost shot Naomi.

"You did what?"

"She was with a man."

Phillip rose and moved to sit next to Lightfoot. "What happened?"

"I caught 'em together at the old house. I shot. I just wanted to scare off the man, but I came close to killing her."

"Where is she now?"

"At the old place."

"Is she alive?"

"Yeah. But I wanted to kill her. She was fucking that

man. I don't know how she could do that to me."

"Who was the man?"

"I don't know. Never seen him before." Lightfoot had never paid any attention to the man who racked the balls when he shot pool with Slick.

Phillip took a deep breath and pulled at his eyebrows. Troubles were raining down on the family: Lala announced that she was getting a divorce--Rosa was running around with a man wanted by the law, and Lightfoot came close to killing Naomi. His family was unraveling right before his eyes.

* * *

Naomi had to do something. A backdoor man had destroyed her mama's life, and she did not want hers to follow the same path.

Her mind's eye travel back to when she was ten.

The commotion in the back room woke her from sleep. She listened. As best she could figure out from the voices, her papa and mama were fussing about another man. She heard her papa say, "If I ketch y'all, I'll kill you both." She remembered that as clear as day. At that time, she didn't know who her papa was talking about killing. She remembered that several nights later her Papa pulled her out of bed, dragged her outside and left her under a tree.

After the fire, her grandma told her what happened. "Chile, yo' daddy was a cotton picking man. He'd leave town, every now and then and go where the picking was good, and sometimes he'd be gone for weeks at a time. Now, yo' Mama was a good woman, but she needed a man, so she took up with a backdoor man, and when yo' Daddy was away, the backdoor man would come around. One night yo' papa came back unexpectedly and found them in bed asleep. He poured coal oil over them and lit a match. Then he pulled you out of the house and took off."

Naomi remembered hearing their screams over the crackle of the flames, and there was nothing she could do but cry. She never saw her papa again after the night. It was a horrible memory and one that she did not want to have repeated. She didn't know why her grandma told her what had transpired, except as a warning of what could happen if a woman took up with a backdoor man.

Naomi had to do something to get Lightfoot's love back. The affair with SipZu was just to forget about Elvina, but she got carried away and things got out of hand. She had no intention of putting her marriage at risk. Now she had to fix it.

The first thing she did was to redo the hex that had attracted Lightfoot in the first place. She wrote his name on a piece of parchment paper in dove's blood ink. Then she glued the paper to the feet of a voodoo doll made in his image. She sprinkled the doll with French Luv power and anointed it with Luv oil. And while Luv incense burned, she recited the 40th and 41st Psalms. That had worked to get his love in the first place, and she believed it would work to bring it back. But she was not satisfied that that was enough. She had to do more.

The club was closed on Monday nights, and Naomi went in and made the necessary preparations. Then she went home. She quietly entered through the kitchen. When she got to the den, she saw Lightfoot sitting in his Lazy Boy chair. He had not eaten. He had not shaved. He had not slept. He was just staring into space. She stood quietly in the doorway and watched.

Lightfoot sensed that someone else was in the room and he turned. Their eyes met.

Naomi was afraid to say anything.

213

Lightfoot was silent.

For several minutes, they just looked at each other, and private thoughts raced through their minds. Neither would dare express their feelings for fear that all hell would break loose. Naomi did not know if the intention to shoot her was still in Lightfoot's mind, but she wanted the opportunity to say she was sorry.

She approached slowly. Their eyes remained locked. She knelt down next to the chair and gently took his face in her hands and slowly brought his lips to hers. She kissed him and breathed out tearfully, "I'm sorry."

Lightfoot did not utter a word, nor did he return the kiss.

She took him by the hand and pulled him to the bathroom. While water filled the tub, Naomi ceremoniously undressed him and kissed each part of his body as it was stripped bare. Lightfoot remained stoic. He didn't know what to think about what was happening. And because the rage over what he had seen had now subsided, he was numb.

The warm, fragrant water felt good. It was soothing. Naomi knelt next to the tub as if in prayer and squeezed water from the sponge, trickling it gently over his shoulders.

Lightfoot closed his eyes and tried to shut out the vision of her in bed with the other man. He didn't want to know his name, but the picture of his face remained in his memory. Naomi helped erase the image as she soaped and sponged his body. She understood the simple, uncomplicated nature of a man, and she called forth all of her knowledge to save her marriage. She could sense his body relaxing, and she knew that his mind was releasing the angry thoughts that were there earlier.

Lightfoot's thought's were now focused on Martha.

Maybe she had been right all along. Martha had said, "Naomi is low class, and they have no morals." He could hear the echo of his sister's voice, "You gonna find yourself in a whole peck of trouble messing with that woman." And now it seemed that Martha's prediction had come to pass.

The main thing about Naomi that he did not understand was the voodoo. At first, he had accepted it as a part and parcel of who she was. He knew that the practice of voodoo had come from Africa, and like the blues, it grew strength from slavery and oppression. So maybe the voodoo was what had attracted him to Naomi in the first place, and he had accepted it the same way Martha accepted her faith in Catholicism. And although Martha's predictions about voodoo and the devil seemed to be coming to pass, he refused to accept that. There just had to be something else to explain why she had gone to bed with that man.

His mind left Martha's disapproval and traveled the road of self-incrimination. Was there something that he had done or not done to cause Naomi to do what she did? He knew that sex played a large part in their relationship, and they had not been intimate during the entire time Elvina was living with them. And even before that, he was busy with the club, and when he got home late he was tired, and as soon as his head hit the bed he was out like a light. Maybe it was his fault. He was fifteen years older than Naomi, and at sixty-four, fucking was not on his mind as much as it was when they met. Maybe that was the reason. She needed love. So she went outside to find it. Maybe her displeasure with Elvina being in the house was stronger than he thought. Maybe that was the reason. His mind skipped from one possibility to another, like trying to see shadows on a cloudy day.

Lightfoot felt his nature rise, awakened by the gentle

stroking of the sponge. It was reassuring, with all of the other shit on his mind, that his dick could still get hard. Naomi had stirred up the embers of the dormant passion and brought back the fire that forged the bond between a man and a woman. She knew exactly what to do. She understood the power of the sexual instinct that controlled practically all behavior. Slowly, his thoughts left the past and came back into the present. Naomi stood and held a towel open for him. When she had dried him off, she said, "Get dressed. I'll meet you at the club." Then she left.

Lightfoot was confused. He was all primed and ready to make love and she disappeared. He didn't know what to make of what she said. His dick slowly slumped along with his hope that things might be on the road to repair. This woman was indeed mysterious. He didn't even try to figure what she had in mind. He got dressed.

When Lightfoot entered the club his mouth dropped open. Candles lighted the entire place. Candles were on the bar, on stands and buckets, washtubs, and in bottles. Candles surrounded the table in the middle of the dance floor that was set with a dinner of T-bone steak and oysters, okra on rice, baked sweet potatoes, and sliced tomatoes--all of Lightfoot's favorites. He looked around for Naomi and slowly limped to the table. He eyed the delicious food and sat down.

The sound of drumming came from the kitchen, and Naomi jumped out of the flickering shadows, stark naked. She danced around the table in rhythm to the beat of the drums, slowly moving her body and arms in a ritual that symbolized the casting of a spell.

Lightfoot began to eat. He had heard tell stories from early plantation days about the the master of the mansion having dinner served with voodoo dancing to stimulate desire for the mistress of the house. And that was very much like what happens on Bourbon Street every night. Lightfoot figured that Naomi was dancing her way back into his good graces.

He had never before seen such intensity in her dance. She had dance naked many times but never with such solemn movements that seemed to come from an inner passion. The drums were live. Someone was beating in the kitchen, and as the beat of the drums grew faster, Naomi's movements intensified. Lightfoot's stomach and desire were fed at the same time. Naomi's facial expressions grew more and more erotic, and after going on for what seemed like an hour or more, the drums stopped. Naomi collapsed on the floor at Lightfoot's feet.

For several minutes, she did not move, and about the time Lightfoot began to worry, she reached up and began ripping off his clothes. She guided him to the stage and placed him gently on a mattress pallet where she gave him a fuck the likes of which he had never before experienced. She kissed every inch of his body, and when his dick was hard, she thrust her body on top. Then she sucked him alive again and put him on top. And this went on and on until Lightfoot was worn out. He closed his eyes and fell into a dead sleep.

For the next two hours, Naomi rested. Then, as if prompted by an inner spirit, she was abruptly startled awake.

Naomi went into the kitchen and found SipZu draped over the drums. She checked his heart to be sure he was dead. Then she took the bottle containing the remains of the remains of the cyanide-lace liquor and poured it down the drain. She smashed the bottle into smithereens and scattered the slivers among several garbage cans. Dragging his body through the back door of the kitchen into the trunk of her car was difficult but somehow she managed.

On the way to the thicket, her mind's eye went back to the day that Lightfoot discovered her in bed with SipZu. Tears slid down her face along with the memory. She was still trembling in the corner where she was left after Lightfoot pointed the pistol at her. SipZu entered, as naked as he was when he ran out.

He knelt down next to her trembling body, his face filled with hatred, and said with vengeance in his voice, "I ran down the street and all the peoples laughed at me. Then I hid behind the honeysuckle fence until I saw his truck leave. I had to run from one cover to another to come back to get my clothes and my bicycle. And all the while, the people were laughing from behind doorways and curtains. Now I swear to you, on the soul of Marie Laveau, that I will kill that bastard for making me a laughing stock. That, I swear, I will do."

SipZu had every intention of fulfilling his threat, and the plan for him to slice Lightfoot's throat when he was intoxicated with drink was the enticement used to lure SipZu into the scheme at the club.

Naomi did what she did to save Lightfoot. He had been a godsend. He had faced the hatred of his sister to give her love. He had given her a life style that she could only imagine in her dreams. There was no way that she could knowingly allow Lightfoot's life to be sliced away by SipZu. She had to choose between the two, and she made her choice.

When she reached Tante's place, she dragged SipZu's body out of the trunk of the car and rolled it into the alligator infested bayou. For several minutes, under the waning moon, she danced a silent ritual of thanksgiving and praise to the voodoo spirit that had saved her marriage. The backdoor man who threatened her peace and happiness was gone, and she would not be tempted into sin again.

Daylight broke as she headed back to Estilette. It had been an event-filled evening, the likes of which she had never experienced in her life--the voodoo spirit and taken over and guided her back to the road that she should travel. She arrived at the club and set about extinguishing the candles.

The aroma of coffee with chicory opened Lightfoot's eyes, and he turned to see Naomi walking in from the kitchen through a shaft of sunlight. She carried two blue and white graniteware cups of steaming coffee. She sat on the edge of the mattress, passed one cup to Lightfoot, and said, "Good morning, sunshine, hope you're feeling better now."

Lightfoot's mind raced a mile a minute. What should he say? How should he respond to this unfaithful woman who was now being so attentive? She had asked forgiveness, and he decided to let bygones be bygones.

He said, "Yeah, I am. Thank you." He kissed her and took a sip of coffee.

* * *

Two nights later, Rosa walked into the house.

Phillip was in the den listening to the radio. He heard the front door open, and he stood in the doorway as Rosa walked down the hall.

"Where have you been?" he asked.

"Hi, Papa." She stopped and kissed him.

"I asked you, where have you been?"

"I got married."

Phillip was shocked. He was not sure he heard what he heard. He asked, "You did what?"

"I got married."

Phillip walked away and sat on the sofa.

Rosa stood in the doorway. She knew that her Papa's distress had not reached its peak, and she was determined to get it over with once and for all, so she stood waiting.

Phillip caught his breath and said, "I guess you married that. . ."

Rosa interrupted, "Joshua Kane. I am Mrs. Joshua Kane."

Phillip said quietly, "Well, I guess that's that."

Rosa moved to the sofa and sat next to Phillip. "Papa, please try and understand."

"What? That you have thrown away your life on some law-breaking hustler who schemed to marry the finest woman from the best family in Estilette? Were you that desperate?"

Rosa thought for a moment and let the stinging words sink in. She said slowly and thoughtfully, "A few days after you and I had that big fuss over me seeing Joshua, I went to see Mama. She was in a bad way. At first, she said she knew who I was, but actually she did not. And I was lost. I didn't know what to do. I had gone there to talk to her and ask what to do. I'm forty-two years old, and I went to talk to my out-of-her-mind mama about what to do. Now she's dead and gone."

Phillip got up and turned off the radio. He returned to the sofa and sat listening, with his arms folded across his chest.

Rosa continued with a distant stare in her eyes, as if she was directing her comments to someone not in the room. "My papa wanted me to get married, but he didn't approve of the man that I liked." Then she looked into Phillip's eyes. "You realize that I didn't say loved, because I don't know if I love him or not. I like him a lot. He is a decent, kind, and thoughtful man, and he treats me like a woman, and he wants to make a future for us, and he wants to sell my candy. And at this point in my life, that is about all I can hope for. So I'm sorry you don't approve, but I do hope you understand."

Her words sank deep. Phillip thought about the confession and the heartbreak that Rosa had been through. And although she did not know that he knew what had happened, he figured the Father Pat business and the aborted baby was the reason she went to talk with Martha. He felt like jumping into a bayou of alligators.

He put his arms around Rosa and held her close for several minutes. Then he asked, "Where were you married?"

"New Orleans."

"By a priest?"

"No, but we plan to get it blessed by Father O'Riley."

"Is he Catholic?"

"Yes."

Phillip was surprised to hear this. He pulled at his eyebrows and said, "Well, I guess that's that. What now?"

"I'm going to take a few things that I need and get the rest later. Joshua has rented a place over on Boagni Lane, near the city park, and later on we'll buy our own place."

"No Negroes live out on Boagni Lane."

"I know, but somehow he was able to make a deal. He's in the car waiting. Do you want to meet him?"

Phillip thought for a long moment and then said, "Not tonight. A little later, after I've had some time."

Rosa got up and crossed to the door.

Phillip stopped her with his voice, "Rosa! Wait a minute." He moved to his desk and took out his checkbook, signed his name to a check, tore it out, and brought it to her. "Here. Congratulations. You fill in the amount that you need. It's from your mama and me." He kissed her and said, "Good night."

She returned the kiss. "Good night, Papa, and thanks." She continued down the hall to her room to get her things.

Chapter 15

Taking Stock

On Friday May 3, 1963, Phillip and his family sat in front of the television in stunned silence. Fire hoses knocked down grown men and swept young children spinning down the street. The water pressure pinned people against brick buildings until they passed out and fell to the pavement. Those who escaped the water hoses were attacked by vicious dogs. Bull Conner, police chief of Birmingham, was having his day. His words of action were, "Let 'em have it." And the police force and the firemen under his command did just that. The knock-down drag-out was seen all over the world. President Kennedy said the sight of the assault made him sick to his stomach and he could "Well understand why the Negroes of Birmingham are tired of being asked to be patient."

Phillip looked from the sixteen-year-old face of Ann to the face of eighteen-year-old Les and saw the vacant stares of bewilderment. He didn't know what to say or how to explain. When the program turned into reporter witnessed commentary, Ann left the room. Soon after, so did Les.

The next day, Les was up early and walked into Phillip's den. Phillip put down his *Times Picayune.* "You're up mighty early."

"I couldn't sleep."

"That kinda stuff will keep you awake."

"Grandpop, why are those men so mean?"

Phillip didn't have a ready answer. He thought for a bit and said, "What you saw was the result of feelings built up over years and years. It's the anger left when a life-style based on slavery was taken away. Ever since then, white people especially in the South, have been determined to keep colored people 'in their place,' so they call it. When the civil rights movement started and colored people began to demand their rights, the whites got angry and afraid. And this is what happened." Phillip didn't know if he had answered the question or not.

Phillip remembered when Bobby sat at his feet and learned the ways of the world, and now it was the time for his grandson to do the same.

Les looked up at him and asked, "Why were all the children there?"

Phillip cleared his throat in the usual manner and said, "The children's campaign was a strategy that the civil rights leaders made, but it's causing a lot of controversy. They had a problem getting large numbers of people to protest, and they knew if the school kids were involved, the parents would also come out. And from what I've been reading, Dr. King is under criticism for what some people call 'exploiting the children.' King's response to that is, 'Our children have been brutalized by the practices of discrimination for many years. And going to jail is a learning experience about the price of freedom.' It seems to me that the strategy is working because Bull Conner is

showing the world how mean and evil his people can be--
turning dogs and hoses loose against the children."

Les asked, "When is the next protest in Birmingham?"

Phillip looked up and saw Lala standing in the doorway
sipping a cup of coffee. He cleared his throat again and
said, "I don't know.

Without a moment's hesitation, Les said, "I'd like to
go."

Lala made her presence known to Les by interrupting,
"Lester Junior, don't you think it's time for you to get
ready for work?"

He looked around and said, "Oh, yeah. I'll talk to you
later, Grandpop."

Lala moved in closer and stood next to Phillip. With
flashing eyes and clenched teeth, she said, "Papa, what are
you doing?"

"Nothing, why?"

"I heard you encouraging Les to get involved in the
movement."

"I did no such thing. He asked me some questions about
what was going on in Birmingham, and I answered. That's
all."

"I heard him say he wanted to go to Birmingham."

"That was something he said. I did not encourage him."

"It's too dangerous. Have you forgotten what happened
when you tried to register? And that was child's play
compared to what's happening now. I will not let him do it.
He's my only son, and I'm not going to let him be exposed
like that."

"Now hold on, Lala. You're jumping the gun. The boy
just said he'd like to go. He didn't say he was going to."

"Well, I just want to be sure that you don't encourage
him."

Phillip took a deep breath and didn't say anything more.

After a few seconds, Lala asked, "You ready for some breakfast?"

"That'll be nice."

Lala drained her cup and left Phillip with his thoughts. He watched her disappear, went over to his desk and looked through a stack of clippings. He found what he was looking for and placed the article, *Letter from a Birmingham Jail*, in the center of the desk and went to breakfast.

* * *

Opposition to the Civil Rights Movement continued to grow, spread, and worsen. In addition to the responses in Birmingham, the governor of Alabama, George Wallace stood in the doorway of The University of Alabama to prevent the enrollment of two Negro students. And the next day, June 12, 1963, Medger Evers, field secretary of the NAACP, was killed in the carport of his home in Jackson, Mississippi.

Phillip put the paper down. He couldn't read anymore. It was all too depressing. And as much as it pulled him down, it fired up Les. He had read Martin Luther King's *Letter from a Birmingham Jail*, and now more than ever, he wanted to go to Birmingham to take part in the protest. Lala was more determined than ever that he should stay safe and away from the conflict.

Later that day, Phillip got up from their dinner table discussion of protest events and went to his den.

Les caught his mother's eye before she moved from the table and said, "Mom?"

"I told you no!" She was emphatic.

Ann thought she should intercede. "Mom, let him go. He can take care of himself."

"And that's what scares me. The movement is non-violent, and Les is hotheaded. He'd just get himself killed."

Les said, "No, I won't, Mom. I'll go through the process of self-purification."

"You'll do what?"

"Take some workshops, so I can learn to get hit without hitting back. It's called self-purification."

"Where did you hear about that?"

"It was in Dr. King's *Letter from a Birmingham Jail.*"

Ann joined in, "I read it, too, Mom. I believe he can do it."

Lala closed her eyes, clenched her teeth, and said, "Don't tell me. I know where you got that letter!"

Phillip could hear what was going on from his den. He stood and made a move to rejoin the discussion, but he changed his mind and returned to his seat. It was better if he stayed clear of the attitudes now being aired.

Lala went on, "Let me tell you about your Grandpop." She took a deep breath and looked into the waiting eyes of her children. "When you were just babies your Grandpop almost got himself killed."

Ann's eyes widened and she looked at Les.

Les leaned in with his arms crossed on the edge of the table.

Lala continued, "I had just brought you back from Kansas City. When I got home, I found out that Papa had gone down to the courthouse to register and vote. They beat him to within an inch of his life . . . and he still suffers with pains in his chest. And that was nothing compared to what they are now doing in Birmingham."

Phillip sat as still as death and listened.

Les said, "Wow. Grandpop got beat up trying to vote!"

Ann added, "You didn't tell us this before."

Lala continued, "No, I didn't. There was no reason for

you to know before. He's been working for years, in his own way, to get justice. Now I know he means well by giving you this information about the letter and all, but there's another side to this integration coin. Dr. King is a Baptist preacher. And the Catholic church feels that this is a Protestant church-led protest."

Les interrupted, "Mom, that's. . ."

Lala would not let him talk. "Let me finish. The Catholic church does not endorse what is going on."

"Mom, that's what I wanted to say. They are coming around. That was in the letter. All the religions, and the Jews too, are getting involved. They support it now, because it's the right thing to do. But on the other hand, the whole movement is about us, whether the Catholic church backs it or not. We have to do something."

Phillip smiled and turned in the direction of the voices. His eyes grew a little moist.

Lala took a deep breath. "Look, I know all of that. But my biggest concern is for your safety. You're my only son and Papa's oldest and only grandson. I just don't want anything to happen to you."

Les reached across and held his mother's hand. "Mom, if I lived to be as old as Mr. BoBo and ended up being as scared of white people as he is, then my life would not have meant very much. And I know you wouldn't want that. Well, I'm not afraid of them, and I want us to have all the rights they have. I tell you what, I'll make a deal. If you let me go to the march in Washington, I'll forget about going to Birmingham."

Phillip turned his head toward the dining room expectantly. He waited. There was silence.

After a while, Les added, "Everybody says it's going to be a peaceful march."

Finally, Lala said slowly, "If you can convince your

Grandpop to go with you, it's all right with me."

Ann asked, "Can I go, too?"

Lala answered immediately, "Absolutely not."

Ann shrugged her shoulders and said, "Just thought I'd ask."

Les kissed his mother and ran into the den.

Phillip's eyes met Les when he came through the door. He smiled and nodded his head. Les knew that his Grandpop had heard it all.

Now Phillip had a problem. After Martha's death, Phillip had promised Alicia they would travel to Haiti this summer. But Alicia knew how important the commitment to Les was, and said, "Go with the boy. It's only for a week. When you get back I'll have everything planned and ready."

So, on August 27th, Phillip and Les got on the bus to Washington D.C. It was an experience that Les would never forget and one that Phillip wished he had had years earlier. They joined the thousands of other blacks, whites, Indians, Jews, Protestants, Catholics, men and women marching for justice. It was the culmination of the protest that had begun in the 1955 bus boycott and had continued through school integrations, riots, sit-ins, freedom rides, jail-ins, and the death of Medger Evers.

The opposition was great, and the price was high. But finally, the leaders of the country had been made to pay attention and now realized that the promises of freedom and justice for *all had never been fulfilled.*

Phillip remembered the price he had paid just to register for the vote that he did not get. Being at the march was a deep, soul-stirring experience for him that ended with the unforgettable *I Have a Dream* Speech. Phillip watched, as Les was moved to tears. Phillip was too.

When they returned from Washington Alicia had bad

news. The United States had suspended all diplomatic relations with Haiti. Papa Doc Duvalier, who had been elected several years earlier, subjected the country to his absolute dictatorship and many people were killed opposing him. So travel restrictions were imposed.

Phillip's response was, "Where else would you like to go for a honeymoon?"

Alicia looked him in the eye and asked, "Do you really want to do this?"

"Don't you?"

This was a question Alicia dreaded she would some day have to answer. As long as Martha was alive, she knew the question of marriage would not come up. Now, her fears were realized. Alicia took Phillip's arms, put them around her waist, and kissed him. She looked deeply into his eyes and said, "Thank you. I really appreciate the proposal. Now, don't misunderstand what I'm about to say. I want you to think seriously about this."

Then she went to the cabinet and took down a bottle of Old Taylor and poured a couple of drinks.

Phillip said, "Oh, it's going to be one of these you-listen-better when you're-drunk sessions."

"Will you please be quiet? I'm in charge here. I want you to relax. Now drink this and listen." She kissed him on the forehead, placed the glass in front of him, and sat across the table.

"I love you. And I've loved you since we were at Iowa. That was over thirty years ago. Then when I came to Southern, we were reunited and that was about seventeen years ago. In all of that time, there has been only one other man in my life."

Phillip said as he swallowed down a drink, "Ah, so there *is* another man."

Alicia playfully slapped his hand. "Will you be quiet

and listen?" She continued, "The other man was that fool I was married to while I was at Iowa. That was just a stupid interval in my life, and I've tried my damndest to forget it. The truth is, you have been the only man I've ever loved. Right now, you are approaching seventy, and I am sixty-five. You have three grown daughters and two growing grandchildren, and none of them need to start worrying about their inheritance. And whether you know it or not, that has been on their minds since their mother died. We don't have to get married to be together. In three years, I plan to retire, and I'm going to buy a house out there in Southern Heights and live there, with you, for the remaining years I have left. Now, if you still want to go to on a trip without being married, we can make it a celebration."

Alicia drained her glass and brought it down on the table with an ending thud.

For several moments, there was silence. Flashing through Phillip's mind were thoughts of how fortunate he was to have someone to love and be with as he approached his twilight years. He would not be alone like his brother. He drained his glass and brought it down on the table with a thud. And that was the end of that.

* * *

Two weeks later, Phillip got a call from Elvina. She had bought a house near the French Quarter and invited him to come for a housewarming.

"Shall I bring anything?"

"Whatever you want that would make a good memory."

"Shall I bring anyone?

Elvina answered without hesitation, "My brother and Naomi."

Phillip felt he was now on notice that he should not bring Alicia. Elvina knew that he was seeing her, and because she did not mention her name, he felt the housewarming was a family affair, so he did not question the invitation.

Lightfoot drove into the yard, and Phillip came out with his present wrapped, looked into the car, and asked, "Where is Naomi?"

"She's not feeling well."

Phillip did not know about the problem that Naomi had with Elvina reminding her of Martha, but apparently she had decided not to resurrect those feelings.

Phillip and Lightfoot arrived at the address on St.Claude near the intersection of Esplanade. It was a charming two-story brick Creole cottage, with a one-step-up entrance from the street. It had green functional shutters that concealed the main entrance and closed off the windows to the sidewalk traffic.

Elvina proudly showed off the five rooms: the living room, kitchen, and library on the first floor, and upstairs, connected by a wrought iron spiral staircase, the two bedrooms, and a bath. The floors were original pine, restored and covered with elegant rugs that she had purchased in the Quarter. Out back was a secluded garden filled with banana trees, ferns, azaleas, and other flowers. It was a delightful and cozy place. She had made an excellent buy and smiled from ear to ear as she showed it off.

Phillip waited for other guests to arrive but soon realized that there would only be the three of them. Dinner was served in the garden on an antique wrought iron table covered with Elvina's best linen cloth and set with silver and crystal, the likes of which Phillip had only seen in magazines.

He and Lightfoot presented their gifts. Lightfoot brought a patchwork quilt that Naomi had selected and sent with her regrets. When Elvina unwrapped Phillip's gift, the large portrait of her father, she burst into tears. It was more than she could have hoped to receive after the many years of having only the small photograph from her mother's missal.

As darkness fell, the gaslight torches transformed the garden to the days of 1806. Lightfoot looked around and said, "All this is nice, but the night time is the right time to hear some blues. I'm going to Bourbon Street. Y'all coming?"

Elvina was the first to respond. "I'd rather stay here and enjoy the phantoms of yesteryear."

Phillip chose to remain with the ghosts rather than fight the spirits on Bourbon Street.

When Lightfoot left, Phillip walked to the edge of the garden, attracted by the light dance on the banana leaves. He heard the melodies of Mozart join the flickering shadows, and turned to see Elvina emerge from the doorway with two brandy glasses of liqueur. For a brief moment she seemed like a delicately carved statue of Carrara marble, highlighted by the soft yellow light, from the interior of the house. As she approached, she reminded him of Martha come alive. She stood face to face as she extended the glass of Drambouie. She was close enough for Phillip to feel her breath as she spoke.

"I've been waiting for this moment for months."

Phillip asked, "What do you mean?"

"Last year when I came to say good-bye, I kissed you while your were asleep, and you thought I was Martha. I got the feeling that you wished I was."

Phillip was lost for words, and his mind's eye quickly went back to the conversation that he had with Luther. He felt uncomfortable. He did not want to believe that Luther was right.

He walked back to the table and took a seat. Elvina followed. He said quietly,"I think you might have gotten the wrong impression."

"Oh, come on, Phillip. We are both adults, and we've been around the barn many times. How often does a man get a second chance to be with the woman of his dreams? I know that you loved Martha, and when she died, you were devastated. I was reluctant to say anything earlier because I thought it might be too soon, but it's been almost two years now."

Phillip was still lost for words. But since the idea was planted, it was food for thought. Yes, he loved Martha, and Elvina did have a point. How many chances does a man get to have the woman of his dreams? Martha was his dream, but she had turned into a nightmare. Now here was Elvina, the shadow of Martha, yet she was everything that Martha was not. Maybe, just maybe, there was a possibility.

Phillip said haltingly, "I guess that's something to think about."

Elvina laughed and ran her fingers seductively through her silky flowing hair. She said, "Oh, you poor baby. You don't have to make a decision this minute. I just wanted you to know that I would be your Martha, when you are ready." And after a couple of moments, she added, "If that is what you want." Elvina leaned over and kissed him lovingly to let him know that she was sincere.

For the next two hours, until Lightfoot returned, they talked trivia, history, life in New Orleans, laughed and enjoyed being with each other. Yes, being with Elvina *was* food for thought, and thoughts of Alicia were blurred and shadowy.

On the drive home, Lightfoot expounded about his sister's new home, the New Orleans blues, and his plans for future visits.

Phillip's mind was frantic with the possibility of a reincarnation of Martha. Luther was right: he did love Creole women.

Chapter 16

Scared Stiff

September 23, 1963 - Les and BookTau heard the music as they rode up on horseback. When they cleared the curve around the elderberry bushes, they saw Lightfoot's truck. Mr. BoBo was in his rocking chair keeping time, his feet stomping the floor and his hands slapping his thighs. Lightfoot stopped playing his harmonica and watched them dismount.

As they walked up to the porch, BoBo asked, "Where y'all goin' on them horses?" BookTau fell out laughing, pointed his finger at Mr. BoBo, danced around, and said, "You don't know the difference 'tween a horse and a mule!"

"I know you riding 'Fessors's mule. He ain't got no horses strong enough to hold yo' heavy ass."

Les laughed. Lightfoot played a musical accent.

BoBo went on, "That boy is riding da horse. That's Quickstep, the Tennessee Walker that 'Fessor bought after Betsy died. You think I don't know what I'm talking 'bout,

236

but I do. And you would too if you'd listened, but you don't. Jus run yo' big mouth and don't know what you talking about."

This shut BookTau up. He dropped his head and ran his foot across the dust.

He was in his early forties with the mental age of a teenager. He was six feet ten inches tall and weighed 270 pounds. He was the strongest man in Estilette and could lift anything that wasn't nailed down. BookTau would do anything that he was told, especially by Phillip, who he loved. He enjoyed playing children's games, so people in the community said he was not "all there," but no one in their right mind would make him mad because he could change from pussycat to lion in an instant. He chewed tobacco, never wore shoes, and had a husky laugh that could be heard for a country mile. Although simple, he was fearless and always told the truth about how he felt.

BoBo realized that because of the silence he might have hurt BookTau's feelings, so he softened his voice and continued, "Now where y'all goin' riding that mule and that horse?

BookTau said, "To the bayou."

"Now, what y'all gonna do out there?"

Les spoke up, "BookTau's gonna show me how to catch a 'gator."

"He gonna show you how to get bit. You be careful back there at that bayou."

BookTau defended himself, "I know what I'm doing. Used to catch 'gators with Bill Blue before that deputy shot him."

BoBo decided he had better stay on BookTau's good side and said, "I know you do, but this boy don't." Then he shook his finger at Les. "Boy, you listen to what he tell you to do so you'll come back with yo' hands and feet intact."

BoBo reached down next to his rocker and picked up his bottle. He took a deep swallow and extended the bottle to BookTau, who spit out his wad of tobacco and took a swig.

Les made his way up the steps and disappeared into the house. He came out with a Nehi and joined the men on the edge of the porch.

BoBo said, as he reached to retrieve his bottle, "Since Lightfoot stopped me from working in ma garden and y'all stopped me from my entertainment, I'm jes gonna have me another drink."

Lightfoot headed for his truck. "I gotta go."

"Why you leaving, Uncle Johnny?"

"Got lots of work to do. Can't lollygag all day."

"What were you playing when we rode up?"

"Muddy Waters."

"Lemme hear you play it again before you go."

"Now if I do that, I'll need another drink. To play the blues right, you gotta be drunk."

BookTau laughed and slapped his legs while he turned in small circles.

Lightfoot played the introduction.

BoBo started singing.

"A gypsy woman told my mother . . . before I was born . . . I got a boy chile comin' . . gonna be a son-of-a-gun . . . He's gonna make pretty womens jump and shout . . . then the world wanna know what's this all about . . . but you know, I'm here . . . everybody knows I'm here.

Well, you know I'm your hoochie-coochie man . . . Everybody knows I'm here."

BookTau danced.

BoBo kept time slapping his thighs with his phrasing, then he and Lightfoot went into the second verse, which listed the special traits that the hoochie-choochie man was born with.

Les applauded.

BoBo said, "The hoochie-choochie man was born at the seventh hour of the seventh day of the seventh month, jes the same as me. Now y'all get on away from heah and lemme take my nap."

He watched as Lightfoot sped away and Les and BookTau galloped off in the direction of Bayou Coutableau, then he closed his eyes.

* * *

The slamming doors of a truck aroused BoBo from his nap, and he watched as two white boys made their way across the yard with shotguns. He stood next to the porch roof post and yelled across at the boys, "Dis is private land. Ain't no hunting allowed."

One of the boys yelled back, "Shut up, old man, and mind your business."

"Dis is my business. I'm caretaker of dis here property."

The other boy yelled, "Nigger, shut the fuck up!"

With that, the boys continued their trek into the woods.

Phillip didn't allow hunting on his property because of the proximity to the surrounding homes. He had told Mr. BoBo to watch out because, "A stray shot could accidentally hit or kill somebody." BoBo shrugged his shoulders and returned to his rocking chair and his bottle. There wasn't too much he could do but tell them. In no time at all, he had fallen back to sleep.

Karl Rubin and Eric Schultz were two of a kind. They both disliked Cajuns and niggers, and both had ancestors from Germany who had settled in Teche country to farm the fertile land.

Karl, who had a deceptively friendly looking face, was the quarterback and captain of the football team.

Eric was less handsome, with a face full of pimples, and was also a capable athlete and the star running back. He was plain-spoken with a vulgar mouth and the one who yelled back, "Nigger, shut the fuck up." He and Karl made a winning combination on the football field and were heroes to the white people of Estilette.

Karl's father was an oil field rigger. Eric's father was a plumber and long-distant trucker. The boys had learned to use guns at an early age and were as fond of hunting as were their fathers. Both men were away most of the time, leaving the boys on their own to do mostly what they liked--playing practical jokes on their schoolmates.

They had recently won a hard-fought game against the Istrouma Indians, a rival school from Baton Rouge. In order to win, they knew they needed the cheering support of the entire student body as well as the townspeople. And as sometimes happens, there was a conflicting school activity scheduled on the same day and at the same time as the big game--a play, *The Importance of Being Earnest.*

As they wove their way around and through the briars, palmettos, and tall grasses, they laughed and talked about their most recent prank.

Shouldering his shotgun as he walked, Karl asked, "How did you know about that sewer line?"

"I was with my daddy one day when he was fixing the hot water tank. He called Mr. Wilson in and showed him that clay pipe. Told him it was ready to break, and it was in a bad spot when it did."

"And I know what dumb-ass Wilson said." Karl did an impression of the school principal, " 'It'll cost too much money, and the school board just don't have it.' "

"That's just what he said. Did I tell you this before?"

"Naw. I know him. He says that about everything. The coach tried to get us new uniforms, and that's what he said."

"Well, I knew that utility room was right next to the stage."

"Man, that's the best trick you ever pulled."

"Don't I know it. All that shit just slid out under the door and all over that auditorium." The two boys laughed, and Karl continued, "I sure wish I had been there to see Wilson's face. That dumb-ass Cajun. Where he go to school?"

"LSU."

"That's supposed to be a good school, but it didn't help him any. I'm gonna get a scholarship and play for them when I finish."

Eric decided to also reveal his future plans. "When I finish, I'm going to Alabama to play for Bear Bryant. I was hoping to take you with me, that is, if you can graduate the same year as me."

The boys exchanged playful blows and continued on their way.

* * *

Not far away, Les and BookTau sneaked up on the sleepy alligators sunning themselves on the bank of the bayou. BookTau put his finger to his lips for silence and motioned Les around the back of a drowsy beast. He crawled up in front with a rope, planning to snare the mouth while Les grabbed the tail. Just as they were about to make their move, a shotgun blast thundered through the woods. The alligator woke up and opened his mouth to greet BookTau, hissing and snarling as it slowly backed toward the safety of the water. All of the other alligators followed and the sluggish stream was turned into an instant sea of mud.

BookTau threw down his rope in disgust. "Shit. Missed him."

Les turned and looked in the direction of the sound. "Somebody's hunting over there."

"Ain't supposed to. 'Fessor don't allow hunting."

Another blast sounded off. Les said, "Let's go see." He started in the direction of the horses.

BookTau stopped him. "Naw, we gotta stay low. They might be shooting this way."

The two left their mounts and made their way stooped over for cover in the high grass.

*　*　*

Meanwhile, Eric broke open his gun and reloaded the shot. "Goddammit, missed another one."

Karl sat down under an oak tree and said, "Let's give 'em a chance to settle down." He took out a pack of Camel's and lit up, then he flipped the pack to Eric. "I sure am glad that shit drove everybody out. They had no other place to go but the game."

Then Eric said in a wistful manner, "Especially the cheerleaders. All five of 'em was in that fucking play. If I hadn't busted that pipe open, we woulda been playing without any cheering." Karl's mind shifted from the game to the head cheerleader, his former girlfriend, who was now dating his best friend. "You get any of that?"

Eric lit up and blew smoke in Karl's direction. "What are you talking about?"

"Jan. Didn't y'all go out after the game?"

Eric smiled and asked, "You jealous?"

"Naw. I'm through with her. Just wanted to know if you

scored with her, too."

Eric stood and looked down at Karl. "You really want to know if I'm getting your leftovers, right?"

"Man, I don't care. I got mine. Just wanted to know if you got yours."

"Shit, you was there, you figure it out."

Karl said, "I don't know what y'all did after you took off in the truck. Maybe y'all just held hands."

With a telling smile, Eric said, "Why the fuck you think I got them blankets in the back."

"I thought they was your daddy's blankets."

Eric decided that the focus of the conversation needed changing. "When he goes out to fuck, he goes to the Downtowner Motel. Where does your daddy go?"

"I dunno. I guess he fucks on the oil rigs."

"Ain't no women out there. But on the other hand, maybe he fucks the men."

That pissed Karl off, but before he could reply he said, "Sheee, I hear something." The two boys remained still and quiet.

Les and BookTau stood tall in the grass.

Les said, "I don't see nothing."

BookTau pulled at his pants leg and whispered, "Get down and stay down. Jus' wait till they shoot again. I figure we're pretty close to where the shots come from."

Karl crushed his cigarette into the ground and picked up his gun. "You hear that?"

Eric picked up his gun, and his cigarette dangled from his lips. "What?"

"The rustling. Look over there, I see two of 'em." Karl pointed in the direction of a briar patch.

"I don't see nothing."

"You go around that way, and I'll wait here. We'll have 'em surrounded."

Eric crouched down and quietly made his way around in the direction that Karl had pointed. After several minutes Karl figured that Eric was in position. Karl rose up, shouldered his gun and yelled, "I see 'em," blasting both barrels. A voice in pain cried out from the direction of the shot.

BookTau whispered, "What happened?"

Les peeped out from behind the tree and said, "I dunno. Sound like somebody got shot."

At that moment, Les saw Karl run in the direction of a large briar bush. He motioned for BookTau to follow as he crept through the grass to another tree for a better view. On the other side of the briar patch, Les saw Karl kneeling over the bloody body of Eric. Les pointed in the direction and said to BookTau, "Look there." Then he stood and started in their direction.

BookTau grabbed his legs and pulled him down. "Where you going?"

"To help."

"Naw, you better not do that."

"Why?"

"They white."

"I don't care."

BookTau shook his head and said, "They'll put the blame on us. Let's get on away from here."

For the moment, Les didn't know what to do, but he remained hidden along with BookTau.

Karl watched as the smoke from the cigarette in Eric's mouth drifted into his water-filled eyes. The rabbits that were the object of the blast lay on the ground in front of the body.

Karl cried out, "Eric, Eric, speak to me man! Say something. Man, I'm sorry. I didn't know you was so close." Karl stood, a terrified look was on his face. Then he started running back toward the road.

BookTau said, "Let's go. He killed that man."

BookTau and Les hastily made their way back to their mounts and rode away in the opposite direction.

Karl's thoughts came a mile a minute while he ran. *How can I explain what happened? No one will believe it was an accident . . . especially since Eric was fucking Jan, my old girlfriend . . . we had an argument over her in the lunchroom just two days ago, and everybody heard. And how am I supposed to explain that we were hunting on nigger property without permission?"*

By the time he reached the truck, he had it figured out. He turned and ran to the shotgun house. He shook Mr. BoBo awake.

"Old man, I need your help. My friend is hurt."

Mr. BoBo looked up at Karl with fear mounting in his eyes and asked, "What happened?"

"He's hurt."

"How?"

"Fell and broke his leg. I need some help to get him out."

Mr. BoBo got up and followed Karl into the woods.

When they reached the spot where Eric lay, Mr. BoBo knelt down next to the body, removed the shotgun from Eric's hands, looked up, and said, "This boy's dead."

Karl had retrieved his shotgun and stood looking down at BoBo. "And you killed him." Karl pulled both triggers then realized that the gun was empty. He swung the shotgun and hit BoBo in the head, knocking him out. Then he hightailed it back to the truck and sped off to the sheriff's office.

Karl led Sheriff Cat Bobineaux to the scene of the crime. Mr. BoBo was on the ground next to the body, the shotgun across his lap, his head dripping blood. The sheriff took away the shotgun and put it into a burlap bag, then he instructed BoBo, "Go sit under that tree over yonder."

Mr. BoBo, still holding his shirttail against the bleeding wound, did what he was told. Sheriff Cat examined the body and noticed that the cigarette in Eric's mouth had burned through his lips. He picked up the two dead rabbits and put them into another burlap bag, then he turned to Karl and said, "Go on home and wait till I call you." He watched as Karl made his way through the grass, looking back over his shoulder every now and then.

The sheriff went to BoBo and asked, "What happened here?"

Fear consumed every wrinkle of BoBo's face. "Sheriff, I didn't kill that boy."

"I asked you what happened."

BoBo looked up pleadingly into the Sheriff's eyes, "As God is my witness, I don't know. I was sleeping on my porch and that boy that jus' went away come over and woke me up, saying dat his friend had a broke leg and he needed help. When I got here, dat boy dere was dead."

"Why was you holding that shotgun?"

BoBo shrugged his shoulders and explained as best he could. "It was in his hands, and I took it away, and that's how I knowed he was dead."

"How did you get a bloody head?"

"I was jus lookin' at the dead boy dere and next thing I knowed, the other one said I killed the boy, and then he hit me. I woke up from being knocked out jus' befor' you come."

"I'm gonna have to take you to jail. The boy says you killed his friend."

BoBo just shook his head, and on the verge of crying he said, "Lord, Sheriff, God knows I didn't do that."

Bobineaux watched the tears form in the old man's

eyes, picked up the pieces of the broken shotgun butt, and then took BoBo to jail.

It wasn't long before word of what had happened was all over Estilette. Phillip was very upset and went to the jailhouse immediately. He was allowed to visit with BoBo, who told him exactly what he had told the sheriff. Phillip believed him.

Then Phillip went in to see Cat Bobineaux, who leaned back in his chair, put his feet on the desk, and asked, "What can I do for you, Professor?"

"Sheriff, the old man says he didn't kill that boy."

"He told me the same thing."

"Do you believe him?"

"It ain't for me to say. That's for a jury. He gonna have to stand trial."

"Can I pay his bail so he can go home?"

"Not till the judge set it. And that won't happen till tomorrow or the next day."

Phillip took a deep breath and said, "That old man is frightened to death."

"I know he's been crying, but he's gonna have to stay in jail till the judge lets him go." Phillip knew any appeal was hopeless, and he went back to the jail cell. When he approached, Mr. BoBo stood up and pressed his face against the bars. Phillip could see the fear in BoBo's eyes.

BoBo reached out, took Phillip's hand, and asked, "What he say?"

"Not much, but you're gonna have to stay in jail until the judge says you can go."

"How long that's gonna be?"

"I don't know. Maybe tomorrow."

"Lord, I can't stay in this jail. Did Sheriff Cat believe I killed that boy?

"He said it wasn't for him to say. You might have to

stand trial."

BoBo's eyes rolled around in his head and fear mounted in his voice. "Trial? For what? I didn't kill that boy."

"I believe you. But when somebody is charged with a crime, they have to stand trial. That's why we have to wait for the judge to have his say-so."

BoBo reached out and grabbed Phillip's arm. " 'Fessor, I beg you, don't let 'em do to me what they did to those mens in Kirven, Texas."

Phillip could feel the trembling in Mr. BoBo's hands that now squeezed his arm. He asked, "What's this about Kirven, Texas?"

"That's where they burned them mens alive and stood around laughin'."

Phillip remembered immediately. Mr. BoBo had told about this incident at a hog killing several years back, and it was still etched in his memory. He knew that Mr. BoBo was frightened, but he didn't know what he could say to calm him down. He gave as much assurance as he could.

"That's not going to happen here."

"'Fessor, you don't know white folks like I know 'em."

"I'll be back to see you tomorrow."

A depressed Mr. BoBo shook his head without saying another word.

Phillip left with a heavy heart.

* * *

At supper that evening, Phillip told the family about the incident.

Les asked, "Why did they put *him* in jail?"

"They say he killed a boy."

"Mr. BoBo didn't kill that boy. Karl Rubin shot him."

248

Phillip stopped eating and looked inquiringly at Les. "How you know?"

"I saw when he did it."

"Where were you?"

"Me and BookTau was out hunting 'gators and we heard shots, so we went over where they was coming from, and we saw Karl shoot the other boy."

"How you know it was Karl?"

"His picture's in the paper every week. He's the quarterback."

Phillip's heart began racing, and he put his hand on Les' arm. "Son, I want you to tell that to the city attorney. But don't tell anybody else, you hear me?"

"Yes, sir."

Then Phillip turned to Lala and Ann. "And y'all, too. Don't breathe a word of what this boy saw to anybody."

Phillip didn't sleep very well that night.

Neither did BoBo. He never closed his eyes; he just stared up at the dark ceiling of his jail cell.

His mind traveled back to 1922. He was thirty-five years old. He didn't know how he ended up in Kirven, Texas, but he reckoned it was because when he finished the cotton-picking season in Shreveport, someone said there was off-season work around Waco, Texas. He had to travel to the work so he could earn a few dollars to make ends meet. He boarded a bus and finally ended up in Kirven, a small dusty town on Highway 84, a few miles from Fairfield, which was the closest town big enough to have a Sears, Roebuck.

He had only been in Kirven a few months when a young white girl was found raped and decapitated in the nearby woods. It created quite a stir, and over one thousand men combed through the woods to find evidence that would lead to the killer. What they found caused the sheriff to arrest two white men who had carried a grudge against the murdered girl's family. They were put in jail.

Then the hearsay of a disgruntled wife got back to the sheriff. A colored lady told a neighbor that her husband, McKinley Curry, came home bloodied from a rabbit hunt in the same woods, on the same day that the girl disappeared.

That was all the evidence the sheriff needed to change the focus of his investigation. McKinley Curry was arrested, and after interrogation it was learned that Curry had had dealings with the white men arrested earlier. Curry was forced to make a statement, and he implicated two of his friends, Johnny Cornish and Mose Jones.

BoBo knew Mose, they had chopped wood together, had drinks together on the weekends, and BoBo had taken a room in a house not far from where Mose lived.

Tears slid down BoBo's face as the events tumbled back into his memory. And just like Mose, he was in jail but not guilty of anything. He kept staring into the darkness, and he could see, as clear as day, what he saw from his hiding place high in that oak tree.

That night, forty years earlier, BoBo had been awakened from dreams of what he planned to do with the money he would make. There were sounds of cars and trucks and loud talking and cursing. He got up, put on his clothes, and went outside to find out what the ruckus was about. He saw a crowd of people gathering on an empty field not far away.

BoBo climbed into an oak tree to get a better look. By this time, the mob had built a huge bonfire, and he could make out three colored men tied up like hogs lying on the ground. The crowd cursed, kicked, and spat on the men. One member of the crowd knelt down between the legs of one of the bound men, and BoBo had a suspicion, from the way the man yelled out, that his manhood was being cut away. Then the crying, screaming man was doused with gasoline and set on fire. As the flames roared, the crowd cheered.

Now attention was paid to another of the bound men, and BoBo recognized his friend Mose. They cut loose his feet and tied a chain around his hands, soaked him with gasoline, then pulled him through the fire, from one side and then the other. He was made into a running torch until he could no longer stand up, then his body was dragged to the center of the flames and left to burn.

The third man, Johnny Cornish, was the youngest of the three--nineteen years old--and like Mose, he was there only because he was a friend of Curry's. Cornish was the most enraged of the three. He fought back furiously, lunging his body against his attackers, kicking, cursing, and yelling at the sadistic, bloodthirsty mob. One of the gang had heard enough and hit Cornish across the face with an iron pipe, and then others joined in the beating until he was unconscious. He was thrown into the fire along with Curry and Mose, and the crowd applauded.

BoBo's nostrils were singed by the stench of burning flesh carried by the breeze. The laughter and merriment of the crowd made his blood boil; his heart pounded in his head, and a shiver of goosebumps caused him to tremble as if struck by lightning. He was so overcome with horror, he almost lost his grip and fell, and he could do nothing but watch through tear-filled eyes. He remained cramped in a cradle of tree branches all night, fearful that he would be spotted if he came down.

As the morning sun rose over the smoldering funeral pyre, BoBo could see a church on one side of the field, and not far away was another on the other side. He wondered how those white people could do such a horrible thing in the shadow of two churches.

Now, all was quiet, and except for the distant approach of the sheriff's car, there was no one to be seen. He watched as the sheriff kicked around in the ashes. When it was safe, BoBo climbed down and headed away from Kirven. He didn't even go back to his room to get his belongings, nor did he catch a bus. He walked. He stayed hidden under the cover of the trees and bushes that paralleled the highway, and when he got to Fairfield, he caught a bus to Shreveport, Louisiana.

From his seat in the back of the bus, he overheard the white people telling how the crystallized livers from the niggers found guilty of killing Eula Ausley were being sliced up and passed out as souvenirs. It was a memory that would remain in his mind's eye for the rest of his life.

Just like the night in that tree forty years earlier, BoBo did not close his eyes. He just stared into the black ceiling of the jail cell. After a few hours of silence, his attention was drawn to loud voices coming from a room at the end of the hall. He got up from his bunk and went to the bars closest to where the voices were heard. It was clear that someone was being questioned.

What he heard curdled his blood, and he could feel his heart pounding in his chest.

"Nigger, I'm gonna ask you again, what were you doing with that lady's purse?"

"Jus'like I told you before, I found it in a trash basket."

"And what was you doing on Garland Avenue at two o'clock in the morning?"

"I wus goin' home."

"Through the white area?"

"Yes, sir. Jus' like to told you, I wus taking a shortcut cuz it was late."

"Where you say you live?"

"Near the cotton mill."

Then another voice chimed in, "Nigger, I'm gonna give you something to think about tonight, then we gonna ask you again in the morning."

The sounds of a beating filled BoBo's ears along with the moans, groans, and pleadings from the man. After about five minutes, it was quiet again.

The door at the end of the hall opened, and light from the outer room shot into the jail area. BoBo hustled back to his bunk and pretended to be asleep with his face turned to the wall. He heard the door to his cell open, and the semi-conscious man was pushed in and fell to the floor.

The two deputies departed with words of wisdom. "You better pray that we find that woman alive and well, or your ass is gonna belong to us."

When the darkness returned to the jail cell, Bobo kept his face to the wall. He wanted to turn around and look at the man, but it was too dark and he was too scared.

He could feel his heart drumming in his head along with the images of the lynching in Kirven, Texas.

He sealed his eyes shut--forever.

*   *   *

Early the next morning, Phillip headed to the jailhouse. As he walked up the steps, the coroner and his staff were wheeling out a body.

Phillip approached and asked, "Dr. Pavy, who died?"

"That old man BoBo." Phillip was so shocked he could hardly speak, but he was able to get out, "What happened?"

"Just died, far as I can figure out."

"Can I see him?"

"You know him?"

"He sharecrops for me."

Dr. Pavy stopped his assistants and pulled back the

253

blanket. "Is that him?"

Phillip could not speak. He nodded his head as tears filled his eyes. He was unable to move from the spot for several minutes after the coroner's hearse had pulled away. He felt like he wanted to throw up.

Phillip's minds' eye traveled back in time. He had known BoBo over forty years. He was a gentle spirit who had had a hard life. He had worked the land since he was able to walk, and somewhere along the way, his life had taken the true direction: an acceptance of the basic values-- truth, honesty, and integrity without compromise. It was written in his face.

Phillip felt there was something that he had to do. He did what he had asked the others of his family not to do. But he could trust Stephen, and he knew that being white and the editor of the town paper, Stephen could get things done in the tradition of the way things had always been done in the South. He figured this was the best way to get Mr. BoBo's name cleared.

Stephen took a sip of coffee and said thoughtfully, "I'm going to ask Pavy to do an autopsy just to make sure there was no foul play. Then I'm going to do some investigating of that Rubin boy. Now that BoBo is dead, he could get off scott free if, like you say, he killed the other boy."

"Thank you, Stephen. I knew I could count on you."

Phillip stood to leave. Stephen put his arm around Phillip's shoulder and said, "Come back tomorrow. I'll have something to tell you."

The next morning, Phillip sat in the same seat and listened.

Stephen revealed, "Pavy found nothing to indicate the old man was harmed in any way, except that blow on his head. It was a superficial wound that caused a slight concussion, and he was knocked unconscious for a while.

But that didn't kill him, and there was nothing else found. Pavy figured his time was up and he just died, like we all got to do."

Phillip stared into space and said, "He died of fright."

Stephen looked at Phillip and asked, "What was that?"

"He must have willed himself to death rather than be lynched."

"What are you talking about?"

Phillip told the story that Mr. BoBo had told at hog-killing time.

Stephen concluded, "Well, I guess if enough fear builds up it will kill you."

Phillip's eyes glistened.

Stephen went on, "I spoke to Lazzaro. The only way he can do a full investigation is to have somebody charged with murder. And there's no evidence to charge the boy, so he suggested that Mr. BoBo be charged so the case against him can be tried, and with your grandson and BookTau as witnesses, his name can be cleared."

Phillip had his doubts. Too much depended on too many unknowns. He said, "That is, if a jury goes along."

Stephen echoed Phillip's skepticism. "Yeah, if a jury goes along. But I don't see why they wouldn't. They'll have testimony from two eyewitnesses. Should I tell Lazzaro to go ahead?"

With some hesitation, Phillip nodded his head. He figured there wasn't too much to risk, since BoBo was already dead.

* * *

Phillip arranged Mr. BoBo's funeral. He was able to get him buried in the Mount Calvary Baptist Church cemetery although he was not a member.

It was hot and muggy, a typical summer day in Louisiana. Present at the funeral were Phillip, Lightfoot, Les, Ann, BookTau, Lala, Rosa, and Lilly Ellis. BoBo had no family, and his few friends were all present. Reverend Promise didn't see any point in passing him through the church, so he said a few last words over the open grave.

When he finished, Phillip said, "I'd like to say a few words."

He shook out the handkerchief that was balled up in his hand and wiped away the perspiration on his face. His short-sleeved white shirt was sticking to his back. He looked up at the sky and said, "We are committing the soul of Mr. BoBo to your care. I know that he's up there with you now. He used to talk to you a lot, so I know you must remember him. He said that you knew everything that he was about to say for us to hear. So I guess I don't have to tell you that he was a good man. But I know, as you do, that he had a hard life, and it was written in the lines on his face."

Phillip wiped his eyes, and then he continued, looking down at the box that held the body of Mr. BoBo poised over the hole in the ground. "It was a good face. A face that had seen more than his share of hard work and trouble. A face that had experienced only a few moments of joy and pleasure in all of his seventy-five years on earth. And I would like to think that at least a few of the hours that I've spent with Mr. BoBo over the last forty years were some of those pleasant moments he enjoyed. He loved his neighbors, and he never had an evil thought in his head about anyone except white people. He couldn't love white people, because he believed they were out to do him harm. He was afraid of them. And it was that fear that took him away from us. He willed himself to die because he was so fearful of what white people might do. Now I know you have your reasons for everything that we do here on earth, but I am hard pressed to figure out why you let white people do so much evil. Why did you let this good man die with so much fear of them in his heart? It would have been better if he had died like Jesus, with too much love."

Phillip had reached the end of what he wanted to say. He passed his handkerchief over his face to wipe away the sweat and whatever tears that had formed. He looked around at the small group of mourners. "Anybody else want to say something?"

Les raised his eyes to meet Phillip's.

He glanced over at his Mama and then walked toward his Grandpop and stood next to him at the edge of the hole in the ground.

He began slowly, as he lifted his eyes to the clouds. "Mr. BoBo I didn't know you as well or as long as my Grandpop, but I did know that you were a special man. I'll never forget the first time we met and you made me stand next to you as you took my measure. That was a very important moment for me."

There was a pause as Les brought his eyes away from the clouds and down to where the coffin lay over the hole in the ground. He continued softly, "And as I stood there and looked down into your eyes, I saw all of the years of hard work that you had done--all of the cotton you had picked, all of the fields you had plowed. I saw all of the years of injustice and insults that you had suffered, from the hands of white people, and the fear of them that had replaced the twinkle in your eye. And yes, I also saw all of the love that you had for the people who treated you with the respect that you were due as a human being. I thank you for telling me about the blues and all of the people that you knew who played and sang the blues...This will always be a part of my life. I thank you for sharing the adventures of

257

your life with me and for being a friend to my Grandpop, and all of the people gathered here to say goodbye."

Les took his place next to Lala. She wiped her eyes and enclosed his body with her arms. Ann joined the two of them in the embrace. Then, one after the other, starting with Rosa, Lilly Ellis, BookTau, and Lightfoot all walked past and patted Les on the back. Phillip watched and then wrapped his hands around his face, concealing his eyes.

Reverend Promise cleared his throat and said, "Earth to earth, ashes to ashes, dust to dust."

Chapter 17

Trial by Jury

In February, 1964, Stephen asked about the investigation that had been scheduled to begin six months earlier. Mario Lazzaro had dragged his feet and made a lame excuse that things were moving along. Stephen and Phillip got together and decided that they should hire a lawyer to represent Mr. BoBo and move the case to trial.

Stephen located a lawyer friend who agreed to take the case.

Kenneth Malveau was a native of Opelousas who practiced in Lafayette. He and Stephen had first met at LSU when Ken was in law school and Stephen was studying journalism with the intention of starting his own newspaper. Ken took the case because of its unusual nature--a dead man being charged with a murder that he didn't commit. Except for expenses, he agreed to do the case pro bono, out of friendship. Both Stephen and Phillip were delighted with the arrangement, and the ball started rolling.

First, Ken talked with Les and BookTau and then filed the necessary papers with the city attorney's office.

Mario Lazzaro, city attorney, was shocked and wanted to know, "Why the hell you wasting your time with this shit?"

"The old man needs representation."

Mario agreed and said, "He's gonna get a court appointed lawyer. It's an open and shut case."

Ken said, "That old man didn't kill that boy. And his name needs to be cleared."

Mario shuffled papers on his desk and said matter-of-factly, "Well, I got an eyewitness that says he did."

"And I've got two eye witnesses that say he didn't."

Mario stopped shuffling papers, looked up and asked, "Who?"

"Now, Mario, you know better than that. You'll find out in court. In the meantime, I'd like to see the evidence from the crime scene."

All of the evidence that Sheriff Bobineaux had so carefully bagged, along with the autopsy report from Dr. Pavy, was made available. A trial date was set.

One year after the death of Eric Schultz, the trial of Mr. BoBo was scheduled to begin.

It was headline news in *The Chronicle*. A special news reporter was assigned to the case because Stephen had excused himself. He did not want any public perception that he might be considered biased because of his vested interest. The assigned reporter was impartial and reported fairly. He interviewed the accuser, Karl Rubin, in a featured article. The town was ready to hear what the star quarterback had to say at the trial.

All of the necessary preliminaries were rapidly dispensed with, and a jury of eight white men, two white ladies, and two colored men were selected. Ken was pleased with the speed with which things finally got moving. And so was Mario, who, after initially putting the case on the back burner, was pleased with the newspaper coverage. It was timely and developing into the most prominent case during Mario's term in office. But the best news of all was he believed he had a sure-fire winner.

After a routine opening, Judge Milton Perrodin was ready for the prosecutor to present his case to the jury.

Milton Perrodin was a fixture in the judicial system of Estilette. He had heard, since he was a young boy, about the legendary legal precedents set by Judge Estilette. His family had lived in the area as long as Stephen's family, which is to say even before the town was named Estilette. He was in his early seventies, and his wild bushy eyebrows frequently tangled with his eyelids, which caused him to constantly brush them back. That and cascading hair along with the growth of a white unruly beard gave an appearance of wisdom--the image that he wanted to project. He liked the idea of being as old and as wise as Solomon.

He loved the law and considered himself a fair and impartial judge, particular in matters that had to do with "our colored citizens." He was also the judge that heard the case *Fergerson vs. the School Board,* which Phillip had brought years earlier. He was well acquainted with both City Attorney Lazzaro and the defense attorney Kenneth Malveau.

It was hot and muggy. The heat clung to skin like a shroud. If not for the fans that created a breeze through the opened windows, it would have been unbearable.

Judge Perrodin rapped his gavel several times; he liked to hear this symbol of authority that got immediate attention. The courtroom was crowded and abuzz with the speculation of an open and shut case.

The colored people were there because they were

shocked that this kindly old man could have been charged with a crime, plus there were rumors circulating that the old man had been framed, and they were curious about how that happened.

The white people were there to see their star quarterback up close.

Karl's father had taken off from work on the oil rig to be there.

Eric's father was also there, and to emphasize that his son was dead and that "the nigger killed him," he wore a black armband on his right bicep.

Phillip watched him settle next to the Rubin boy's father, and he nudged Stephen and nodded his head in their direction.

When everyone was settled, the judge said, "I'm not going to tolerate any talking or noise in my courtroom. Y'all just sit and be quiet, if you can find a seat. If you can't find a seat, just go on out to the hallway or outside and hear what you can hear from there. Now, Attorney Lazzaro you can start."

Lazzaro stood and glanced at the wall-to-wall audience. He smiled, and his moving eyes paused briefly on the front row where the reporter from the *Chronicle* sat, then his eyes moved to the jury.

"Ladies and gentlemen of the jury, good morning. We will be brief. This is a simple case. A young boy, Eric Schultz, was shot to death with a shotgun, and the man who shot him has since died. Karl Rubin and his friend Eric went hunting on private land that the deceased was caretaking. And because they had been told that they could not hunt on this property but ignored the warning, the deceased man followed them into the woods. When Eric put down his gun to take a smoke, the deceased man, who went by the name BoBo, picked up the gun and shot him dead.

"Then Karl ran off, just like his friend Eric had done so many times on the football field. But it was a different run this time. Karl ran off to save his own life and to get the sheriff. My only witness will be Karl Rubin, who will tell you, in his own words, what happened."

He sat down and defense attorney Malveau stood.

"Good morning, ladies and gentlemen of the jury. It may not be such a good and simple morning as the district attorney would have you believe. Mr. BoBo, who is charged with this crime, does not have any other name. For all of his seventy-five years, he was known as BoBo. There is no birth certificate, no baptismal record, and no other document to establish any other name. He is simply known as BoBo, and he is not here to defend himself. A couple of his friends want his name cleared and the truth of what happened brought to light, and they have asked me to defend Mr. BoBo of these charges. We are asking you to keep an open mind, and we ask your indulgence as the facts of this case are presented.

"Mr. BoBo did not kill Eric Schultz. True, Eric Schultz is dead, but Mr. BoBo was not the one who killed him. This is all that we have come here to prove. Thank you."

Judge Perrodin smacked down his gavel and said, "Attorney Lazzaro, call your first witness."

Karl Rubin was called. The heads of the people turned when the clerk opened the double doors and Karl entered. He walked down the aisle to the bench, was sworn in, and took his seat in the witness chair.

He smiled. He was the good-looking all-American hero, and his friends and admirers, including Jan, the cheerleader, were there to give him support.

Lazzaro asked Karl to tell what had happened on September 23rd, 1963.

Karl told his story. He and Eric went to hunt rabbits on

the private land. There was no sign, so they parked their truck on the road, and while they were walking back to the woods, a colored man yelled at them that they could not hunt on this land.

Karl continued, "We didn't pay him no mind and continued on our way. While we were hunting, about an hour later, I was sitting under an oak tree, waiting for the rabbits to settle down. Eric had just lit up a cigarette, and he heard a noise like the rabbits were moving around. He put his gun on the back of the tree where I was resting, and he crept around to the briar patch. The next thing, I hear this blast and I jumped up, and then I saw that old colored man with Eric's gun headed over to where Eric was lying. I guess he was going over to find out if he was dead. Well, I crept up behind and hit him in the head with my gun. Then I took off running back to the truck, so I could get the sheriff."

Lazzaro got up to ask questions. "What was your relationship to Eric?"

"We were best friends."

"You were on the same football team, right?"

"Yes, sir."

"You were the quarterback, and he was the star running back, right?"

Ken was on his feet, "Objection. Relevance?"

Judge Perrodin, asked "What's your point, Mr. Lazzaro?

"Your Honor, this witness was deprived of a friend and the school was deprived of a star football player."

The judge continued, "I know, Attorney Lazzaro, but what does this have to do with your case?"

"Your Honor, I want to establish the urgency that was in the mind of my witness that made him choose to run away and get the sheriff and not to shoot back in self-defense."

Judge Perrodin pulled at his eyebrows then leaned forward and said, "If you want to pursue this line of questioning, go ahead, but you must understand you're opening a door."

Lazzaro continued, "Why did you hit the killer in the head?"

"Because he had killed my friend."

"Why didn't you take your gun and shoot him down like he had shot down your friend?"

"I couldn't kill anybody. I was just scared that he was going to kill me, too. He had just told us not to come on the property, and I guess he was mad because we didn't pay him no mind. After he shot Eric, I just hit him in the head and high-tailed it out of there."

"Are you sure that the man who killed your friend is the same man who told you not to hunt on the property?"

"Yes, sir."

"How are you so sure?"

"He was the only nigger we saw all day."

"That's all. Thank you."

The judge said, "Your witness, Attorney Malveau."

Ken stood and walked up to the witness chair. He turned slightly so that the jurors could look directly into the face of the witness as he answered questions. "Tell me, Mr. Rubin, what caused you and your friend to go hunting on this private property?"

"I dunno, we just did. It was a good place to hunt."

"Had you hunted this land before?"

"No, sir."

"Why not?"

"'Cause, I dunno. We just didn't."

"So you really didn't know whether it was a good place to hunt. Is that right?"

"I guess not."

"Where did you hunt before?"

Lazzaro interrupted, "Your Honor, I object."

"Overruled."

Ken continued, "Please answer the question, Mr. Rubin. Where did you hunt before?"

"Cross town on the Wyble place."

"Did Mr. Wyble give you permission to hunt his land?"

"Yes, sir."

"Why did you stop hunting there?"

Karl looked around and then shrugged his shoulders. "I dunno, we just did."

"Could it have been because Mr. Wyble told you that there was nothing left to hunt? That you boys had killed all the rabbits and squirrels?"

"I guess."

Ken had to be sure he pinned him down. "What does 'I guess' mean?"

"He told us there was nothing left to hunt."

"Now when you and your friend decided to hunt on the Fergerson land, did you have permission?"

"No, sir."

"Did you see a sign?"

"No, sir."

"Did anyone tell you not to hunt the Fergerson land?"

"We didn't know it was Fergerson land."

"Did anyone tell you not to hunt?"

"Yes, sir."

"Where was the person who told you this?"

"Standing on the porch of a shack."

"About how far away was he from you when he told you? Would you say it was a football field away?"

"About a half a field."

"So he had to yell. Is that right?"

"Yes, sir."

"Tell the jurors what he said and what you and your friend said. And remember you are still under oath."

Karl told that the old man had yelled at them. "He said, 'Ain't no huntin' allowed.' Then I yelled back and told him to shut up and mind his own business. Then he said he was the caretaker, and then Eric told him to shut the fuck up."

The audience reacted to the colorful language.

Judge Perrodin banged his gravel for silence.

Ken went on with his cross examination. "So, you ignored the old man and went hunting anyway. Did you realize that you were trespassing?"

"I guess."

"What does that mean?"

"Yes, sir. We were trespassing."

"Did you shoot anything?"

"No, sir."

"Did you shoot at anything?"

"Yes, sir. I shot at some rabbits but missed."

"How do you account for the fact that the sheriff found two dead rabbits?"

"I dunno."

"Did you shoot them?"

"I shot at some rabbits, but I don't remember hitting any."

"Where was your friend Eric when you shot at the rabbits?"

Karl was beginning to show signs of nervousness. He looked down and away and didn't answer.

Ken continued, "Well, where was he?"

"I don't remember."

"Could he have been on the other side of where the rabbits were?"

"I dunno. I don't remember where the rabbits were."

Ken crossed over to the table and reached down into a

267

burlap bag and took out a large jar containing two rabbits floating in formaldehyde. "Your Honor, I'd like to present in evidence these two rabbits that were shot by the witness. The sheriff picked them up on the day of the shooting. If necessary, I can put the sheriff on the stand to testify that these rabbits were found approximately five feet away from the body of the dead boy."

The judge said, "So done."

Lazzaro went over to examine the evidence, realizing now that he had overlooked the fact that the boys had indeed bagged some game. He then addressed the court. "Your Honor..."

"Settle down, Mr. Lazzaro, it's just evidence."

Lazzaro hesitated a moment, then he returned to his seat.

Ken continued. "Mr. Rubin, would it be fair to say that when you shot and killed these rabbits, your friend Mr. Schultz was in the line of fire?"

"No. The old man shot him."

"Now, Mr. Rubin, after the old man shot your friend, as you say, what did you do?"

"I sneaked up behind him and hit him in the head with my gun."

"About how far away from you was the old man when you say he shot your friend?"

"Oh, I dunno maybe about ten feet."

"And you picked up your gun and crept up behind and let him have it?"

"Right. I knocked him out."

"Are you right-handed?"

"Yes sir."

"Now, let me see." Ken took a right-handed position like he was holding a bat and made a swing. "Like this?"

"Yes, sir."

"Then the blow on the head of the old man would have been on right side of his head. The autopsy shows that the blow from the gun was on the left side of the old man's head. How do you account for that?"

Karl was now truly flustered. He shifted his position in his chair. He glanced over to where his father was sitting, as if to ask for help. He took a deep swallow of water from the glass sitting on the ledge next to the witness chair. Ken noticed that the jurors were showing some real interest in the line of this cross-examination. There was no response from Karl.

Ken waited for a few moments, then he asked, "Could it have been that the old man was facing you when you hit him with your gun?" There was no answer. Karl stared blankly into space and passed his hand across his forehead and shook off the sweat.

Ken continued, "Is it possible that the old man was kneeling down on the ground when he was hit?"

All of a sudden, Karl seemed to come alive. He responded with conviction and increased volume. "No. I hit him from the back, and he was standing up. He musta got a bruise on the other side when he fell."

Ken turned to the judge and said, "Your Honor, at this time I have no further questions for this witness, but I reserve the right to call him back to the stand."

Karl left the stand and took a seat next to his father who proudly patted him on the shoulder.

Jan, the cheerleader, turned around, smiled, and caressed his hand.

Two teammates reached over from behind and jostled his hair.

Karl's face was a mass of confusion. He was truly shaken. He stared blankly into space, showing no signs of acknowledgement for the supporting gestures from his friends.

The judge banged his gavel and looked down at Lazzaro who said,"I have no further witnesses.

The judge looked at Ken, "Mr. Malveau?"

"Your Honor, I'd like to call my first witness."

There was a stir at the city attorney's table. Mario Lazzaro stood and said, "Your Honor, may we approach?" The two attorneys went up to the bench. Lazzaro said, "Your Honor, I was not informed about witnesses for the defense."

Ken pushed a sheet of paper into the judge's hand. "Your Honor, when I filed this case with the city attorney's office, I informed Mr. Lazzaro I had witnesses. And this is a copy of the list of witnesses that was delivered to the prosecutor's office yesterday at twelve noon."

Lazzaro reacted, "Twelve noon. My lunch time."

The judge handed the list to Lazzaro. "This is a timely notice. It's not my fault or Ken's that you didn't get back from lunch. It's admissible." The judge smoothed his eyebrows away from his lashes and banged his gavel. "Call your witness, Mr. Malveau."

Lester Martel Junior was called.

Ann reached over and squeezed her mother's hand. Lala's eyes were glued to his face as Les walked in with confidence and raised his hand to be sworn in. Phillip leaned across Ann and whispered to Lala, "Don't worry, he'll do fine."

A cold chill ran down Karl's spine.

As Les sat in the witness chair, Karl got a good look at Les, but he did not remember seeing him before and was very confused.

Ken began, "Where were you on September 23, 1963?"

"I was over near Bayou Courtableau on my grandfather's property." Les went on to say he and his friend BookTau were trying to catch alligators when they heard a shot. They knew that his grandfather did not allow hunting because the houses were too close to the woods, so they went over to investigate. When they got near to where the shots were coming from, they saw the two boys. One of the boys was creeping around in back of a briar patch, and then they heard two more shots, one right after the other. Les told how he and BookTau moved to get a better look and saw Karl Rubin kneeling over the other boy, who was lying on the ground.

Les went on, "He was crying something awful. And he said, Eric, Eric, speak to me, man. I'm sorry, I didn't know you were so close."

Ken asked, "Why didn't you go over to help the boy that was shot?"

"I wanted to but BookTau said, 'No. They white boys, we gotta leave 'em be.'" When we saw Karl run away, we left."

"How did you know it was Karl Rubin that you saw?"

"He's in the newspaper every week during football season. He's captain of the football team. I'd recognize him anywhere."

"Do you see him here today?"

"Yes, sir. He's right over there." Les pointed him out sitting next to his father.

Ken went on, "Did you see Mr. BoBo that day?"

"Yes, sir."

"Where was he when you saw him?"

"He was on his front porch. We talked with him before we went to the bayou."

"When was this?"

"Oh, I guess about an hour before we heard the shots."

"When you left him to go to the bayou, where was Mr. BoBo?

"On the porch in his rocking chair. He had been

working in his garden, so he was tired. I think he was planning to take a nap."

"Now let me get this straight. You said Mr. BoBo was not in the woods with the boys at the time you saw Eric Schultz get shot?

"Naw. Mr. BoBo was not in the woods. He was on his porch sleeping."

Ken said, "Thank you, Mr. Martel. Your witness, counselor."

Lazzaro stood and said to the judge, "Your Honor, I'd like a recess to confer with my client."

The judge looked puzzled. "Your client? I was not aware that you had a client, Mr. Lazzaro. The person charged in this case is Mr. BoBo, and he's Mr. Malveau's client. If you would like to cross-examine the witness, now is the time to do so."

Mario Lazzaro had made a big mistake and everyone knew it. His function as the prosecutor was to bring the city's charges against Mr. BoBo. Karl was a witness, not his client.

Lazzaro walked towards Les. "How long have you known Mr. BoBo?"

"As long as I can remember. He's caretaker for my grandfather."

"And did you like him?"

"Yes, sir. He was a good man."

"So you'd do or say anything to protect him?"

"No, sir. That wouldn't be right."

"Are you sure you didn't see him in the woods that day?"

"I am positive. He was on his porch asleep. Not in the woods."

"Why are you so sure?"

"He was tired cause he'd been working in his garden,

272

and he'd been drinking."

"Oh, so he was drunk?"

"No, sir, he wasn't drunk. He'd had a drink of whisky and that made him sleepy."

"Did you have a drink?"

"No, sir, I didn't."

"Did your friend have a drink?"

"BookTau?"

"Whatever his name is. The man who was with you that day."

"Yes, sir. He and Mr. BoBo had a drink together."

"How much did they drink?"

Ken was on his feet. "Your Honor, I object. The witness is not on trial here, and the city attorney is harassing him."

The judge looked from Ken to Mario and asked, "Mr. Lazzaro, where are you headed with this line of cross-examination?"

"Just trying to establish the state of mind that the witness was in when he saw what he said he saw."

"Seems to me you are asking questions about somebody else, not the witness. The witness testified that he didn't have anything to drink. Sustained! Mr. Lazzaro, if you have further cross for this witness, you may proceed."

"Nothing further, Your Honor." Lazzaro sat down. He realized that there was no place to go with a cross, and he could not discredit the witness.

Then Judge Perrodin banged his gavel and said, "Mr. Malveau."

Ken stood and said, "Your Honor, I'd like to call Mr. Rubin back."

Every eye in the courtroom turned to look at Karl. He was petrified. He rose slowly. The members of the jury watched as he took the witness chair again. He looked at them and then quickly away. His eyes focused in space.

Ken's voice was very gentle now, and he thought it wise not to give the impression that he was accusing the boy of any crime. "Mr. Rubin, you've just heard testimony that Mr. BoBo was not seen in the woods at the time your friend was shot. Do you want to add anything to your testimony?"

Karl thought for a long second, his eyes now focused in the direction of his father and Mr. Schultz. "Yes. The old man did come into the woods."

"And when was that?"

"When Eric got hurt. I went to the porch and woke him up."

"Oh, this is new testimony. We haven't heard this before. We didn't know that you had gone to the porch. Tell us what happened."

"Well, my friend hurt his leg, and I ran back to get the old man to help me bring him out. When the old man got to where Eric was, he took Eric's gun and shot him, and then I hit the old man in the head with my gun, and you musta been right, he was facing me then."

Ken knew that he had caught Karl in a lie. Then he piled it on. "Now, Mr. Rubin, I'm going to share with you some of the information that the sheriff found and that the city attorney was not at liberty to share with you. The sheriff found that Eric's gun had shells in both barrels, and that your gun was empty and the butt was broken. Therefore, would it be correct to say that, maybe, Eric was accidentally shot when you killed the two rabbits?

The silence in the courtroom could be felt. Karl didn't say anything. Nothing and no one moved. Then, after what seemed like five minutes but in reality was only about fifteen seconds, Ken continued, "And would it be correct to say that Mr. BoBo was hit in the head by you while he was examining the body of your dead friend?"

Karl dropped his head and started crying. Mr. Rubin and Eric's father shook their heads at the same time. Jan covered her eyes with both hands, and his teammates looked at each other dumbfounded.

Ken waited a few seconds and then he said, "Mr. Rubin?"

There was no answer. The silence of the courtroom prevailed, and the only sounds were Karl's weeping and the hum of the fans.

Ken addressed the court, "Your Honor, I see no reason to carry this trial any further. It has been established without a doubt that my client Mr. BoBo was not responsible for the death of Eric Schultz, so I am requesting that my client be cleared of all charges."

The judge looked down and said, "Mr. Lazzaro?"

"Your Honor, I concur."

The judge banged down his gavel once more, " The case against Mr. BoBo is dismissed with prejudice. The jury is dismissed with thanks."

The entire courtroom was stunned. For several minutes, no one moved. Gradually, a few people at a time got up and left. Karl remained in the witness chair. Sheriff Bobineaux went over and talked with Mr. Rubin and Mr. Schultz.

Les, Phillip, and Stephen left down a side aisle and joined BookTau in the hallway. BookTau asked when would it be time for him to have his say. He was told that he didn't have to testify, and he let out a yell. That caused several people to look in his direction.

At this time, Mr. Rubin, tightly embracing Karl's shoulder, Eric's father, and their friends and relatives passed on their way out. Mr. Rubin stopped and looked long and hard look at Les. Then he spat on the floor. One of the group grabbed Mr. Rubin's arm and led him away.

Chapter 18

The Cost of Justice

February, 1965 - It was almost eighteen months since Eric Schultz had been killed.

Foot-dragging in a case that could indict a white boy was the order of the day.

Mario Lazzaro had more than he had bargained for. He had prosecuted Mr. BoBo for the crime, and now he had to prosecute Karl Rubin for the same crime. Although confusing, it was his job as city attorney. However, many in the community, especially the relatives and friends of Karl could not understand how Mario could charge two people with the same crime, but it was something that could not be ignored or avoided. The facts of Eric's death had been brought out in the BoBo trial, and the forces of justice could not turn and look the other way.

The Rubin family was furious, especially Karl's father, Walter Rubin. They were angry because they believed that "the nigger boy lied." So Les was blamed for the problems they were having. It didn't matter to them that Karl's story about the events of that fatal day did not support his plea of innocence. He was their hero on the football field, and he was their hero in the court of their opinion.

The Rubin family had to engage a defense attorney. It would not be an easy task. The best defense counselors in the area were ACLU and civil rights lawyers, and they did not answer the needs of the Rubin petition. Consequently, the family was forced to look at criminal defenders who had experience in cases that were settled by plea bargains. During the interviews, the attorneys quickly realized the difficulty of attaining an innocent verdict and proposed a plea of manslaughter as a defense strategy. This, of course, did not sit too well with the family, so Karl's father, Walter, had strong leanings toward an attorney who said, "If we can make it look like the nigger witness is lying, we're likely to get a favorable ruling. Consequently, attorney James Patterson, who had previously defended Klansmen, was engaged.

There was talk around town that Les and BookTau had made up lies to convict a white boy. Phillip and the family were not very happy about this turn of events. Lala was a basket case and shadowed every move Les made.

Once again, the courtroom was packed. However, this time there was racial tension in the air. Because Judge Perrodin would not allow anyone without a seat to remain inside, speakers were put in the hallways, which were also packed. The standing whites and coloreds had separated themselves on either side of the courtroom door, and as people arrived they gravitated toward the group that matched their skin color.

Judge Perrodin banged his gavel.

Mario opened.

"Ladies and gentlemen of the jury, the State will prove that the accused, Karl Rubin, did on September 23, 1963, shoot to death Eric Schultz. It was a hunting accident, we admit, but it was nevertheless a crime, a crime to which the defendant has pleaded not guilty. So the state will prove beyond a shadow of a doubt that it was Karl Rubin who committed this crime and tried to cover it up. We will present evidence from eyewitnesses who saw Mr. Rubin shoot Eric Schultz. I do not feel it is necessary to go into a lengthy opening statement, because the truth of the evidence will show beyond a shadow of a doubt that Mr. Rubin is the guilty party. Thank you."

Judge Perrodin smoothed down his eyebrows, banged his gavel, and pointed the handle in the direction of James Patterson.

"Thank you, your honor. Ladies and gentlemen of the jury, I am James Patterson. Just think of me as Jimmy, like I was an old friend and neighbor of this fair city. I have come here today to see that justice is done. I heard my esteemed colleague say something about truth. That is also what we are seeking. He tells you that there are witnesses who claim they saw what happened and are accusing Mr. Rubin of killing his friend.

"Mr. Rubin is a fine young man with a bright future as a football player. He is of sound mind and impeccable character. There is no motive here. Mr. Rubin and the deceased were teammates. Together they put their school on the athletic map of the state. So he had no reason to kill his friend. We will show that the prosecution witnesses are trying to frame my client for the ghastly deed of murder. They are lying when they say they saw Mr. Rubin commit this murder. They are lying to cover-up for the true killer of Eric Schultz. We will show that the witnesses have concocted their testimony to go along with the climate of hate that is now sweeping the country. The witnesses are hoping that their story will be believed because of what might happen if it turns out, and we will prove that it is true, that a Negro shot and killed a white man. These witnesses are counting on the tumultuous situation that the country is now experiencing. They are counting on the proposition that you would rather find a white man guilty than to convict a Negro, because, as they figure it, if you convict a Negro, it would be like pouring kerosene on the smoldering embers of our racial situation. So they are counting on the fact that you will find my client guilty in order to keep the peace. It is a terrible thing to bring in the race issue to overrule justice. But these witnesses are lying when they say they saw Karl Rubin kill his friend Eric Schultz. They have a motive. My client does not. Thank you."

When Jimmy Patterson completed his opening, even the judge was confused. He had never, in all of his years on the bench, heard such an expeditious proposal for racial backlash in a court of law. He stroked his beard and said, "Attorney Lazzaro, call your first witness."

Lazzaro called Sheriff Bobineaux, who testified to the evidence that he had gathered: the dead rabbits, the broken shotgun with the empty barrels used by Karl Rubin, and the fully loaded shotgun that was used by Eric Schultz. He explained the location and the condition of the body, that the shots came from the front and a cigarette had burned through the boy's lip.

Patterson decided that he wanted to ask the sheriff a few questions. He intended to make his observation of the cigarette seem frivolous.

"What did you make of that cigarette burning the lips?"

Sheriff Bobineaux answered quickly, "That tells that the deceased was killed immediately. Otherwise, the heat from the cigarette would have caused him to brush it away."

279

Now Patterson had to move in another direction. After a deep breath he asked, "What do you make of these dead rabbits that you found?"

"The rabbits were lying five feet in front of the body, and the shot that killed the rabbits killed the boy."

"Did you take fingerprints from the guns?"

"Yes, I did."

"What did you find?"

"On the broken gun, I found Karl Rubin's prints on the barrel and the stock. On Eric Schultz's gun, I found his prints on the stock and BoBo's prints on the barrel."

"And what conclusions were you able to reach?"

"Since there was only one set of prints on Karl Rubin's gun, he was the only one to have used it for any purpose. On Eric Schultz's gun, the prints of BoBo were in a position on the barrel that shows it was held with the stock away from the person handling it. The only sets of prints on the stock were those of the deceased."

This was not getting Patterson where he wanted to go. As a matter of fact, it was hurting his client, so he ended his cross.

Lazzaro called his next witness.

BookTau was dressed in a new pair of bib overalls with a red plaid shirt. He wore shoes and approached the witness chair walking lightly with shortened strides as one does when their shoes hurt. He raised his hand slowly as he took the oath; his eyes were glued to Phillips' face for confidence. He took his seat in the witness chair and let his eyes roam the faces of the people in the jury box who stared back at him.

When Lazzaro asked his name, he said, "Booker T. Washington." This came as a surprise to the colored people present. He had always been called BookTau, and no one ever suspected that his mama had named him after the great educator, no doubt hoping that the character of his namesake would influence his life.

Lazzaro asked BookTau to tell what he saw happen. It was the same as Les had told in the first trial. BookTau began to feel at ease in the witness chair because Lazzaro had not questioned any of his testimony. When Jimmy Patterson began his cross, however, BookTau was uncomfortable and did not understand why this man was asking questions about everything he had just told to the other man.

Patterson continued, "Now, Mr. Washington, you said that you had been drinking that day, is that right?"

BookTau answered, "Yes, sir."

"Were you drunk?"

"No, sir."

"How do you know you were not drunk?"

" 'Cause after one drink I had a chaw, and I don't drink nothing with chaw in ma mouth. Yo' supposed to spit not swallow."

The courtroom laughed.

Judge Perrodin banged.

BookTau was startled and looked around at the source of the hammering.

The judge yelled, "Silence!" And immediately there was. His eyes met BookTau's, and he said, "You may continue."

BookTau kept his eyes on the judge and continued explaining, "I nebber drinks when I chew. And it take a hellava lot more than one drink to make me drunk."

Patterson's next question caused BookTau to turn and face him. "How did you know that the man you say shot Eric Schultz was Karl Rubin?"

BookTau pointed at Karl. "That's him right over there."

Patterson continued, "Had you ever seen him before?"

"Yeah, the day he shot that boy."

Patterson was getting a bit perturbed, "I mean had you seen him before that day?"

"No, sir."

"How did you know it was Karl Rubin?"

"Les told me."

Patterson felt he now had a nibble in the right direction. "Oh, someone else told you what to say, is that right?"

"No, sir."

"You just said that Les told you who Karl was."

"Yes, sir, he did. He said he was the same as the picture in the paper."

"Did Les also tell you to say what you saw Karl do?'

"No, sir." BookTau was emphatic, and he went on. "Don't nobody have to tell me what to say, 'cause I always tells the truth."

The courtroom laughed, and again the judge rapped his gavel.

Patterson decided that he should try another line of questioning. "Mr. Washington, how far did you go in school?'

"I stopped in the seventh grade. Why you wanna know that?"

Patterson looked up at the judge and said, "Your honor?"

The judge looked down at BookTau and said, "You are not supposed to ask questions, only answer them."

BookTau nodded his head that he understood, and the judge continued, "Mr. Patterson, I am also curious, why *do* you want to know this?"

Patterson responded immediately, "credibility, your honor."

The judge caressed his beard then slid his hand down and twirled the end. With a tone of admonition in his voice

282

he said, "All right, if that's where you want to go. Continue."

Patterson asked, "Why did you stop in the seventh grade?"

"Had to pick cotton. Dat white man say I didn't need to go to school as much as he needed me to pick his cotton."

Patterson would not be outdone so quickly. He was looking to find evidence of imbecility or incompetence, so he kept pushing. "How long did you pick cotton?"

"Til I was 'bout twenty."

"How old are you now?"

"Forty-one."

Lazzaro stood and said, "Objection."

Judge Perrodin hesitated a few moments. He was curious about what Patterson would find traveling his chosen line of cross-examination.

The judge said, "Overruled."

Patterson dug his hole deeper. "What did you do after you stopped picking cotton?"

"Worked on construction with Lightfoot, sawing, nailing, and building houses all over town. Then I worked for Bill Blue . . . I helped him catch 'gators for the meat that he sold and cut down trees for his firewood yard. When he was shot dead by Sheriff Cat's deputy, I didn't have a job no more. Then I started working for 'Fessor Fergerson. He right over dere." BookTau pointed to where Phillip sat with a subtle smile on his face. "He's real smart, and he taught me a lot . . . book learning and stuff like that . . .and I still work for him, and I do just about everything he needs me to do, like killing hogs and planting crops and things like dat. So I didn't have to pick cotton for dat hateful white man I told you about. He wasn't paying me much anyway."

Patterson realized that he had come to a dead end. It

was clear he was not making any progress trying to establish incompetence, so he decided to end. "That is all, your honor."

Lazzaro had learned from the previous trial to present all of the evidence before calling his final and strongest witness.

Les gave the same account that he had given in the first trial. His testimony and BookTau's were consistent with everything that the evidence showed.

Patterson knew that this was his last chance to execute his strategy. He began, "Mr. Martel, did you see Mr. BoBo in the woods?"

"No, sir."

"Did you know he was in the woods?"

"No, sir."

"Where was Mr. BoBo when you saw him?'

"On the porch of his house."

"Now you have testified that you saw Karl Rubin shoot Eric Schultz. And where were you at that time?"

"In the woods, about fifty feet away."

"Now remember, you're under oath. Who told you to say this?"

"Nobody. I saw it with my own eyes."

It was becoming more and more clear that Patterson was not accomplishing his strategy. But he kept on digging, hoping that something he could use would surface.

"Describe what you saw."

"I saw Karl Rubin fire two shots in the direction of a briar bush. And I heard a voice yell out. I moved closer to get a better look, then I saw Karl run behind the bush and he knelt down next to the dead boy and cried. And I heard him say he was sorry he didn't know he was so close."

Patterson went over to Karl and whispered something,

then he turned back to the judge and said, "No more questions, your honor."

Lazzaro stood and said, "Your honor, I would like to enter into evidence a tape of the testimony that Karl Rubin gave in the previous trial."

Immediately, Patterson stood and objected, then he said, "Can we approach, your honor?" Judge Perrodin allowed them to come to the bench. Patterson wanted to know if this kind of presentation was allowable.

The judge asked, "Have you listened to the testimony from the previous trial?"

Patterson answered, "Not lately, your honor."

The judge surmised that he had not heard it at all. Then he advised that Patterson might like to take some time and talk with his client and consider whether a plea bargain was agreeable.

"The mercy of the court might be more preferable than for you to continue your line of defense."

With that the judge declared a recess.

Patterson was able to convince Karl that a plea of accidental shooting with a jail time of two to three years was in his best interest. This was done.

When the judge announce the verdict, Walter Rubin jumped up and yelled, "Hell no!"

The judge banged his gavel, and said, "silence."

On the way out of the courtroom one of Karl's football friends charged Les, yelling "You nigger bastard!"

BookTau stepped in, picked up the young man, and hurled him against a wall. That was all there was to that. No one tried anything else.

Sheriff Bobineaux urged everyone to go home in a peaceful manner.

* * *

When President Lyndon Johnson signed the Civil Rights Act into law in 1964, he hoped it would "close the springs of racial poison."

That was not the case in Estilette, nor was the advice of the sheriff taken seriously.

Two weeks after the trial, Les was on his way to work at the Black Eagle. A car containing three boys passed him, traveling in the opposite direction. At the end of the block the car turned around and followed.

Les was sure that he recognized the driver as one of the faces he had seen at the trial. He turned a corner and hid in the doorway of the dry cleaners. The car drove by, slowed down, and stopped when he was no longer in sight. Les was convinced they were looking for him. The car backed up. Les ran out of the doorway and high-tailed it the opposite direction. Two of the boys got out of the car and gave chase. Les took the back alleys and shortcuts through neighborhood yards and empty lots.

The boys followed, and their football conditioning paid off, because they were gaining on him. Les was cornered near a stack of lumber in the Prudhomme yard. He grabbed a two by four and swung it at the first boy, who ducked, and it slapped the second boy in the head. Les made it out and kept running. He found himself heading in the direction of the Sugar Patch pool hall.

Slick was shooting pool with a friend when Les ran into the men's room.

A few moments later, the two boys ran in, out of breath. They stood in the doorway and looked around.

Slick approached the boys and, with his pool stick across his body asked, "What y'all want?"

"You seen a boy run in here?"

Slick looked them in the face, eyeball to eyeball. "Maybe, y'all hard of hearing? I asked what you want."

286

One of the boys answered, "We're looking for a friend."

"You ain't got no friends in here."

The boy with the swelling knot on the side of his head said in a challenging manner, "We saw him run in just now."

"Like I say, you ain't got no friends in here. Now if you boys know what's good for you, I suggest you look for yo' friends on the other side of town. Yo' ain't gonna find none in here."

Slick followed the boys outside.

They crossed the street and got into the car that had just driven up. They glared at Slick, and Slick glared back, as the car sped off.

Slick opened the door of the men's room. It was empty. The window was open. He went to the phone and dialed.

Chapter 19

Intrusions

L ala was a basket case as a result of Slick's call, and she refused to allow Les to leave the house, for any purpose. She also refused to let him live in Frilotville with his father because that would mean renewed contact with Lester, and she did not want to go through that again. Les refused to be a prisoner in the house, with claims that he could protect himself. Even though Les had demonstrated in the past, *that he was a kick-ass kind of guy*, Phillip knew that Les had to leave Estilette to be safe. History was repeating itself. Like with Bobby, twenty seven years earlier, Les had to be protected from the ugly shadow of racism.

Phillip got on the phone to Velma.

"Vel, we have a situation here and Les needs a place to live for a while. Do you have space for him with you in Chicago?"

"What kind of situation?" Vel asked.

After a full explanation of everything that had happen,

she paused for a few seconds. This meant that her entire operation, of love for hire, had to be to be relocated. There was no way she could get out of the business entirely, she was only teaching part time to keep up appearances.

"I need a few days to fix up a place. I got clothes and junk all over."

"Vel, we've got to get this boy away from here as soon as possible."

"Papa, that's the best I can do. I'm really very busy with school and everything else, and I need the time to make a place."

Patience and compromise prevailed and they agreed that Les would come to Chicago in two weeks. In the meantime Vel rented a house and moved her entire evening activity to another location.

Lala insisted that Phillip take Les to Chicago. Two weeks later they boarded the train.

Lightfoot met Phillip upon his return. He could tell that Phillip was weary. It seemed that in the short time he was away he had grown older. However, Lightfoot was full of curiosity.

"What kinda house she got?" Lightfoot asked.

"It's a large place. Five bedrooms."

Lightfoot exclaimed, "Five bedrooms? Why she need such a large place?"

"I haven't figured that out, but there's enough room for Les to stretch out."

Lightfoot was persistent, "Why then she had to take so long to fix up a place for him?

Phillip breathed out, "I don't know."

"How long he gonna stay?"

"I don't know that either. But he's already thinking about going to school at Northwestern University."

"Maybe it's a good thing this happened. It got him out of Estilette, and if he can get into that school, maybe he'll be a doctor."

"That's not what he wants to do. He's thinking about being an actor. I've done all I could to put doctor in his head, but he's determined to be in the movies."

"Well, it's good he's got away from here. They still got some evil white people in Estilette."

For the trip home there was silence, and Phillip felt his eyelids drooping. But before they closed, Lightfoot asked, "Did you get to go to a blues club?"

"Naw, there wasn't enough time."

Phillip lied. He didn't tell Lightfoot that he had gone to hear Buddy Guy at Big John's. Buddy Guy was another of the many Louisiana bluesmen attracted to Chicago. And if Lightfoot didn't know him personally, he sure knew of him and would have wanted a detailed explanation of each song. Phillip didn't want to get into a detailed discussion of anything just then.

His mind's eye drifted back. It was a couple of days after he got to Chicago, and he had gone to Big John's alone. He had planned to take Les with him, but at the last minute, he decided not to. While he sat on a stool with his back to the bar, and facing the stage, a fancy-dressed man in a gray suit, black shirt, and gray tie with a diamond pinky ring on each hand squeezed in next to him. The man called the bartender over and asked where he could find high-class entertainment for the evening. The bartender said, "You wanna see Vel the Belle." The name caught Phillip's ear, and from that point on, the blues music of Buddy Guy was less compelling than the conversation he was overhearing.

He learned that Vel the Belle had recently moved her "pleasure palace" from Ashland Avenue to 55th Street.

The bartender continued, "Here's the new address, and tell Vel that Red Rooster from Big John's sent you."

Phillip was familiar with the Ashland address and the eavesdropping explained Vel's need for so many bedrooms. It also explained why she needed the time to, "fix up a place," before Les came.

For the remainder of the evening at Big John's Phillip debated his decision to leave Les in Chicago. His first impulse was to take him back to Estilette, but his better judgment could not expose him to the threat of harm from the Rubin clan. And in the few days he had been in Chicago, Les seemed motivated to attend Northwestern. So he had no other choice but to leave him with Vel. As much as he disliked him being exposed to the life she led, Phillip breathed a sigh of relief to hear that Vel had moved her evening pleasures to another location. So he was comforted by Vel's apparent attempt to shield her nephew from the shadows of her life.

Phillip felt that Lightfoot did not need to hear any of this, and of course Phillip was not pleased about what he had overheard. Vel had not turned out to be the kind of person he had hoped--nor had any of his other daughters. Lala was getting a divorce from an abusive husband, Rosa was married to a hustler and con-artist, and there was nothing that he could do or say about any of it. He had to accept the fact they had made their own choices.

When Phillip got out of the car, he stuck his head through the window and said, "Send BookTau over here. I got a present for him from Les."

Phillip entered the empty house. Lala and Ann were still at school. He figured to take a rest before they came home. He was weary.

He wasn't even dreaming yet when he heard footsteps in the hallway. They were heavy, slow, and reluctant--a man's strides. It sounded like it could be BookTau, but there was not enough time since Lightfoot had driven off. Phillip decided to investigate. He got up from the sofa, and as he turned into the hallway, he came face to face with Walter Rubin, who was pointing a pistol at him.

Phillip yelled, "What the hell?"

Rubin's face was a mask of anger. He snarled, "Where's that boy?"

Phillip, incensed by the intrusion, pointed toward the door and shouted, "Now you just get the hell out of my house!"

Rubin brought the gun closer to Phillip's face and yelled back, "I'm looking for that boy." Phillip knew that the man was enraged, and he didn't want to infuriate him further, so he toned down his response and said, "You've got no business here."

"Who's upstairs?"

"Nobody."

"Let's go see."

Walter pushed Phillip ahead of him up the stairs. He went through each of the bedrooms and the bathroom but found no one. Then Walter pushed him down the stairs, and Phillip had to grab the banister to keep from falling. He remembered the same hateful treatment from the hands of the white ushers who pushed him out of the white church, when he went to worship.

Walter Rubin was in his mid-forties, and the years of working on the oil rigs had made him rugged and as strong as a horse. Phillip was no match for this intruder, so he felt it best that he not antagonize him any more than he already had.

When they reached the first floor, Rubin searched each room and then pushed Phillip back towards the den. During the entire search, Phillip was silent, and every time he got a chance, he looked into Rubin's eyes. They were the same squinty, hate-filled eyes that he had seen years earlier at the courthouse when he had tried to vote. There was something unforgettable about shifty eyes filled with contempt for Negroes.

The audacity of this man coming into his house, demanding Les, told Phillip what kind of person he faced, and he became frightened. At first he was angry and insulted by the intrusion, now he was terrified.

When they got back to the den, Rubin pushed him to the sofa and stood towering over him with the gun inches away from Phillip's mouth. He shouted, "Now, where is that nigger boy?"

Phillip's response was almost a whisper: "He's not here."

"I know that. I wanna know where he's at."

Phillip felt maybe a conversation might bring some form of sanity. He asked, "Why? What do you want with him?"

"I wanna know why he lied, and I don't want no more stalling."

"What was done in court is over and done with, so let it be."

"Nigger, I know you know better than to tell me what to do. They say you one of them smart-ass niggers, but I ain't about to take none of your sass. Now where is the boy?"

Phillip's strategy had backfired, so he remained silent.

Rubin continued, "I'm gonna ask you one more time, then I'm gonna beat it out of you." Phillip knew the man meant what he said, and he prepared himself. He remained silent.

Rubin kept repeating over and over, "Where's he at?" The rapidity of the questions and the silence that followed seemed to infuriate him more.

He swung the pistol against Phillip's head, and the blow stretched him out on the sofa.

Rubin pulled him to the floor and began kicking him. After the fourth or fifth kick to the stomach and chest, he knelt down on one knee and brought his face close to Phillip's and screamed, "I'm gonna ask you again, where's the boy at?"

Phillip's face was covered with blood oozing from the left side of his head, and he wiped his eyes with the back of his hand, looked up into Rubin's face, and said as strongly as he could, "I'll never tell you that."

Rubin kicked him repeatedly in the groin.

Phillip groaned and cried out.

A voice from the hallway yelled, "Fessor, you in here?"

Rubin jumped up and quickly hid behind the door that swung into the den from the hallway.

BookTau yelled out again as he walked down the hall. When he passed the den, he saw Phillip on the floor.

Phillip, unable to catch his breath from the last kick, raised his hand and pointed in the direction of Rubin behind the door.

BookTau rushed in, knelt next to Phillip, and asked, "What happened, 'Fessor?"

Rubin rushed out and pushed the gun against BookTau's head. "Don't turn around, nigger."

BookTau responded instinctively, and he swung his mighty arm around, catching Rubin's legs, which brought him crashing to the floor. Then, as quick as lightning, BookTau threw his two hundred seventy pounds of pure muscle on top of Rubin, pinning his gun hand to the floor. Rubin was simply not strong enough to get it free, so he spat in BookTau's face, causing him to recoil enough to break free.

Rubin headed for the door with BookTau right behind.

Rubin swung the door against BookTau's, head but that only stunned him for a moment. BookTau kept coming.

Rubin backed out down the hall, yelling, "Stop, nigger or I'll shoot."

BookTau was as unceasing as the mighty wind of a hurricane. He kept coming. Rubin fired randomly without taking aim, and one of the bullets hit BookTau in the shoulder. Rubin fired again and hit him in the leg, but he kept coming. Since bullets did not stop him, Walter Rubin felt that it was time to abandon his mission. He ran out with BookTau in hot pursuit.

Ann walked up as the truck sped away. She saw BookTau leaning against the opened doorway and knew something was wrong. She ran to the porch yelling, "What happened?"

BookTau pointed into the house and said, " 'Fessor."

Ann found Phillip struggling to pull himself onto the sofa. "Grandpop, what happened?"

Phillip said, "Call Bobineaux."

Sheriff Cat Bobineaux listened to Phillip's description of the attack, examined the gunshot wounds, turned to Ann, and said, "You'd better get 'em to the hospital. I've got to catch up with the Rubin fella."

Ann immediately called Uncle Lightfoot, then she put pressure bandages on their bleeding wounds. She watched with mounting anxiety as Phillip, holding his aching chest, struggled to his desk, picked up the gift from Les, and put a Chicago Cubs cap on BookTau's head. Then he gently caressed BookTau's face and said, "Thanks for coming to get your present."

BookTau smiled and responded, "Everything's gonna be all right, 'Fessor."

Ann insisted that Phillip lie down and be quiet. Phillip was impressed with her calm, take-charge behavior in a crisis, and he began thinking that maybe *she* had the makings of a doctor. Phillip felt maybe some good had come out of this attack. Otherwise, he would have never seen the possibility of Ann being a doctor. Having not fulfilled his dream, he would die happy if one of his grandchildren followed in Bobby's footsteps.

Lightfoot pulled up into the yard just as Lala arrived from school. With one of the injured men in each car, they drove to the hospital.

BookTau's gunshot wounds were not serious. They were bandaged and Lightfoot took him home.

Phillip was examined, and the X-rays showed that his ribs had been reinjured. Two of Phillip's ribs were broken by the mob that beat him when tried to vote. Dr. Rossini had treated that injury in 1948, and now he ordered that Phillip remain in the hospital until other tests were completed.

Lala and Ann were with Phillip when Sheriff Bobineaux came. He walked over to the bed as he nodded politely to the two women. "How are you feelin', Professor?"

"A lot better, thanks to BookTau."

"Yeah, I'd say that big guy just about saved your life. How is he?"

"He'll be fine. Lightfoot took him home. What about Rubin?"

"He's in jail. I arrested him for breakin' and enterin' and attempted murder. Now that family's got more troubles than they know what to do with. When you get out of here, come by my office to sign the complaint."

"I'll be happy to do that."

As Bobineaux turned to leave, he looked at Lala and said, "I sure am glad it didn't turn out any worse for your family."

"Thank you, Sheriff."

Dr. Rossini entered the room with a worried look on his face. He went over to the bed and stood silent for a few moments then he said, "Phillip, I've been treating you and your family for over thirty years, since Martha began nursing for me."

Lala didn't like the sound of the doctor's opening statement, and she interrupted, "What's the matter, Doctor?"

Dr. Rossini turned to Lala and calmly said, "Lala, would you and Ann step outside for a few minutes so I can talk to your papa?"

Lala reluctantly complied, taking Ann by the arm and closing the door as they left. Dr. Rossini turned his eyes to Phillip and said, "When I was checking your lower intestines and bladder for bleeding, I found a large growth that I think is cancer."

"Cancer?"

"It seems to me that it's an advanced case, but I still have to do other tests, so for the time being I'm gonna keep you here a few more days." Phillip took a deep breath and closed his eyes.

* * *

Four weeks later, as usual, Phillip sat in his chair at the window with his cup of coffee and the *Times Picayune.*

It was 1965, and President Johnson's Great Society had taken a back seat to Vietnam. There was growing opposition over the country's involvement in the undeclared war, and one woman even doused herself in gasoline and lit a match in protest. This news did not make Phillip feel very good, nor had the news from Dr. Rossini. Phillip folded the paper and dropped it to the floor. He took a long swallow and a deep breath of air and thought back to that day in the hospital. He replayed the events in his mind's eye. The doctor's voice was still clear.

"It's cancer of the Prostate."

"What's that?"

"It's a gland at the base of the bladder, and it's gone bad.

"What does it do?" Phillip asked.

"It squeezes out that milky fluid during ejaculation."

"Maybe that's why I've had some pain when I come."

"How long has this been going on?"

Phillip knew his answer would reveal his sexual activity and he was not too anxious for Dr. Rossini to know that he was having an affair. After a moment, he said, "Can't rightly say, since Martha's been gone, but sometimes I masturbate, and when I do I get this pain between my legs near my butt."

"Any pain when you urinate?"

Phillip answered with a slight chuckle, "Yeah, a little, but I just thought that was because I was getting old."

The doctor was serious. "I'm afraid that the cancer has spread to several vital organs. If we had found it in time, we might have been able to treat it with some hormones, but now it's too late to contain it."

"How much time do I have?"

"It's hard to say for sure. Maybe eight months . . . or a year at most."

Phillip did not expect to hear this.

Dr. Rossini watched as Phillip's expression changed and a cloud of depression swept across his face. It was clear that the news had struck a nerve. Phillip repeated slowly, "A year. . . at most?"

The doctor was quick to respond, "Don't let it get you down. We all will die someday, but most of us don't know when. But now that you know, I think you oughta live each day like it was your last." He didn't know if his words would change Phillip's outlook or not, but he said them anyway.

Phillip let the words sink in, and he asked softly, "Do I have to stay in the hospital?"

"There's not much we can do for you here except make you comfortable. And knowing you, you'd rather be comfortable at home. I'll give you something for the pain and let you go about your usual activities. I'll drop by and check on you once a week."

Phillip nodded in agreement with the memory, put down the empty cup, and got dressed for the day.

Alicia drove, and Phillip gave directions. She had prepared a picnic lunch and Phillip wanted to go to his fishing spot on the bank of the bayou.

He had not told her about the cancer. He had not told anybody. All she knew was there were complications as a result of the kicks in his genitals, so she understood that sexual activity would be on hold for a while.

Alicia laid out the picnic on the blanket-covered grass, and they settled down for a peaceful day. She smiled lovingly as she looked at Phillip's gaunt face. It seemed that he had changed overnight, and his once full jaws had begun to sink into the cavities of his mouth.

Alicia spoke softly, "How long is this going to last?'

"How long is what going to last?"

"Your condition."

Phillip paused to think. The question sounded as if she knew about the cancer. And for a brief moment, he thought he should tell, but then he decided there was no point; she would know soon enough. So he said, "The doctor didn't say. He just gave me medicine for the pain."

"Did it hurt the last time we were together?"

"Some. But not too bad."

"Well, I guess we'll just cut back on doing it until the pain goes away."

Phillip smiled, reached over, and patted her hand. She was compassionate, and that was what he needed.

After a moment, Alicia said, "Last week I saw a house in Southern Heights that I think would be just right for us."

Phillip kept his eyes focused in the distance and said softly, "Why don't we wait a while before doing something like that?"

"It's the perfect house, a place where we can live out our lives together."

Phillip could not look her in the eye, so he said without turning his head, "Since that beating, I can't be driving as much."

"You wouldn't have to drive at all. You could move in with me."

"Dr. Rossini wants to see me every week, so why don't we wait until my condition clears up before doing something like that?"

Alicia was heartbroken. She didn't understand his reasoning. She figured he could see a doctor in Baton Rouge if he had to see one. She was ready to make a move and wanted it to be soon.

She said with sarcasm, "Well, maybe I'll just stay in my little ol' house until I die."

Phillip realized that at some point he would have to tell her, but he didn't want to do it right now. He touched her arm lightly and said, "Let's not talk about dying."

"So what do you want to talk about?"

"Nothing. Let's just be."

And that's what they did. Their minds sailed along with the clouds, and they watched the butterflies and listened to the birds and the crickets and the bees. They stayed until the sun set.

* * *

Phillip figured it was time to get his soul ready to meet his maker. He got up early and walked to Holy Ghost Church. He didn't trust himself driving anymore, plus he needed the exercise. He was early enough to make his confession, and before the bell signaled the six o'clock mass, he was in the pew where he had sat before he stopped going to church.

He felt someone slide in next to him, and he turned to look into Rosa's eyes. Tears slid down her cheeks, and she kissed him and whispered, "Good morning, Papa."

They received communion together, and after the service they headed to the cemetery. Rosa was as happy as a lark, and she walked stride for stride with her arm locked into her papa's. She said softly, "Papa, I'm happy that you came back."

"A little angel told me that you'd be here to greet me."

"It took a long time, but it finally happened, and just in time for Christmas."

"Well, I figured I might as well come back to the family's church, where I've spent most of my life."

Rosa hugged her papa and started crying again.

Phillip patted her shoulder and said, "Now you stop that. I'm not dead yet." Phillip knew if he had mentioned the word cancer, not only would it have announced a sentence to death, but it would also bring a stigma that most Creole families did not want anyone to know. So he was thankful that he had decided to spare her this pain and humiliation.

She said, "I'm sorry, Papa. But I've been crying since

the day that man assaulted you."

When they reached Martha's tomb, they stood in silence. Rosa picked up the flowers that had blown over and stuck them back into the vase.

Phillip ran his hand over the chiseled inscription in the headstone: *Martha Broussard Fergerson, born 1894, died 1962.* He turned to Rosa and said, "Put my name right here in this vacant spot."

After silent prayers, they walked to the large crucifix in the center of the graveyard.

Phillip said as he sat, "I've got to rest a spell. I'm not as spry as I used to be."

Rosa looked at her father's frail face. Unknown to her, the onset of the final stage of the disease was taking its toll. She remembered when that face was alive with energy and drive. She also remembered the gulf that had grown between them, which began when she had the abortion. Although it was her mama's idea that, "Papa should not know," it was not the only reason she hadn't told him; she was ashamed and didn't want him to know about her relations with Father Pat, who was the reason that Phillip had left the church in the first place. Everything was so interwoven; if she had shared one thing, she would have to share it all, and it wasn't something she was prepared to do. So over the years, the chasm between them continued to grow, and when she married Joshua it became a bottomless pit.

Phillip broke the moment of silence. "How are you and, er . . . Joshua getting along?"

It was spooky, almost like her papa knew what she was thinking. For a brief moment she wanted to tell him all of everything that she had not told him before, but she only said, "So far so good."

"What does that mean?"

Phillip's question gave her a chance to bring a small measure of closure to the separation between them. She began slowly, "I married Joshua because I was getting to be an old maid and I wanted to give you grandchildren. Love was not a major concern. But he was nice and he had ideas for a business, and it seemed like a good thing to do. I guess I had as many reservations about marrying him as you did for me seeing him. Although my reluctance didn't have anything to do with what Uncle Johnny found out, I was feeling desperate and felt that Joshua was my last chance, even though his background was so different. So all I can say now is so far so good."

"How's the candy business?"

"Growing. I'm spending more and more time making it, mostly, late at night after I finish my schoolwork. If it keeps on growing, I'm gonna have to get some help."

"Still thinking about children?"

"Still thinking." Rosa was not sure she should tell her papa that they had been trying for over a year without success. Then she realized there had been enough secrets between them. After a moment's hesitation, she continued, "The doctor said there would be no children."

Phillip looked at her with surprise. He knew that she had been pregnant before, but he couldn't let her know that he knew. So he voiced the only conclusion that he could make. "Sorry to hear that Joshua is sterile, but maybe it's a blessing in disguise. I don't think your mama would like for you to have children with, as she would say, 'a kinky-headed nigger.' "

Now Rosa had arrived at another crossroad. She could let her papa think what he was thinking or tell him the truth. She wanted to close the gap. She looked into his eyes and said, "Papa, it's not him, it's me.

Phillip looked back in disbelief. He wanted to say out

loud, "But you were pregnant for Father Pat," yet he would not dare.

Rosa continued, "Years back, I had an abortion, and my uterus was damaged. I didn't know that until my doctor told me a few months ago."

Phillip's eyes said what his mouth could not. His mind's eye flashed back to what Lightfoot had told him about the confession: "And then she fixed it so she wouldn't get pregnant again." He shook his head and wondered what kind of mother would do such a thing.

Rosa continued, "At the time when that happened, Mama thought it best not to tell anyone. So now you are the only one alive who knows."

Phillip dropped his head and focused on the ground between his clinched fists that rested on his knees.

Rosa continued, "Papa, I'm not going to say who the father was. There is no point, and now you know as much as I am able to tell. The rest is too embarrassing."

Phillip's tears puddled the dirt between his feet as he felt Rosa's hand slide across his shoulders. At that moment, he felt closer to her than he had ever been.

Chapter 20

Giving up the Ghost

965 - A few weeks later, Phillip walked into Stephen's office and dropped a document on the desk.

Stephen turned from his typewriter and said, "Have a seat. What brings you here?"

Phillip said in a business-like tone, "Read it."

Stephen picked up the papers and read, "Last Will and Testament? What's going on?"

"I have cancer."

There were several moments when neither Stephen nor Phillip spoke.

Then Phillip continued, "So now only you and Dr. Rossini know. I want you to be the executor of my estate and I'm asking that you see to it that all of this is carried out."

Stephen was silent.

Phillip saw the same glistening in Stephen's eyes that he had seen when Kennedy died.

Stephen walked to the window and for several minutes

did not say a word. Finally, he picked up the papers and began reading out loud. "I want BookTau to have the house that Mr. BoBo lived in, along with the parcel of land it sits on. To my grandson, Lester Martel Junior, I give five acres of land along Bayou Courtableau where we went fishing. To my granddaughter, Ann Martel, I give five acres of land adjacent to the family house. The remaining thirty acres and the family home are to be divided equally between my daughters, Rosa, Lillian, and Velma along with whatever cash is left in my account."

Stephen dropped to his chair and put the document on his desk. "You've thought it all out."

"Yes, I have. There's no point in denying dying. I've just got to accept."

"I know it's hard and it's something we all have to do. I hope when it's my time I am able to accept it as bravely as you."

"You're a good friend, Stephen, and color has never mattered. Your friendship has meant a lot to me over the years."

There was pain and joy in Stephen's heart, and tears filled his eyes as he said, "I'll always remember and cherish our years of friendship, along with all of the good things you did for the people around here. You're one of a kind. So I guess maybe I should tell you this now, before you run off and leave us. A few years back, when Alex finished her book about the Creoles, she started writing a book about you."

Phillip was flattered. And after it sank in, he repeated, "A book about me?"

Stephen passed the back of his hand across his eyes. "Yeah. About your life. It's called *The Man Who Made a Difference*. It was going to be a surprise, so remember, you don't know anything about it." Stephen smiled, winked, and continued, "Now, let's go over to the house and drink some wine."

* * *

Naomi prepared a special meal for the opening of Silas Hogan's concert at the Black Eagle.

Lightfoot wanted this to be a family dinner, and he invited Lala, Rosa, Joshua, Elvina, Luther and Stephen, who was considered family--and he was asked to provide the wine. Lightfoot did not invite Alicia because she was not family, and in the minds of Lala and Rosa, she still remained the "other woman." The only person invited who was considered a stranger was Joshua, and during most of the pre-meal chatter, the smooth-talker remained silent. However, from time to time, Rosa would explain Stephen's long association with the family, Aunt Elvina's relationship to her mama, and Uncle Luther's estrangement from the family, just to keep him from feeling like an outsider.

Lightfoot had pushed together several small tables on one side of the club where Naomi could spread out her luscious meal of gumbo, T-bone steak, home fried potatoes, fried shrimp, eggplant, string beans, and macaroni.

She announced, "This dinner is going to be a celebration feast."

Phillip thought of it as the last supper.

After Naomi had placed the last dish on the table, Lightfoot said the blessing and Stephen gave a toast: "Here's to Phillip my brother, the head and progenitor of our family, the man who made a difference in all of our lives." Everyone raised their glasses and drank to the toast, and the meal was eaten and enjoyed.

While they were having coffee and pecan pie, Sheriff Bobineaux entered.

Lightfoot limped over to the door and they exchanged whispered greetings.

Then the sheriff approached the gathering with Lightfoot following. He nodded his head around to the gathered assembly and said, "Phillip...y'all...I hate to break this up, but I got some business to attend to."

Stephen spoke, "What's the problem, Cat?"

"I got a call from Chicago to pick up Joshua Kane."

A hush descended over the table. All eyes focused on Joshua. Rosa gasped and covered her mouth.

Joshua stood and asked, "Sheriff, what is this about?"

"I've got to arrest you."

"For what?"

"Fraud, extortion of insurance money . . . something about a Cadillac car and some other things. I got the call to pick you up and hold you 'til somebody comes down here to get you."

Joshua turned on the charm, he smiled and said, "Well, Sheriff I guess you've gotta do what you gotta do. Know what I mean? But I'm sure there's a mistake. How did you know where I could be found?"

"I went out to that rental you got on Boagni Lane and nobody was home. Then I went over to the Fergerson house, and Ann told me y'all was over here."

Joshua laughed, "Thanks for a small town."

Rosa exclaimed, "Oh, Joshua." Then she started crying.

Joshua looked at the sheriff and asked, "Can I have a minute with my wife?"

The sheriff nodded.

Joshua took her by the arm and walked her away from the group. With his index finger, he wiped away the tears and said, "Don't cry, baby, everything's gonna be all right."

"What is this all about?"

"Just a mistake. I'll get it straightened out and be back before you know I'm gone. Know what I mean?" Joshua planted a kiss on her forehead, and Rosa ran off to the ladies room, followed by Lala. Joshua watched them disappear then shook his head.

The sheriff said, "Let's go, boy." He escorted Joshua out of the Black Eagle while everyone looked on in silence.

Naomi was the first to speak, "Ain't this some shit!"

Lightfoot said, "I knew it was just a matter of time."

Phillip pulled him close and whispered, "What did Cat have to say, back there at the door?"

"That he put a tracer on the plate of the pink Caddy and then got a call from the police in Chicago to pick him up."

Phillip response was, "Just like Slick said."

"Yeah, everything Slick said is comin' true."

Elvina strained to hear the conversation between Phillip and Lightfoot, then she looked from face to face and asked, "Will somebody please tell me what's going on?"

Lightfoot took his seat and said, "It's more than we know, but you just seen a bad apple plucked from the family tree."

Stephen turned to Phillip. "Is there anything you want me to do?"

"No, thank you, Stephen. Just leave it be."

Elvina asked, "Should I go to Rosa?"

Phillip said, "Lala is with her, that's enough."

Everyone was looking to Phillip for what to do or how to feel about what had just happened.

Naomi asked, "What do we do now?"

Phillip said, "Finish our coffee and dessert." Then he opened his arms in her direction.

"Naomi, come here so I can give you a kiss. You did a beautiful job on this meal."

The others applauded and added their comments.

Then Phillip set the tone for the remainder of the evening. "All right, Lightfoot, bring on the Blues."

Lightfoot jumped up. "Damn, it's almost time."

Rosa and Lala came out of the ladies room and approached the others at the table. Rosa said, "Will y'all excuse me? I don't feel much like staying for the music."

Phillip hugged and kissed her. "It's all right, baby. Go on home."

Lala volunteered, "I'll go with her."

Phillip watched them leave, took a deep breath, and sighed, saying to no one in particular,

"She's had to carry a heavy heart all of her life."

* * *

Silas Hogan was one of the few bluesmen who used his own name. He didn't have a moniker or use a nickname--he was just plain Silas. He was raised in Scotlandville and played mostly around Baton Rouge, Crowley, Opelousas, and New Orleans. Every now and then he would tour Texas, and a couple of times he went as far away as California, but basically he was just a local bluesman.

After getting everything started, Lightfoot came over and sat down at the table. There was not much to do. The crowd was slight, and everything was running smoothly for both the bar and the kitchen, so he and Naomi joined the others and enjoyed the music.

At intermission, Lightfoot asked Phillip, "Well, what do you think?"

Phillip thought for a few seconds, then said, "He plays the guitar and the harp all right." Elvina added, "Just all right? I thought he was great."

Naomi said, "That's 'cause you ain't never heard many great ones before."

Lightfoot laughed and said, "She's heard Clifton Chenier."

Naomi shook her head from side to side, "And that's all she's heard."

Elvina came back with, "Well, his *Honey Bee* and *So Long Blues* sounded fine to me." Naomi, still regarding Elvina as Martha's ghost, refused to let her off the hook.

"Somebody please educate the po' chile."

Stephen stepped in, "As far as I could tell everything he sang about was lost love."

Naomi said, "Maybe that's why Elvina thinks he's so great, 'cause she needs to find love."

Elvina was unaware that she could not say, think, or feel anything that would meet Naomi's approval. She looked at Phillip and said, "All right, Phillip, you started this, what do you have to say about lost love?"

Phillip's mind's eye immediately went to lost love for Martha, being asked by a Martha look-alike. The appearance of Martha's ghost on the day of her burial was too eerie. An apparition. Luther was right. He did love Creole women. As he looked across the table at Elvina it was like seeing a new Martha. A godsend—a prophetic foretelling of the direction his future life should take. Although it was not finalized in his mind, he could not ignore the possibility that everything that he had wished and hoped Martha to be, could be realized by her ghost.

He shook his head to clear the hopeful fantasy, and addressed Elvina's question.

Phillip was shrewd and said, "Y'all all right." They laughed and he continued, "While I was listening to y'all, I thought of something that Mr. BoBo told me before he died. He said, 'Nowadays, bluesmen play in the shadows of the blues.'"

Elvina asked, "What does that mean?"

"It means they don't really know what it feels like to have the blues. They have not experienced the trials and tribulation of being hungry or going without a job. And they've never felt the pain and suffering of a broken love life, bad living, or unfair jail time. The early blues people experienced all of that firsthand, and you could feel it when they sang about it. But they are dying out, and nowadays the bluesmen sing what they were told about, so they are just singing in the shadows. Mr. BoBo opened my eyes to that. He said it just don't feel the same."

Stephen remarked, "Phillip, I don't think those shadows will ever go away. I think they'll be with bluesmen for years to come."

Lightfoot slapped the table, stood up, and added, "As long as we're black, we'll sing the shadows." Then he picked up his glass and said, "I'll drink to that."

Naomi added, "Take it from one who knows, he's a black Creole and don't know shadow for shinola." Everyone got a good laugh, including Lightfoot.

The rest of the evening was spent listening and enjoying just plain Silas Hogan.

As they got ready to leave, Elvina volunteered, "Phillip, I'll drive you home."

When he realized they were headed to New Orleans, he did not protest. This may be the chance to have a life with, or to exorcise this ghost.

When they arrived at the St. Claude Creole cottage, Elvina took him by the hand and led him upstairs. She said with mischief in her voice, "You can sleep with me."

"Why?"

"Why what?"

"Did you bring me here?" Phillip wanted to find out, once and for all, how she really felt about the possibility of them being together.

She explained, "I wanted some private time with you, and the opportunity presented itself."

"So here I am. now what?"

"Are you afraid of being seduced?"

Phillip laughed and said, "I've never been seduced before. Are you sure you are ready to do this?"

"Are you ready for me to try?"

Well, I don't rightly know."

"When you came for the housewarming, I told you I could be your Martha, if that was what you wanted."

"I remember."

"Since that time, you have not made a move in my direction, so tonight I thought I'd give a little push."

Phillip wanted to tell her about the cancer, and he wanted to tell her about Alicia. But he felt that she already knew about Alicia and it didn't seem to matter or make a difference. However, he was curious about how it would feel to make love to a kind, considerate Martha. He searched his mind for the wrongness of sleeping with his dead wife's sister, and the only wrong he could reckon had to do with his feelings for Alicia. Since he would be dead soon, it did not seem to matter that much. He kissed Elvina with the passion that he had kissed Martha when they were first married. His body responded with vigor.

Elvina said, "I see you are eager to be with Martha again." After a slight hesitation and a very gentle pass of her hand over the growing bulge between his legs, she said softly, "And I am honored."

Phillip could not figure why she felt honored to be thought of as Martha. Was it just her way of saying that she was in love with him? Or was it because her resemblance to Martha induced her to take her place? Maybe it was her way of trying to experience life as a Creole. Although her heritage had made her one, she had never lived as one.

Now she lived in New Orleans, had a Creole cottage, entree to the husband of a dead sister, and all in the tradition of Creole life as it was known and lived. It was also life as told in the bible when the sister of a deceased wife was expected to take up with the bereaved husband. Phillip surmised that all of this could just be a fantasy that both he and Elvina were playing out.

His mind had drifted from the matters at hand, and Elvina said, "Come back to me. I hope your thoughts of Martha are not making you feel guilty."

He responded quickly, "No. It's not that at all. I was thinking about Rosa and the shock she experienced tonight."

Phillip lied. He hadn't thought about Rosa; he was wrestling with the rightness or wrongness of what he was about to do.

Elvina said, "She's a big girl now. I'm sure she will be all right."

She kissed him again, and his mind stopped wandering, thinking, and reasoning about anything other than the basic instinct, the urge to make love. And nothing else mattered.

His desire to be with Martha again outweighed his feelings of righteousness. He looked at Elvina's black hair spread across the white pillow and he thought of Martha. He looked into her deep-set gray eyes and thought, *God she is beautiful.* His hands glided lightly over the milky skin of her body and the soft luscious mounds of her breasts, and he rolled her nipples between his fingers as he was accustomed to doing, and he had the same feelings that he had when he looked into Martha's eyes and kissed her soft lips. Their passions grew and grew and mounted higher and higher until they exploded.

Phillip yelled and rolled over and away from Elvina.

She sat up in bed and turned on the light. She asked,

"What's wrong?"

Phillip was so overcome with pain he could not speak. As the agony faded, and when he could catch his breath, he said slowly, "The pain from that attack has come back."

Elvina looked down at his penis and said, "You're bleeding all over!"

He ran to the bathroom. It was difficult to suppress the urge to explain and tell about the cancer, but he felt there was little point in bringing it up now. The pain had taken away whatever pleasure he had hoped to receive from being with Elvina. In that one quick moment, the distress had brought back the joyless memory of Martha's ghost. She was still haunting his life.

In the morning, Elvina served breakfast in bed and watched from the rocker as Phillip drank his juice. "Are you still hurting?"

"No."

"Has the bleeding stopped?"

"Yes." Phillip knew that the bloody discharge came from the cancerous prostate.

Elvina sipped from her cup of coffee and said, "I'm so sorry. Life does play tricks on us." Phillip bit into his toast, and after a moment he asked, "What do you mean?"

"I had laid out my life to include you. I felt that because I looked so much like my sister that you could continue loving her through me, and that was fine with me. I wanted to bring you that happiness, and since I was alone and lonely, I felt that maybe this was a divine prophecy that we should spend our remaining years together." After a moment of contemplation she said sadly, "But it seems I would only bring you pain."

Phillip said sincerely, "You should not fault yourself. You had nothing to do with that. I guess that assault was more serious than I thought. I'll have to see my doctor when I get back."

Phillip took his last bite and drained his cup. "I think I should call Lala and tell her where I am."

"She knows. I called while I was fixing breakfast. And Rosa's all right. She stayed over with Lala."

"You are so thoughtful." Then he tried to make light of the situation and continued with, "How long am I going to be held captive here?"

"I'll take you back when you are ready to go."

"That should be soon, because if I stay away from my medication too long, the pain will come back. Have you finished with me yet?"

"Not yet." Elvina put the tray on the floor, sat on the edge of the bed, and gave Phillip a long loving kiss. She picked up the tray and went downstairs.

Phillip got dressed.

* * *

It was spring, 1965. The trees were flowering and the bees were working and the air was warm and comfortable.

Luther came for a visit. The brothers sat on the porch and let the rays of the sun bathe over them. Luther asked, "Did you read about that Liuzzo woman?"

"The one killed in Alabama?"

"Yeah! Man, I tell you, them crackers are somethin' else. That woman was only driving people back to Selma from the march, and now she's dead. Leaves her family in Detroit without a wife and mother."

Phillip said with a distant look in his eyes, "They don't care who they kill. If you're colored, they kill you. If you're white and helping coloreds they kill you. It's like all those people live for is to take life."

Luther was silent for a second and then asked, "You

think they were behind killing Malcolm?

"I don't know what to think. He was having problems with his own people, ever since he went to Mecca. But you never can tell, and I guess we'll never know."

"How are you doing?"

"As fine as anyone my age can be."

"I see you're not too old to still have fire in the furnace."

"What you talking about?"

"That night several weeks back when you were supposed to be dropped off at home."

"Now what's that supposed to mean?"

"You didn't come home."

"So?"

"So, Lala said you went to New Orleans with Elvina."

Phillip didn't answer.

Luther continued, "I know you. I told you some time back that you would be getting next to this Martha look-alike. You just can't let them Creole women alone. They got their hooks into you."

"Luther, you don't know what the hell you're talking about."

At that point, Alicia walked out, carrying a tray. "Lala made some teacakes and lemonade for you and your brother."

Luther's mouth dropped open. Phillip said, "I don't think that you two have met. Alicia, this is Luther. Luther, Alicia."

Luther stood and extended his hand. "Pleased to meet you. Phillip talks of you often."

"All good, I hope."

"Oh, yes. All good."

"And he's told me a lot about you. . ." she added with a twinkle in her eye. "All good. I'll leave you brothers alone

317

to enjoy your conversation and the teacakes."

Luther watched Alicia disappear into the house, then he turned to Phillip, shook his head, and chuckled. "Man, you're somethin' else."

"How's that?"

"Made a liar out of me again."

Phillip smiled. He knew what Luther was talking about. However, after that evening's experience with Elvina, he was done with Creole women for good. What was left of his life would be spent with Alicia, whose love he knew was boundless.

He had finally told Alicia about the cancer, and she decided to stay with him in Estilette until the end. The day she arrived at the Fergerson house, Phillip had arranged for Lala and Rosa to be there and he told them also. It was not easy, for him or for them, but they accepted the inevitable and promised to help him live each day as his last. But he had not told Luther, and he enjoyed the amusement as he listened to him draw conclusions.

Phillip commented on Luther's last statement. "Now why would you say that? I know you've always had your own ideas about what I did, but how did I make a liar out of you?"

"I thought you was going for the Martha look-alike."

"That just goes to show you can't judge a man by the women he keeps company with." Phillip chuckled.

"That woman that brought the teacakes is brown sugar."

"And just as sweet."

"Are you sure Alicia's not a black Creole?"

"Not a chance. But she's just as beautiful on the inside as some of them are on the outside."

"Same with Helen. When that woman died, I thought I'd die, too. But I had them children to look after."

Phillip had no idea that Luther had taken the death of his wife so hard. He wished he had been with him in his time of sorrow; he was a good man whom Martha had kept him from fully knowing.

Luther broke the silence. "You ever think of dying?"

Phillip was tempted to say, *I'm thinking about it now.* But he didn't. He said, "Sometimes. And you?"

"All the time. Don't have much to live for anymore. Children gone. Don't hear from 'em. Don't even know if I have grandchildren or not. I'm all by myself shut up in that house. Only time I go out is to fetch groceries or come over here to visit with you."

"Yeah, that's the way it is. You live your whole life and by the time you know what it's all about, it's time to die."

Lala came out. "Hello, Uncle Luther. Papa, Alex called. She's coming over to read her book."

Luther reached over and poured a glass of lemonade and said, "Them teacakes taste just like Martha used to make. I'll have a couple more and then be on my way."

Lala said, "I'll wrap up some for you to take."

* * *

The warm sun had lulled Phillip off to sleep.

Alexandrine said softly, "Professor."

Phillip stirred and then opened his eyes, "Oh, Alex, just taking a little nap while I was waiting. Have a seat and a glass of lemonade."

Alex had not seen Phillip for several months. She was shocked at how much he had changed. It seemed he had aged ten years. His face was sunken, and the light in his eyes did not have the sparkle that was so characteristic. Her father, Stephen had told her Phillip was not well and if she wanted him to hear what she was working on she should hurry and get it finished, and this she did. Now she was anxious to hear what his response would be.

"Professor, I don't want to bore you. And if you fall asleep, I don't mind. I was going to surprise you with my book, but I'd like for you to hear it before it is published, so anytime you have any questions, just stop me."

Phillip nodded his head. Alex took a swallow of lemonade and opened the folder of her manuscript. She began, "The title is *Phillip Fergerson: The Man Who Made a Difference*." Alex looked at him, and he smiled. She continued, "He was a man of vision. Born only twenty-seven years after the Emancipation Proclamation, he was determined to make a difference in the lives of the people emerging from the shadows of slavery. His great grandfather was an Irish slave owner who gave life to a slave son and his name to Christopher Fergerson."

Phillip opened his eyes and waved his hand in a halting gesture. He said, "His name was Crispin not Christopher. That's from a Latin word meaning 'one with curly hair.'"

Alex said, "Thank you, Professor."

While Alex was making the correction, Alicia came out and took a seat on the opposite side of the porch.

Alex continued, "And it was Crispin Fergerson who fathered Henry, who fathered Phillip. And Phillip Fergerson grew up with a burning desire to be a medical doctor, but he fell in love...Phillip opened his eyes and halted her again. Alex waited. For several moments, Phillip didn't say anything. Alex looked intently into his eyes and thought she saw a slight indication of a tear.

Finally Phillip lowered his hand and said, "Put someplace in your book that my granddaughter will be the doctor that I never got to be."

Alex dropped her mouth open and asked, "Ann is going

to be a doctor? I didn't know."

"Just put that somewhere in your book that you think it will fit."

Without hesitation, Alex made a note. A subtle smile played on the face of Alicia.

Alex resumed reading."And Phillip grew up with a burning desire to be a medical doctor but he fell in love and married a beautiful Creole lady and became a teacher instead. It was as a teacher that he changed the lives of hundreds of young people, who were students at one or the other of the elementary or the high school that he started. Not only did this 'Professor,' as he was referred to by both coloreds and whites, bring in-service teacher training to Estilette, he was also the driving force for civil rights. Phillip Fergerson was the first Negro in Estilette to attempt to register for the vote, and he was met by a mob. The beating he endured almost killed him. Undaunted and fearless, he continued his mission to bring light to the shadows of ignorance and prejudice."

Alex stopped reading. She sensed that Phillip was too quiet.

Alicia took a step closer.

Phillip's eyes were closed, and his head was slumped over to one side. There was no sound of snoring.

Alex reached over and touched his arm. There was no response. She called out softly,

"Professor? Professor?"

Alicia came over, knelt at his feet, shook his shoulder, and said louder, "Phillip. . . Phillip?" His body slumped into Alicia's arms.

Alex jumped from her seat and covered her mouth with her hands as the manuscript fell from her lap, and scattered. She ran to the door and called out, "Lala, Lala!

Come quick."

Alicia pulled Phillip to her breast and rocked him like a baby as the tears streaming from her eyes spattered the top of his head.

CPSIA information can be obtained at www.ICGtesting.com
Printed in the USA
270392BV00001B/31/A

9 781432 714758